AURORA 7

Books by Thomas Mallon

AURORA 7

THOMAS MALLON

TICKNOR & FIELDS
NEW YORK 1991

For information about permission to reproduce
selections from this book, write to Permissions,
Ticknor & Fields, Houghton Mifflin Company,
2 Park Street, Boston, Massachusetts 02108.

Library of Congress Cataloging-in-Publication Data

Mallon, Thomas, date.
Aurora 7 / Thomas Mallon.
p.   cm.
ISBN 0-89919-938-0
I. Title.
PS3563.A43157A9   1991   90-47867
813'.54 — dc20   CIP

Printed in the United States of America

BP 10 9 8 7 6 5 4 3 2 1

The author is grateful for permission to
quote lyrics from the following songs:
"It's a Lovely Day Today," by Irving Berlin.
Copyright 1950 by Irving Berlin.
Copyright renewed. Used by permission.
All rights reserved.
"Maria," by Leonard Bernstein and Stephen
Sondheim. Copyright © 1957 by Amberson,
Inc.; Copyright renewed. Jalni Publications,
Inc., Publisher, Boosey & Hawkes, Inc.,
Sole Agent. Used by permission.
"Sugartime," by Charlie Phillips and Odis
Echols. Copyright © 1956 by Nor Va Jak
Music, Inc. Sole selling agent: Melody Lane
Publications, Inc. Copyright renewed.
International copyright secured. All rights
reserved. Used by permission.
"He's Got the Whole World in His Hands."
Copyright © 1982 Warner Bros. Inc. All
rights reserved. Used by permission.
"You Belong to Me," by Pee Wee King, Redd
Stewart and Chilton Price. Copyright 1952
(renewed 1980) by Ridgeway Music Co., Inc.
All rights reserved. Used by permission.

For Seán and Christina

A U T H O R ' S   N O T E S
A N D   A C K N O W L E D G M E N T S

The *Aurora 7* was launched at 8:45 EDT on May 24, 1962.
Throughout the novel, words preceded by a note of the hour,
minute and second of elapsed flight time (e.g., **03 08 35**)
are taken from the transcript of Air-Ground Voice Communications between pilot Scott Carpenter (**P**) and the Capsule
Communicators, or Cap Coms (**CC**), at various tracking stations around the globe. On May 24, 1962, New York City and
its suburbs were on eastern daylight time, whereas Cape
Canaveral was on eastern standard. Unless otherwise noted,
references are to daylight time.

Throughout the novel, words and images specifically attributed to Mercury Control and to CBS' television coverage
on the day of the flight are authentic. Other reports are ac-
curate in terms of information, but the reports themselves
have been composed by the author.

In addition to such obviously historical figures as President
Kennedy, the characters Walter J. Hammill (the condemned
murderer), Ian Shelton (the Canadian astronomer), Everett
Knowles, Jr. (the recovering accident victim) and Kenneth
Shickley, Jr., are actual people. Other characters are ficti-
tious.

Almost all the incidental events of May 24, 1962, that are portrayed or referred to in the novel did indeed occur on that day: President Kennedy dedicated the Rayburn Building in Washington; Korvette's opened on Fifth Avenue in New York; Lee Harvey Oswald applied for permission to leave the USSR and return to the United States; the *Leonardo da Vinci* docked at West 44th Street. The statements written for Vice President Johnson are authentic and are now part of the National Archives. The loggerhead turtles' eggs were laid on Saturday night, May 19, and the evening storm depicted in the Epilogue would be remembered for its severity in the next *Britannica Book of the Year*. The airplane crashes of March 1 and May 22, 1962, took place as described. Advertisements and news clippings are for the most part authentic. Michael Collins's *Liftoff* and *We Seven*, by the original astronauts, have been my chief sources for knowledge of the workings of the Mercury capsule. Thoughts and actions attributed to Rene and Scott Carpenter are based on their own accounts written for *Life* magazine and *We Seven*.

The Peninsula campaign of the Civil War was, on May 24, 1862, at roughly the stage described here, and there was indeed a Union observation balloon called the *Intrepid*. The names of the ships wrecked during the hurricane of August 23, 1758, are real, as is the date of John Wesley's revelation. Coventry Cathedral was reconsecrated on May 25, 1962; the TWA Terminal at Idlewild and the memorial for the USS *Arizona* were dedicated the following week. The police chase through Grand Central Terminal on May 13, 1962, happened as described.

Having established these authenticities, I hasten to add that I have taken a number of small liberties — geographical, logistical and historical — throughout the novel.

I am grateful to the following people for help in researching the events of May 24, 1962: Alexandra Isles, Assistant

Curator, Museum of Broadcasting, New York City; Marjorie H. Ciarlante, Civil Archives Branch, National Archives, Washington, D.C.; Lee D. Saegesser, Archivist, NASA History Office, Washington, D.C.

And thanks to Bill Bodenschatz.

New York City
June 23, 1990

Who can tell if God will turn and repent, and turn away from his fierce anger, that we perish not?

— Jonah 3:9

I want to say that the effort involved in one of these missions is such that, at the end, we often feel emotionally drained, and we tend to fall back on the comfortable phrases, and words, like "happy," "proud," "thrilled" — and we feel so much more . . .

— Rene Carpenter, at a press conference in Cocoa Beach, Florida, on May 24, 1962

T MINUS 8 45 00

A t the bottom of the Pumpkin Patch Channel of Jamaica Bay, a burnt piece of seat belt decomposes. It has been there for seven weeks, since 10:07 A.M. on March 1, 1962, when an American Airlines Astrojet bound for Los Angeles took off from Idlewild Airport and crashed into the water fifty feet from the shore. No one survived, and some of the ninety-five bodies remained underwater for days after the first distress call went out from the airport and fifty-six policemen from the Tactical Patrol Force were shifted from Battery Park to Jamaica Bay.

They had been stationed at Battery Park to help, oddly enough, with crowd control during John Glenn's ticker-tape parade through Manhattan, which began just an hour after the crash. Afterward, at the Waldorf-Astoria, Cardinal Spellman finished the luncheon, whose participants included not just Colonel Glenn but his six fellow astronauts and all of their wives, by praying for "the victims of the tragedy of the skies this morning." It was a sunny morning, a lovely day, just nine days after Colonel Glenn had run three rings around the earth. The crash and the prayer were strangely humbling, some people thought.

Now, seven weeks later, at 11:11 P.M. on Wednesday, May 23, 1962, an air traveler passing over the town of Melwyn Park, in Westchester County, New York — a traveler beginning a peaceful descent toward Idlewild after a peaceful flight from Vancouver — might look out the window of his Boeing 707 and pick out one small light among those in the nebula on the ground between Pleasantville and Valhalla. It would be coming from the living room window of 111 Fillmore Terrace in Melwyn Park, the home of James and Mary Noonan and their eleven-year-old son, Gregory. Part of the light is being made by the Noonans' RCA blond-wood color television, which is tuned to the news, which is now reporting on one more air crash, the one involving "a Continental Airlines 707 jet, en route, you'll recall, to Kansas City from Chicago when it went down last night, killing all forty-five people on board and scattering wreckage over a sixty-mile stretch of Missouri and Iowa. A thunderstorm is still believed to be the cause of the crash, but Civil Aeronautics Board investigations remain incomplete."

(In fact, the CAB will soon know what it already suspects: that the crash was caused not by a thunderstorm but by Mr. Thomas G. Doty, who boarded the plane with some powerful explosives and $275,000 in flight insurance, and who was wanted for armed robbery in Kansas City. His wife, the beneficiary of his insurance policy, is pregnant.)

Only the thunderstorm, not the sabotage, would qualify to insurers as an act of God, but most other people, like the moderately religious Noonan family, wouldn't be so sure.

And just why this year does God seem to be knocking planes out of the sky with such frequency, just when men are being so newly successful in their weightless cartwheels above the atmosphere He gave them to breathe? They've been like boys these last ten months, recklessly testing His limits.

That boys are always testing them is to be expected, though the story coming out of the Noonans' TV just now involves a form of daring commenced, like the space shots, only in 1961. A fifteen-year-old boy attempted today to swim from East to West Berlin when East German border guards began firing at him. West Berlin policemen shot back and killed one of the East Germans. The boy was rescued from the canal and pulled into the British sector — but only after he was hit by seven bullets.

The Noonans, as they usually do in these tense months of the Cold War, watch and listen to these items in silence. But at 11:13 P.M., after the air traveler overhead has passed beyond the lights of Melwyn Park, voices begin to speak in the living room of 111 Fillmore Terrace.

"Here you go, Gregger," says Jim Noonan, noting that what his son has waited up for is finally on.

"Mmmn," says Gregory, lying in front of the TV on the braided colonial rug. He will not let his excitement about it keep him from signaling to his father that he really doesn't need *him* to tell him what is now up on the screen — namely, news that "preparations for the blast-off of tomorrow's three-orbital Mercury space mission are, according to NASA officials, proceeding A-OK. Smoke from some nearby brush fires is giving Cape Canaveral scientists some minor concerns about visibility, but not enough for them to foresee a postponement of tomorrow morning's launch. CBS News will be on the air all day bringing you coverage of . . ."

Jim Noonan thinks of the space capsule that will be going around the globe, which makes him think of the baseball that has been sitting in the empty ashtray over near Mary ever since he and Gregory came in from their silent after-supper catch. That's how it's been between them for the last few weeks: his son has been moving farther and farther into some spooky, sullen world of his own. Gregory has always been dreamy, hard to reach, but until recently you could always catch him on the wing, when one of his occasional bursts of chatter and warmth made him briefly available, like a radio station you passed in and out of as the dial kept scanning. But no more. In these last few weeks his son has been cold, out of contact. Jim wonders: Is it maybe just Gregory's boredom with his nonheroic father, who's about to go to bed before his eleven-year-old son?

Their catch ended tonight when Jim Noonan's slightly wild throw went bouncing out into the street. When Gregory went after it, Jim called out, "Look both ways!" and that had been it, Gregory's small frame stiffening into a signal that as soon as he retrieved the ball he would be calling it a night. Was it just that he resented his father's treating him like a baby, reminding him to look out for cars? No, it was something more: another reminder that the boy his father had known is, for reasons unclear to both of them, inaccessible, gone.

The fifteen-minute-long newscast is ending with a shot of the huge Westclox Big Ben in Grand Central Terminal, where, the announcer reminds viewers, CBS will display its coverage of the flight all day tomorrow on a giant monitor. As the camera moves toward the clock, a bit of the vast ceiling over the main concourse is visible. It is painted with a portion of the zodiac, 2,500 stars, the 60 largest of them marked by ten-watt bulbs. The arrangement appears to have been painted backwards, but that is only true for the human observer below. In fact, the reverse arrangement is the one favored by medieval astronomers, who liked to depict the heavens the way God would see them — from above.

Jim Noonan sees the time on the clock on the screen — 11:14 — and thinks of how nine or so hours from now he'll be walking under that same clock. It's time for bed. He gets up from his chair, crosses the room and kisses his wife good night. On his way to the stairs he passes Gregory, still lying on his stomach on the rug. He reaches down toward his son and tousles his hair, and says what he says every night with the same gentle, jaunty smile: "Good night, sweet prince."

Gregory doesn't look up. Jim looks to Mary, rolling his eyes before he turns and mounts the stairs.

It isn't fair, Mary thinks. Six months ago Gregory would have followed him up the stairs, unable to keep from talk-talk-talking about some new planet he'd been reading about. Six *weeks* ago he would have gone down to the Melwyn Park station to meet his father getting off the 6:32, to walk and talk him home to supper. But they are separate now. She thinks about the Berlin story on the TV a couple of minutes ago, and wonders why her family is becoming a divided city, wonders what power is putting up a wall around her son.

At this moment Gregory is looking at the Westclox Big Ben give way to the newscast's credits. He thinks: T minus 8 45 00. In eight and three quarters hours, an hour before he has to go to school, the rocket will rise.

Actually, though he doesn't know it, Gregory Noonan won't be spending the whole day at school tomorrow. He doesn't know what's in store for him, but God has some ideas — has, in fact, had something up His sleeve for weeks.

LIFT-OFF

On his mother's aqua-colored Admiral radio, in the kitchen below his bedroom, Rosemary Clooney is singing Irving Berlin. A middle-aged disc jockey twenty-five miles away in Manhattan has found just the right thing for a sunny May morning.

It's a lovely day today,
So whatever you've got to do,
You've got a lovely day to do it in,
That's true.

He can't hear the words, and he isn't fully awake, but the faraway nearby music opens his eyes enough to let him notice spangles of light through the new green leaves of the apple tree outside the window. Which gives him his first thought of the day, May 24, 1962: a memory, really, of the news announcer last night, just before bed, talking about forest fires in south-central Florida.

And I hope whatever you've got to do
Is something that can be done by two . . .

The broom handle taps on the kitchen ceiling below the bedroom floor. "Gregger, you'll miss it!"

In a handful of seconds and movements he is not only fully awake and fully aware of what she is talking about, but already downstairs in the living room, in front of the television, facing the rocket, the beautiful bridled Atlas booster sweating liquid oxygen, ready to take off, to slip through the tower's worried, restraining arms and fly away.

It vanishes, not off the launch pad but in favor of a film clip made during the night. The announcer explains that the silver man, waving his gloved fingers and smiling through the glass visor of his helmet, breakfasted on filet mignon, poached eggs, orange juice, toast and coffee before being inserted into the Mercury capsule.

Before *boarding*, thinks Gregory. Not being *inserted*.

It is 8:16 A.M., and in twenty-nine minutes the silver man, whose name is Malcolm Scott Carpenter, will leave the earth. Gregory wants rather desperately to go with him.

In the kitchen a clarinet solo comes to a close and Rosemary Clooney resumes radio contact:

> But if you've got something
> That must be done
> And it can only be done by one,
> There is nothing more to say . . .

He isn't going with Scott Carpenter. "Mom, could you turn that thing off!"

> Except it's a lovely day for saying
> It's a lovely day.

"Come have breakfast."

Except it's a lovely day for saying
It's a lovely day.

Five hundred miles above the earth *Tiros IV*, a satellite shaped like one of Mrs. John F. Kennedy's pillbox hats, flies through one of the hundred-minute orbits it's been making for the last 115 days. Its medium-angle lens begins transmitting a picture of hundreds of square miles of cirrus cloud, over which the *Aurora 7*, a few hours from now, will also be flying. *Tiros IV* is performing well, and will still be in the sky twenty-five years from this morning. But however high its orbit, it is slowly, inexorably, being doomed by gravity, which will one day suck it into a fiery death.

"Gregger, will you please slow down?"

He is eating Shredded Wheat, without sugar or interest, in fast robotic spoonings. Mary Noonan is eating Sugar Crisp. Two years ago she'd come home with a box of it, thinking to please her nine-year-old son, who promptly said, "Yuck." He's the strangest boy, really, preferring vegetables to dessert and leaving Mary with the taste for Sugar Crisp, which she occasionally still buys.

"Gregger, stop rushing. There's a hold." The countdown was stopped forty minutes ago at T minus 11, partly so smoke from the brush fires can clear off for better camera coverage of the launch. Still, it's the smoothest countdown so far in Project Mercury, as the television, still on in the living room, keeps saying.

Gregory drinks orange juice and rubs his eyes. Mary, wiping some milk from the oilcloth, says, "That's what you get for staying up to watch the eleven o'clock news. They say Scott Carpenter was in bed by ten last night."

"But Mom," Gregory groans, "he got up at two-fifteen."

"Even so," Mary says. "You could have gotten up a little earlier. He's been gone for half an hour."

Gregory looks confused.

"Your *father,* Gregory. Not the astronaut."

"Oh."

"'Oh.' Well, you might be down here while he's having breakfast a little more often. His train is probably in that hot tunnel under Park Avenue now, with him thinking he's got to put in another day's work without his son even saying good-bye to him."

Gregory says nothing.

A thousand miles to the south, on pad 14, Scott Carpenter resumes his deep-breathing and muscle-tensing exercises and listens for the whir of liquid oxygen. He feels calm now, even detached, as if he's watching himself get ready, more curious than anything else.

A moment ago it was different. He'd decided, because of the hold, to put in a call to his wife, Rene, who is in a rented house several miles down the beach. She was so startled to hear the phone that she'd answered it with her mouth still full of Wheaties. They'd agreed he wouldn't call after he was in the capsule, but the hold made him change his mind. She said she couldn't see the Cape yet because of the haze. Then he talked to his four children, his six-year-old daughter, Krissy, asking how the "test" was going. And that was when, just for a second, his eyes filled with tears.

"Why did God make us?" Mary Noonan asks her son, handing him a wet dish.

"Mom, that's so *easy*," Gregory says, embarrassed, drying the cereal bowl. He races through his answer: "'God made us to show forth His goodness and to share with us His everlasting happiness in heaven.' God, Mom, you must think I'm stupid."

"Of course I don't think you're stupid. That was very good."

Gregory is about a year away from confirmation. Yesterday afternoon he'd had his weekly "religious instructions" with the other Catholic students, who get to leave the public Melwyn Park School an hour early on Wednesdays and go to Saint Anastasia's for an hour with the nuns. "Why did God make us?" is actually a First Communion–level question, from the first page of the Baltimore Catechism, but Mary is always proud and entertained to hear Gregory rattle off any of the responses. A year from now he is supposed to be gently slapped in the face by the bishop, made a soldier of God and given an additional name. They have already settled on Joseph, after one of Mary's half-brothers, from a list prepared by Gregory, a list that contained, among fifteen others, the name Gordo, for Leroy Gordon Cooper, Jr., one of the seven Mercury astronauts.

"There's no Saint Gordo, Gregger," his father had said.

"God, Dad, it was a joke."

"Oh," his father had said, smiling.

Then Gregory had frowned and gone into the other room.

"I give up," Jim Noonan had then said to his wife. "I smiled, didn't I? I don't get it. I don't get him."

The countdown resumes at T minus 11 minutes. Scott Carpenter, who in 1959 could not understand the importance of the written "Who Am I?" test during astronaut selection procedures at Lovelace Clinic in Albuquerque, New Mexico, thinks that he is about to be let in on the great secret.

————————

Crest has been shown to be an effective decay-preventive dentifrice that can be of significant value when used in a conscientiously applied program of oral hygiene and regular professional care.

Gregory rinses his mouth with the fluoridated water that excites the suspicions of Melwyn Park's Republicans. He makes a big smile in the mirror to check that there's no toothpaste left on his front teeth, which are mercifully straight, unlike those of Brian Kearns, who about twice a week on the school playground hears the jingle for one of Crest's rivals chanted in his direction: "Bucky Bucky Beaver uses new Ipana. Bucky Bucky *Brian* uses new Ipana." Gregory, who is cute, almost pretty in his skinny, undersized way, has no vanity where physical appearance is concerned: not to be funny looking is all he would think to ask at eleven years of age.

The water swirls down the drain clockwise, and he watches it, recalling how last night he had climbed up on the back of the sink, mistakenly thinking he'd be able to look at the water go counterclockwise, the way it does below the Equator, the way Scott Carpenter might see it on certain portions of his flight today. Aside from being a mistake, this was hypothetical, of course, since whatever water is inside the Mercury capsule will be trapped and weightless, but last night he realized that Scott Carpenter will be one of very few human beings alive on May 24, 1962, to cross the Equator six times in one day, and the swirling water suddenly seemed interesting, until his father passed the bathroom door and asked, "Gregger, what the Sam Hill are you doing?"

Gregory's more mature classmates are already being caught masturbating behind closed doors, but it is doubtful that any agitated parental knocking has caused them the mortification he suffered in climbing down from the Rheem-Richmond porcelain sink.

It's his father. They're on different planets now, and to be spotted doing something stupid is to be weakened. When he'd seen that his father was not annoyed but amused, it was worse. He recalls this now as he buries his face in the towel.

Back in his room he gathers up what he'll need for school, knowing he actually won't need a lot of it, since Mrs. Linley never gets around to half of what she plans for them to do. They have the play rehearsal today, and even with the flight going on she still wants them to bring their arithmetic, American history and geography books, as well as their stock market charts. (Gregory is tracking McDonnell Aircraft, because they build the Mercury capsule; it closed at 42½ yesterday afternoon on Wall Street.) On top of the pile of textbooks he puts his latest favorite book, *Men of Iron*, by Howard Pyle, which is due back today at the school library.

Possessed of even more than the typical eleven-year-old's animism, Gregory scans his room — his telescope, his Yankees banner, his Civil War centennial commemorative stickers — and says goodbye to everything.

He starts down the stairs at T minus 6 minutes.

Inside the *Aurora 7*, the tape recorder, which will preserve everything Scott Carpenter and his Capsule Communicators say during the next five hours, switches on.

In Gregory's favorite book, now going down the stairs with him, page 243 reads in part:

And now, at last, had come the day of days for Myles Falworth; the day when he was to put to the test all that he had acquired in the three years of his training; the day that was to disclose what promise of future greatness there was in his strong young body. And it was a noble day . . .

It was also, as Rosemary Clooney had said, a lovely day. Three years and six weeks after being chosen for Project Mercury, Scott Carpenter is ready for it — ready, he realizes, for the ride and morning of his life. And Gregory Noonan, carrying Howard Pyle's seventy-year-old tale of fifteenth-century England, is ready — as soon as he's seen the rocket go up — for school.

"Gregory, please don't shoosh your mother."

The voice of Colonel John "Shorty" Powers, at 8:45:16 A.M., reaching the moment, comes through the television: "T minus fifteen and counting. Ten, nine, eight, seven, six, five, four, three — three, two, one, zero."

Gregory, lying on the living room carpet, is afraid his mother will say something. He needs to be alone at the instant of the rocket's rise, to feel inside himself the moment when the clock will change direction, when the countdown will be over, and time, catching its own baton, will begin moving forward.

But Mary Noonan is silent, having begun — just as Powers stumbled, ahead of himself, on the number three — to make the sign of the cross.

"Ignition."

Everything seems quiet to Scott Carpenter. The signal has been given, but he does not feel the rocket shake, does not hear any machinery start, does not hear the vernier engines light off, does not detect any noise from the liquid-oxygen valve.

But then the main engine ignites. And there is a little bit of shaking. And he feels his body beginning to rise.

"Lift-off," says Powers, and Gregory, looking at the rocket, feels, as everyone always does, that it is somehow rising too slowly, that it won't make it, that it won't come true. The black-and-white picture — LIVE FROM CAPE CANAV-ERAL — seems for a terrible, long instant like a photograph that won't develop, a movie that will break or run backwards, ending in fire and panic.

00 00 01 P
    I feel the lift-off. The clock has started.
00 00 04 CC
    Roger.

But time is running forward, and the rocket is rising, clearing the tower.

00 00 06 P
    Loud and clear, Gus.

Gregory digs into the carpet's braids with both hands, squeezing and pulling as if the *Aurora 7*'s movement into the sky, and dear life, depend on him.

00 00 12.5 P
    Little bit of shaking, pretty smooth.

Gregory trembles.

Down the beach from the rocket, Rene Carpenter, the astronaut's wife, shades her eyes with her right hand and holds out her left, wishing farewell to the Atlas booster, whose tail of flame shines through the remaining haze and is reflected in the green plastic of her wraparound sunglasses. Ralph Morse snaps the photograph that will be on the cover of next week's *Life*. A cry, not of fear but of pain, is all that cuts into her concentration: her six-year-old daughter, standing next to her, has stepped on a sandspur.

Back in Melwyn Park, Gregory Noonan is looking not at the television but into the braided landscape of the rug, feeling a premonition of something, good or bad he doesn't know.

00 00 21 P
Roger, the backup clock has started.

Jim Noonan, emerging from track 28 in Grand Central Terminal, looks at his watch.

00 00 24.5 CC
Roger, Aurora 7.

He sees the great crowd on the main concourse watching the TV screen, and at one point above it an old lady's long white spring glove waving, waving, back and forth, goodbye to the rocket. Cheers fill the great room, cheers that good-natured Jim regrets being too buttoned-down and Sanforized to join. But his heart is excited as he threads his way into the mass of people, finding a place under the great green ceiling, which, though painted with the northern constellations, looks more like an ocean than a sky. He stands under the bulb that is Betelgeuse and looks up at the screen.

Twenty-five miles to the north, on the living room floor of their house in Westchester County, his son, Gregory, closes his eyes. And 1,500 miles to the south, 9,000 feet in the air, and 29 seconds into his flight, Scott Carpenter looks out the window of the *Aurora 7*.

00 00 29 P
Clear blue sky . . .

Mary Noonan looks at her son. The television keeps talking:

Walter Cronkite: Thirty-five seconds. He's getting up towards that maximum —
Colonel Powers: Trajectory okay.
Cronkite: Maximum vibration force. He's just about in it. If all's going well up there, he's getting just about through that maximum vibration force now. He should be through it in another ten seconds.

"Gregger?" Mary asks her son, who seems to be shaking.

He opens his eyes and jumps to his feet. "I have to be gone."

Gone where? she thinks. He doesn't have to leave for school for another twenty minutes or so.

But before she can ask, he isn't there.

———————

00 00 46 CC
Roger. You're looking good from here.

President John F. Kennedy, satisfied that the rocket is on its way, steps back from the bedroom television set and puts on his two-button suit jacket. He looks out the second-floor window and notes with pleasure that the day is looking good. It will be nice to get out in the sun an hour or two from now.

His gaze moves from the green White House lawn below to the window pane a few inches from his face. He sees his reflection, ghostly in the glass, and decides in the course of a self-amused smile that he is looking pretty good, too.

———————

Cronkite: It looks like it is "go, baby, go" all the way. It's looking very good. He's through the maximum force now, or should be. At that point you see a vapor trail as he goes through the condensation layer.

Powers: MA-7 trajectory is okay. We are now one minute and seventeen seconds into the flight. Scott Carpenter reports his fuel and oxygen quantity steady. The cabin pressure decreasing on schedule.

Eighty thousand feet above the Florida coastline, Scott Carpenter thinks, "What an odd place to be, and going straight up."

Mary Noonan has left the living room to look for her son. She goes to the screen door between the kitchen and back yard and sees him climbing the apple tree, grabbing on to the second big branch. From the television two rooms away she hears, faintly, the voice of Colonel Powers:

This is Mercury Control. The United States launched its second manned orbital spaceflight with astronaut M. Scott Carpenter at the controls at 0745 A.M. eastern standard time here today. Purpose of the flight is to continue the investigation of man's capabilities in space, leading toward manned flight to the moon and return. This is Mercury Control.

Scott Carpenter's sky has turned black.

00 01 59 CC
    Stand by.
00 02 08.5 P
    Roger. There is BECO on time, and —
00 02 14.5 CC
    Ah, Roger. Understand BECO.
00 02 16 P
    Roger, I felt staging.

The *Aurora 7*'s booster engine, having fired and pushed the capsule closer to the arc it seeks, falls back toward the earth. The little Erector Set of an escape tower, which it would now be too late to use, has also fallen away, leaving only the small bell that is the capsule, flying toward the captive freedom of orbit.

Gregory, now nestled in a crook of the apple tree and trying to make himself as small as possible, closes his eyes to the yellow sun and green leaves that he awoke to half an hour ago.

Back in the living room, Mary hears an excited Cronkite verify what television viewers have seen through CBS' long-range camera:

> You saw it happen on that telescopic camera. You saw those boosters drop away with a burst of flame and a trail of smoke. That was forty miles high and forty-five miles from the launch pad here —

But *he* didn't see it, Mary thinks, wondering why Gregory, her space-crazy child, didn't want to.

---

00 05 09 P
    Okay, there is SECO [sustainer-engine cutoff]. The posi-
    grades fired. I am weightless . . .

Gregory's body stops shaking; he feels the pleasant limpness that follows a long stretching. He looks up to see light and bark and blossoms, and all he knows is that he's stopped feeling some tremendous, unspecified fear that shook him, like a warning, for minutes on end.

A child who has never spent a night away from his parents,

he has known more wonder than fright, the secure wonder of the protected dreamer. He has never been lost and never been taken, never been, even while toddling, more than a supermarket aisle away from those entitled to him. In the past few minutes he has not been lost, just aware of hands, somewhere in the dark, somewhere in the far sky, capable of seizing, hiding, burying things that are simply heading for home.

He climbed the tree because it was something to hold on to, to hide in, and yet even now, calm in his skin, he isn't sure that the tree has done its job. He isn't certain that he's come through whatever it was; he thinks he may only have stepped aside from it temporarily. It's not as if a bad dream has ended, for good, with the morning; it's more as if a strange ringing in his ears had sounded, grown and subsided, leaving him to fear it as a symptom of something still to come, and soon.

But for the moment the feeling has gone far enough away that he cannot imagine what he is doing, on this lovely day, this day of all days, sitting in a tree. As excitedly as if someone had just shouted, "Look — up in the sky — it's a bird — it's a plane —" he climbs back down to earth, realizing, remembering, knowing what he's missing: the chance to follow the progress of a man flying the planet, spinning it centrifugally, as free and as fixed as when he himself, on summer nights, has held on to the poles on the merry-go-round at Playland.

He dives for the living room rug. "I'm back, Mom."

---

00 05 32 CC
  We have a Go, with a 7-orbit capability.

00 05 36 P
Roger. Sweet words.
00 05 38.5 CC
Roger.
00 05 52 P
Okay, turnaround has stopped.

Waldy Munoz looks away from the television and back down at the newspapers spread out on the kitchen table.

"You boys get going. Don't you stay in front of that television set all day!" shouts his mother, Alicia, from the hallway of the apartment on East 117th Street.

"Tel-e-*vee*-sion," whispers Waldy's friend Ramón Arroyo, making fun of Alicia's accent. Ramón is the newest arrival of the three, up from Puerto Rico for only four of his seventeen years.

"Don't make fun of my mama," Waldy says, swatting Ramón without looking up from the want ads. The boys hear the door close; Alicia is leaving for her job in the lunchroom of P.S. 13.

"Man, you're missing everything," Ramón implores, swatting Waldy back and urging him to watch the TV again. Though the rocket, despite the wonders of CBS' telescopic camera, is now out of sight, and the network is alternating between shots of Cronkite and the sketch of an astronaut near a digital clock, Ramón is still excited — and late for school.

Waldy, like Ramón, is seventeen. He left school last fall and on Tuesday was laid off from a messenger's job. His mother, eager to see him working again, returned from her trip downstairs to the grocery store an hour ago carrying not just the *Daily News* but the *New York Times*, which she's never bought before. Waldy circles a want ad:

BOYS/MEN elevator oper, fine hotel $67
GOOD DEAL AGENCY, 136 W. 42 St.

"What you want that one for?" Ramón asks.

"Why? What's wrong with it? Steady job in a nice hotel?"

"Oh, man," says Ramón in disgust. "You wanna be ob-solete? There ain't gonna be no elevator operators soon. Everything be push-button, do-it-yourself. No more men and ladies in little gloves. Besides, what you want to do all day? Just go up and down, up and down?"

Waldy tries to ignore him. He looks farther down the column of classifieds.

"Oh, man," says Ramón with his usual animated disgust, smacking Waldy's arm and pointing at the television screen. "You don't want to go up and down like a yo-yo. You want to go up, up, up!"

---

00 06 59.5 P
It's very quiet.

Inside an egg that lies in a cove not far from the Cape, the protoplasm that is spinning itself into the bones and organs of a loggerhead turtle has stopped shaking. The egg has been in the cove since Saturday night, when a dozen two-hundred-pound loggerheads, observed by flashlight-bearing reporters and turtle watchers, came in to lay their eggs. The gestation period for these turtles is fifty-six days, and fifty-one mornings from now, on July 14, as firecrackers pop in Paris, a new loggerhead the size of a quarter will break through the shell of the egg that has just now stopped rocking from the blast-off.

---

00 07 17 P
ASCS seems to be holding very well. I have a small island
just below me.

As Scott Carpenter pronounces upon the fitness of the *Aurora 7*'s Automatic Stabilization and Control System, Mary Noonan looks at her son, who is completely absorbed by the television, and hopes he's back to something like normal. She wonders if she'll tell Jim about this episode tonight. Probably not. He's already stymied by Gregory's stern and distant daydreams, and the peculiar remoteness of the last couple of weeks. Still, this was strange, alarming. What would he make of his son's running away from the television two minutes into a space launch?

Mary thinks about her husband, who is a good, quiet and wry man — shy in his way, a man who wishes he could jolly his son back into relaxed communication; who knows he can't; and who dreads the idea of having a solemn little talk to straighten things out. A respecter of privacy, Jim won't poke and probe an eleven-year-old boy; his modesty makes him cringe from being interrogator and judge of his own son.

And so, at least for now, he will do nothing. Mary, who has gone over it a lot in her mind in the last two weeks, knows this. She knows, too, that Jim is wishing something will somehow come from Gregory's direction, some voluntary surge, like a warm front moving toward New York on Tex Antoine's nighttime TV weather map.

She looks at the Baltimore Catechism lying on the end table against the couch, where it's been since Gregory's arrival home from religious instructions yesterday afternoon. She'd flipped through it while she had supper cooking and was waiting for Jim, and even if it was disrespectful to Father McGuire, she had to conclude that as questions go, number 107 was a stupid one.

What are we commanded by the fourth commandment?
By the fourth commandment we are commanded to respect and love our parents, to obey them in all that is not
sinful, and to help them when they are in need.

She could imagine Gregory pondering all sorts of possible
situations in which you had to decide whether your parent
was asking you to do something sinful — *if Dad were to say,
'Son, stay home from school and mow the lawn,' would that
be sinful? If so, would it be a mortal sin? a venial one?* —
but how could he, how could any child, possibly understand
the phrase "to help them when they are in need"? Sure, help
carry in the groceries from Food Fair, that's clear enough,
but help ease the heart of your father, a man who's shy in a
different way from the way you're shy? How is a little boy
supposed to know that the adult heart has longings? And if
he did know, how could he not be scared to death from the
insecurity that would bring?

The truth, Mary has to admit, is that these priests really
don't understand children.

While Gregory listens to an explanation of the Mercury
tracking network — a rosary of radio stations beneath the
capsule's flight path, successive transmitters to which the astronaut will become faintly audible, then louder and clearer,
and then once more incommunicable, passing in and out and
over each one three times in the next four and a half hours —
Mary thinks of the newspaper clipping from Monday's *New
York Times* (brought home by Jim because the man at his
usual stand was out of *Herald Tribunes*), which she has put
away in a kitchen drawer. An article by Martin Tolchin, from
the food/fashions/family/furnishings page:

PASSIVE MEN SEEN BOUND TO MOTHERS
A child needs an "esteemed" father, a man to admire and respect. The wife who bolsters a husband, treats him as an es-

teemed partner for life, shows affection for and takes pride in him, is also helping her son to become a man.

Mary knew what he was talking about, of course, without his coming out and saying it. But that wasn't what she was worried about — Gregory, after all, seemed no more bound to her than to Jim. She'd clipped it not because it made her feel she was a domineering woman, nor Jim a passive man, but that she herself might be a passive woman. If she bolstered more, would her son be getting up to say goodbye to his father and not just to a spaceman?

Jim must be off the train and in the city now. She pictures him in his drip-dry suit and straw fedora, which he just switched over to today from the felt one. He usually waits until after Memorial Day to make the change, but he needed a lift today. She thinks of him walking through the forest of towers that used to be familiar to her — she'd worked as a typist-biller at Lowndes Brothers Glove Company just after the war; that's where they'd met. But the city is a remote place now. Each day Jim travels down into it while she stays in the quiet yellow house on the green lawn. She goes into New York no more than a couple of times a year, usually when Jim has complimentary tickets to a show Lowndes has provided gloves for. The last time was a few months ago, for *How to Succeed in Business Without Really Trying*, and he had practically had to drag her in to meet him for dinner beforehand. Manhattan is too loud and dangerous now, nowhere she wants to be at night. It's his world, and only a daytime world at that, the place he goes each day, a white-collar hunter after their food and clothing.

Right now, as Mary sits on the sofa, watching Gregory watch the television, the island of Manhattan lies twenty-five miles below them, slim, tapered, slightly tilted, angling and aspiring, like the rocket, upward and toward the east.

O R B I T   1

00 09 32 CC

——— igee 86.

00 09 34.5 P

Roger. Copied perigee 86 [nautical miles]. Did not get apogee.

Perfectly aloft by now, the pilot of the *Aurora 7* calculates the high and low points of his three impending orbits. Scott Carpenter can pitch and yaw his capsule so that he is flying forward or backward — like picking a seat on a train. Birds, of course, can fly in only one direction, and they do not flap their wings, as Leonardo da Vinci thought, downward and backward — a false assumption that made most of his designs for the "ornithopter" useless, and helped doom the human species to another four earthbound centuries. Still, a few hours from now the astronaut will be depending on one of Leonardo's more successful inventions, the parachute, to bring him down in the Atlantic for recovery by the USS *Intrepid*.

His having invented the parachute is only one reason why the boat carrying 1,195 passengers up the Hudson River at this moment — 8:55 A.M. — is named the *Leonardo da Vinci*. Fifteen days out of Genoa, the liner is about to dock at West 44th Street, on time, though on Tuesday it detoured twenty miles to help the injured carpenter of a Liberian freighter, after the man lost a finger in an accident and the *Aegina's* doctors couldn't stop the bleeding. Among the passengers now lining the *Leonardo's* starboard rail is Elizabeth Wheatley, the fifty-year-old American novelist who seventeen days ago left her second husband, after eleven years of marriage, as they stood admiring Bellini's altarpiece in the Frari in Venice. "Yes, Helen," she soon after wrote a friend on the ship's stationery, "you could say I left him at the altar." Left him for good. The immediate gesture could, she supposed, be construed as impulsive, even romantic, but there was really nothing desperate about it. The need to leave poor, bald, ineffectual Robbie had been apparent for years, and somehow, in front of the Bellini, opportunity seemed to meet motive.

It was more rational than anything else, Elizabeth has decided, fully aware of the girlish side of herself (the one loving lost causes and dire emergencies) but always more admiring of the severe intellectual side, the one she likes wickedly to display while undoing the characters in her comedies of manners. They're cruel books, some say, however witty, but she doesn't think so. *Someone* has to point out the world's general falling off in beauty, grammar and good sense.

She smooths her raw silk skirt and, with the hand not holding a copy of *Doctor Zhivago*, puts a strand of gray hair back into her bun. She smiles serenely into the breeze, ignoring the shouts and chatter of her fellow passengers, turning a frosty eye on the green, international-style blunder that is the McGraw-Hill Building. Awful, she thinks, recalling, as a kind of mental cleanser, the outlines of the Florentine Duomo.

Elizabeth is not certain what she will do today, though she knows she won't be shepherding her own luggage. She's arranged to have it sent up to East 85th Street without her. She probably won't even unpack it there; she'll just send it on to whatever hotel she decides to move into before Robbie gets back. (Having left the man himself, she's decided it is only fair to leave him the apartment.) No, feeling well rested, she'd rather spend the day, once she's through customs, just walking in New York. Perhaps she'll walk all the way home; and maybe, since she'll be walking east on 44th Street, she'll go in the back entrance of the *New Yorker* offices and stop up to see her editor. He'll be pleased when she tells him that at breakfast yesterday she saw a passenger, a rather nice-looking young man, reading *The Committee*, her out-of-print satire about the very literary jury that had once awarded her its prize. (Elizabeth had to allow that sometimes she couldn't help herself, couldn't desist from doing what her considerable natural kindness would try to prevent.)

What she will spend no part of the day doing is watching this spaceman. Elizabeth's romantic streak, the wide soft spot in her left-wing politics, will permit her to be enthusiastic over, say, an Elizabethan explorer, but as a lover of scratch cakes, natural fibers and manual typewriters she finds herself unable to care about a sterile man in a sterile can being applauded at this moment by every one of her Catholic Rotarian cousins in Wisconsin.

As the woman next to her begins waving to someone on the pier, she decides finally how she *will* spend the day. She will go up to the Frick and look at *their* Bellini, the *Saint Francis in Ecstasy*, and see if she can't continue the train of critical thought she'd had to interrupt in order to tell Robbie that things were finished between them.

———

00 12 22 P
    ... I'm going to fly-by-wire to track the booster. I will —
this is not a good tracking problem. Our speeds are too
close to being the same ...

Just over the Queensborough Bridge for the third time this
morning — into Manhattan from his house in Astoria; over
to La Guardia with a fare; now back on Third Avenue and
stuck in traffic — Edward Rodwicki looks northward out of
his empty cab and sees the marquee near the corner of 58th
and Third. Starting today, a double feature:

RAY MILLAND
The Premature Burial
and
Journey to the Seventh Planet

Eddie supposes his kid, the eleven-year-old boy, will be
wanting to see that one. His eyes go to the three color school
photos, barely bigger than postage stamps, taped to the
dashboard, left of the meter — the individual ones they take
in the years they don't take class pictures — Eddie, Maria
and Regina.

He inches the cab west onto 57th. More horns. And he's
stuck again, not moving and no fare, traffic everywhere, pedestrians thick on the sidewalks, each with three minutes left
to get to work and none exactly eager to jump into a cab that's
stuck in traffic on a sunny day. The city more of a nuthouse
than usual, he thinks, considering whether to hit his own
horn, deciding against it, deciding to be calm. So he just
drums his fingers on the Checker's steering wheel and starts
to hum the theme song to *Car 54:*

> There's a holdup in the Bronx,
> Brooklyn's broken out in fights,

There's a traffic jam in Harlem
That's backed up to Jackson Heights,
There's a Scout troop short a child,
Khrushchev's due at Idlewild . . .
Car 54, where are you?

He spots a girl, a pretty secretary with a tight, straight skirt and teased hair and a sweater, and thinks about what it would be like to be nuzzling up to her in the little doorway, a couple of steps below the sidewalk, near the lighting shop he's passing. Or not passing.

But then the traffic suddenly clears, the way it always seems to, for no reason, and she leaves his mind. Now he's moving quickly, a regular speedboat, into the richer world of Tiffany's and the Plaza, moving like a force, a fate, past the fancy façades. And the faster he goes the more relaxed he is, remembering what he likes about this job, the what can you call it, unpredictability, never knowing the place you'll wind up, who will suddenly wave you down and where they'll ask you to go. "You're not just taking them," Eddie, in a philosophical mood, had once explained to his wife. "They're taking you, too."

---

00 16 04.5 CC
Please send blood pressure. Over.
00 16 07 P
Roger. Blood pressure start now.
00 16 19 P
I have, west of your station, many whirls and vortices of cloud patterns. Pictures at this time — 2, 3, 4, 5. Control mode is now automatic. I have the booster directly below me. I think my attitude is not in agreement with the instruments.

Jim Noonan, standing at the corner of Vanderbilt and 42nd, facing west at 9:01 A.M., feels, in quick sequence, confused and then irritated. The traffic flow seems abnormal, the Walk and Don't Walk signs uncoordinated, and everybody seems to be jaywalking. What's going on? he thinks, his heart pumping a few extra times, a fine sweat beginning to break out under the collar of his Van Heusen shirt.

Then he remembers: the Barnes dance. He smiles and joins in, diagonally crossing the intersection, moving from the northeast to the southwest corner during the twenty-three seconds allotted for the dance, named for Mayor Wagner's traffic commissioner, Henry A. Barnes, who, if Jim now recalls correctly, is from Colorado, the astronaut's home state. How the hell could someone go from being traffic commissioner of Denver to being traffic commissioner of New York City? Well, when it comes to moving them around, he supposes, cattle are cattle. And the Barnes dance, which began on January 25, is popular, though after four months of it, Jim is still sometimes governed by his older pedestrian reflexes and forgets he can cross two streets at once.

He figures he will arrive ten minutes late for work at Lowndes Brothers, just down from Rogers Peet at Fifth and 42nd, but that's all right, since there will have been lots of people watching the space shot this morning, probably even old man Newman himself. Walking toward Madison, the horns and hooting and mess outside the terminal well behind him, he relaxes a little; his heart slows down. Lately he is feeling his age, which is to say middle age. He is forty-five, eight years older than Scott Carpenter and, to his considerable distaste, four months older than John F. Kennedy, a fact he still can't quite accept, Eisenhower having had a good quarter century on him. He wonders if he isn't a little past it these days. Here is this guy Carpenter just hooking into his first orbit of the planet, and here *he* is doing the goddamned

Barnes dance. You didn't know whether to laugh or cry. Jim, who usually chooses to laugh in situations where the alternatives are such, smiles a little as he continues west toward the corner of Fifth and 42nd.

But he is uneasy about a couple of things just now. For one, business: it's bad. (Even Kennedy's missus can't seem to save it. One shot of her in a hat or a hairpiece and whole industries will revive, like fairy-tale princesses. But pictures of her in white shortie gloves, just like the scalloped ones Lowndes pushes every spring, don't seem to be doing the trick.) For another thing, his son, his only son, Gregory. It's impossible to figure him these past few weeks, off in space, dreaming precise little scientific dreams with his kid's telescope and compass and protractor. Jim Noonan has no desire for an all-American sports hero, like some of the eager-beaver fathers hugging the baselines at Little League games and giving their kids ulcers by braying out encouragement left over from their own shot-to-hell dreams. No, he likes Gregory's brains, likes the smart-as-hell, determined little wooden-soldier ways of his kid. Mary used to call him Mr. Four-Going-on-Forty, Gregory being the only kid she'd ever known who *liked* making his own bed.

So what does he wish from him? Jim doesn't really know. Just that he'd be *there* somehow. Gregory has never been a cuddly kid — he'll flinch like a bunny rabbit when some uncle or aunt goes to touch him. In ordinary conversation, just riding in the car, he can be awfully formal. You can talk to him for an hour about baseball or geography, or even politics now, and he'll amaze you with his statistician's rattle of infield line-ups, foreign populations and gubernatorial nominees. But try to get him to tell you about his dreams, either the ones he's had the night before or the ones he has for himself, twenty years from now, and he'll clam up like a prisoner of war, giving you his just-name-rank-and-serial-number look before darting away through (circa 1952–56) or around (1957–present) your legs.

For the past couple of weeks he's been crazily remote, so faraway and quiet you'd need radar to track him. The only time they've really talked was last Thursday, when they had an argument. He said no to Gregory's request to accompany him on a four-day business trip, a swing through Maryland and Virginia to call on some old stores and buyers. Before he came into the showroom in '55 Jim had been mostly on the road, and old man Newman still sent him out a couple of times a year to milk old connections. This trip coming up two weeks from now would be one of those times, and Gregory wanted to go, to add to the list of state capitals he'd been through, and to have a look at Langley Air Force Base — "That's where they *train*, Dad" — near which Jim Noonan's business would be taking him.

But he'd said no, pointing out that he couldn't just pluck Gregory from school for four days. Gregory, who knew the angles, argued that this would be no problem: he'd just do a report on his trip, write up a few hundred words on the state of Virginia, paste a few postcards on construction paper, maybe throw in a product map. Kids get away with it all the time, he'd argued. Which made his father argue back, of course, that just because you can get away with something is no reason for doing it.

But that was not the real reason Jim had said no to him. He knew this Mrs. Linley — nice girl, blond, bright — wouldn't mind a straight-A kid like Gregory taking off for a week. The truth was that he didn't want to spend four days and nights with his own son. He could picture the two of them driving somewhere between Baltimore and Hagerstown, Gregory rattling off Moose Skowron's batting average and the name of the UN ambassador from Rumania, and then, between, say, Hagerstown and Cumberland, falling stone silent, his mind racing away under his sandy crew cut, already a trillion miles away in some spaceship beyond Pluto, rigid as a stick, untouchable.

The crew cut would have been gotten on the Saturday after Memorial Day. And Gregory, Jim knew, would be the one to remind him and Mary that it was time for the annual American schoolboy makeover from short hair flattened with tonic to shorter hair raised with butch wax in front.

He loved Gregory and wanted to *get to* him, the way he feels he once did the night a couple of years ago, when a boiler in a house a block away blew with an unbelievable noise, and Gregory, standing next to him in the back yard, raking up the crabgrass Jim was mowing, flung himself against his father, white-lipped, head firing into Jim's solar plexus, certain the McLernons' boiler was a Russian hydrogen bomb. But in two minutes the kid had once more gone rigid with dignity and reserve, raking up the grass in straighter lines than his father was mowing it.

Yes, he loved and admired his son, but he didn't want to spend four days in rented cars and motel rooms with him. (Is it, he wonders, that he hopes, once on the road, for adventures of his own, for something out of the ordinary to happen? Some excitement? Not necessarily extramarital, but something for which he'll need to be alone? Something — he really has no idea what — to make him feel a little less middle-aged?)

All this is in Jim Noonan's mind by the time he rounds the southeast corner of Fifth and 42nd, passing a guy selling sweatshirts with the stenciled faces of the seven astronauts making a halo around a Mercury capsule. He feels a prick of guilt, of love, and thinks of springing for the two dollars and bringing a sweatshirt home to Gregory tonight, a kind of peace offering, but he thinks no, the kid's got enough of that junk already and he's got to learn he can't always have his way. Gregory has been so spookily taciturn these last few weeks that it's hard to know if he is *officially* not speaking — childhood's most important diplomatic sanction — but Jim Noonan is fairly certain that when the two of them went to bed last night after the news, verbal relations had been severed.

Jim looks west, across the street, and notices the stone lions outside the New York Public Library. His thoughts return to himself. That's what he feels like these days — a petrified lion. Seventeen years ago he was street fighting, house to house, through Germany. And now here he is, selling women's gloves, denying his kid a little adventure (and two bucks), doing the Barnes dance and not much liking this guy, younger than himself, in the White House. He shifts his copy of the *Herald Tribune* from under one arm to the other. Eighteen months ago he'd voted Republican for the first time in his life, for Nixon. Never mind the Catholic stuff, either; other things were more important. The New Deal had been one thing, and a good thing, too, and FDR had been a great man, but this was another day, another deal. Jim Noonan has done all right, with his mortgaged house and patch of lawn in Melwyn Park. (Would Rockefeller really go through with this idea to have them all dig bomb shelters under the back yard crabgrass? He gives a few seconds of thought to what spending four days in a bomb shelter with Gregory would be like.) Twenty years ago he never would have thought he'd say it, but the Republicans seem to have more of the right answers. Kennedy is draining off too much of his, Jim's, money in taxes for things like this housing project he's coming to dedicate in Chelsea in a couple of days. How the hell is anybody supposed to save any money? Jim nears the entrance to Lowndes and looks across at the library once more, wondering how he's going to send Gregory to college.

OO 20 16.5 P
  Roger, Canary. I'm going to have loss of signal before I
  get these. I want to get some pictures. Have Muchea, or,
  correction, have Kano send these to me in this order:
  Sunset, sunrise, sunset, sunrise, break, break.

Tommy Shanahan — actually Father Thomas Shanahan,
S.J., twenty-nine years old — passes between two small ta-
bles in the sacristy of Saint Agnes's Roman Catholic Church,
on East 43rd Street, in the shadows of the Chrysler Building
and Grand Central. On one table sits a chalice full of hosts,
broken but unconsecrated, and on the other a pile of small
laminated missal markers with color pictures of African missions. Tommy will be distributing both at noon today when
he says a mass for the Society for the Propagation of the
Faith. May 24 is not much of a feast day — Saint Vincent of
Lérins — and at such more or less uncommemorative times
Tommy's pastor is inclined to lay on masses for the Society,
presided over as it is by Bishop Sheen himself, an occasional
terrifying presence here at Saint Agnes's.

Tommy can hear some good-natured shouts coming from
the boys' high school in back and, in front of him, through
the sacristy door, the murmurs of the 9 A.M. Latin mass, just
getting under way. Father White will be standing with his
back to the parishioners, facing the stained-glass window, a
"Gift of the School Children," depicting Saint Agnes, for
some reason without her customary lamb. Yikes, what a story
of martyrdom! Tommy had brushed up on it when he was
assigned here, and what he found in volume one of *The
Catholic Encyclopedia* was not pretty. "We do not know with
certainty," it said, "in which persecution the courageous virgin won the martyr's crown." But having declared herself
a Christian during whichever Roman emperor's tyranny,
twelve-year-old Agnes was, depending on whom you read,
either decapitated or burned to a crisp. Not without a super-

natural fight, however. "The judge," says Saint Ambrose, "threatened to give over her virginity to a house of prostitution, and even executed this threat; but when a young man turned a lascivious look upon the virgin, he fell to the ground stricken with blindness, and lay as one dead." Nice stuff for the kids, thinks Tommy, as he hears more laughter from the school.

Five months before the convening of Vatican II, Tommy is already having his share of modern problems. He was up in Inwood last night, just across from the Bronx, looking in on his mother's old cousin Annie, whose husband of forty-eight years is in the hospital with cancer. Tommy had said the rosary with her, been made much of by other old neighborhood ladies wearing Lily of the Valley toilet water, and come back here late, his brief sermon for today still unwritten.

Tommy knows he is popular not only with old ladies but young ones, too — and with the old men, for that matter. He's proud of his merry disposition and slim figure, and not above taking secret pleasure in the concealed crushes one or two of the aging guys in the rectory have on him. He's beginning, for the first time really, to wonder what sort of figure he could cut in the world, and in the bedroom, wondering what he might be doing if he'd been packed off to law school at Notre Dame, like his brother, instead of to the seminary in Hyde Park.

And he wonders how comfortable he is propagating the Church's faith to a place that Walter Cronkite referred to a little while ago, in describing Scott Carpenter's planned flight path, as "darkest Africa." Are the Church's sad rituals (Christ, the sight of cousin Annie gripping him with one plump, desperate hand and her rosary with the other) really any better, any more useful, than what the Africans already have themselves? Why, he wonders, does the Church have to intrude on them? In one article of faith he feels secure:

man is the most presumptuous of all creations. This morning in the refectory he wondered out loud why Americans had to be spending all this money to put a man into space. "Perhaps," Father Francis had said, hardly looking up from his coffee, "God wants us to meet Him halfway." And then, after a pause, "Literally, I mean."

Life Is Worth Living, according to Bishop Sheen, and Tommy supposes it is, but why . . .

Good God — Sheen! What would happen if the old man himself was to pop into a pew at lunchtime to check out what sort of pitch the new kid was making for his missions? From what Tommy'd heard, it would be like him. So, with less than three hours, and no ideas at all, Tommy decides he'd better head for the library and find a hook.

In less than a minute he's out on 43rd Street — the little block that eighteen years from now Mayor Edward Koch will rename Archbishop Fulton J. Sheen Place — walking west, passing the rectory and then the Provident Loan Society offices, which look tired and dirty, though they were put up only in 1938, five years after Tommy's still young and newly restless flesh came into the world.

---

00 24 16 P

Roger . . . My status is good. The capsule status is good. Fuel is 99–98 [percent]. Oxygen, 89–100. Cabin is holding good. All d-c power is good. All a-c power is good, 22 amps. Everything is green . . .

Having said goodbye to his mother and come through the screen door into the back yard, Gregory checks out his Rollfast bicycle. He adjusts the baseball cards clothespinned near the spokes, then squeezes the tires and finds the pressure acceptable — something he knows he really needn't do every morning, but it's a habit. Last summer when he and his father and mother got into the car for the start of the family vacation, he had felt compelled to ask his father if he'd rotated the tires. "We're going to New Hampshire, Gregger, not New Mexico." His mother reminded his father that Gregory was only trying to be helpful, and his father said he knew that, but Gregory immediately went into his space-dream mode and didn't speak again until they were nearly in Massachusetts.

Now he experiments with his transistor radio, cramming it into the pocket of his dungarees and running the wire leading to the single earphone up through his plaid cotton shirt. It isn't easy; the pocket is fit to burst. He shouldn't have to do this at all, but Mrs. Linley has decreed that there will be no TV until splashdown. Never mind that they got to watch all of Alan Shepard last year and John Glenn three months ago. This time, she said, they had too much to do to take the whole day off. It was almost as if she thought blasting a man into space and making him ride around at seventeen thousand miles an hour before dropping to the ocean at the bottom of a parachute were *normal* now, as if she thought nothing could go wrong. Which was especially unfair to Gregory's informed way of thinking, because he knew Scott had been given more to do than anybody so far: picture taking, experiments with balloons and flares — he even had to eat solid food!

Adjusting the earphone in his pinkish, slightly downed left ear, Gregory figures he'll be able to catch parts of the flight on CBS Radio and remain undetected. When they do stuff like math, he can pretend he's just resting his head on his left palm as his right hand works away with his pencil. Simple. And when it's too risky he can just put the wire under his collar. He has not confided this plan to his mother, but he's got the radio rigged up now, and as soon as he can strap his books under the big metal clip over his back fender he'll be ready to roll. The pile is unwieldy today. On top of the blue cloth loose-leaf, the Ginn arithmetic text and the fatter geography book, as well as the Howard Pyle, is a small biography of the Hoosier poet James Whitcomb Riley, which Gregory also plans to return to the library. He'd read it through, because one doesn't start books without finishing them, but he'd been bored. Part of a large series of American lives, all bound in orange cloth and exactly 192 pages long, it was recommended, sort of pushed on him, by kindly Mrs. O'Hara, the Melwyn Park School librarian. His own tastes in the series run to Civil War generals and the less well known Presidents. In fact, the night after John Glenn returned to earth, Gregory finished reading the life of Warren Gamaliel Harding, who caught cold in Alaska on page 190 and was buried in Ohio on page 192.

00 28 54.5 P

I'm going to be unable to complete the MIT pictures on this pass, I believe. Negative, negative, I can fix the problem. Too much film was out of the canister, that was the problem. Film is now in tight. The small back going on now.

With a little adjustment the orange book is made reasonably secure under the clip. Gregory walks the Rollfast around the garage. An apple blossom falls onto his shoulder. He mounts the bicycle, pedals down the driveway on one side of the oil-stained grass strip that splits it, and turns left into the street. The turn causes the small tuning dial of the transistor radio to brush against his pocket lining and move from a station with the flight coverage to one playing a record made ten years ago by his father's favorite singer, Jo Stafford:

Fly the ocean in a silver plane,
See the jungle when it's wet with rain,
Just remember till you're home again . . .

The *Aurora 7* passes over central Africa, and Gregory reaches into his pocket and returns the radio to CBS.

Melwyn Park is a product of the late Coolidge years, an incorporated village of 3,146 souls in modest shingled houses that, just before the crash, were bought by newly middle-class Irish brokering the boom in the city, whose rougher precincts they'd been born into in the 1880s and 1890s. There are Italians and Jews here now, and postwar arrivals like the Noonans, who had come on the GI Bill. It is full of children, begat by optimism and Catholic law, so many that the village now sends them to its own elementary school, built in 1954.

At thirty-five years of age Melwyn Park has a leafiness and maturity that can't be claimed by a lot of the Levittowns sputnikking the city. Gregory bicycles under strong sycamores that line both sides of the street and whose tallest branches meet above the middle of the road. He passes the house of Mr. Worrell, the jaunty widower whose leaves he rakes for fifty cents each Saturday in the fall, and then the house the McCarthy brothers lived in until last August, when his two best friends' dad received a job transfer to California. Gregory has suffered their loss in silence, sending them three letters on lined paper, mailed with Project Mercury four-cent stamps, and receiving three back; he realizes that he will not write them again.

The Rollfast glides by the Melwyn Park Country Club, which has a big swimming pool but no golf course. The railroad runs right behind it, and it is hardly a country club at all in the usual Westchester sense. Still, the sons of Ireland who hold mortgages here take out memberships and, after the

Memorial Day picnic finishes up in the club driveway, feel good watching the lawn fill up with their sons in Little League uniforms, and their girls in Brownie beanies, all of them eating ice cream. Gregory makes another turn and is on Tulip Street, the main thoroughfare. He rides past the A & P, Spotless Cleaners and Melpark Pharmacy, sponsor of his Little League team, the Comets, named only indirectly for astronomical phenomena. (In fact, they got their name because their founder, the vice president of the Melwyn Park Dads' Club, filled out the sponsorship form while sitting in his new compact car in the parking lot outside the Village Hall. It was a Saturday morning; his daughter was waiting to be picked up from dancing school; the form was due at noon; and, while trying to think of a name, his eyes fell on the chrome insignia glued to the glove compartment. Gregory will never know this.)

00 31 02.5 P
Pitching down, yawing left.

The Rollfast bumps over the railroad tracks and Gregory waves to Mrs. Burke, the crossing guard, as he turns left into the schoolyard. He slows down and pedals carefully on the graveled path running along the chain-link fence separating the playground from the train tracks, over which his father travels to and from Grand Central. A week ago Tuesday the Comets played an early-evening game against the Tornadoes, with Gregory in lonely right-field exile. Jim Noonan's train passed the field at 6:30 and he waved to his son. Gregory's heart thumped with shame and gratitude and what he didn't quite have time to realize was love. It was in the bottom of the fifth inning, when no ball made it out of the infield, that Gregory, ready hands on bony knees, got the idea of asking to go on the trip to Virginia.

Now he recalls his father's wave from the train, but he legislates it out of his mind: he is, after all, angry at him.

He's ten minutes early, ten minutes he could have spent in front of the television back home, but Gregory is not one for cutting things close, and probably, without being aware of it, he was looking forward to doing what he now proceeds to do: locking up the bike and lying down under one of the slides, so he can listen to the radio as if it's talking just to him. He shuts his eyes tight and watches the speckled red glow behind his eyelids.

00 35 02.5 P
> I'm using the airglow filter at this time. Visor is coming open for a better look at that. Hello, Indian Cap Com, Aurora 7. Do you read?

WCBS reports that Carpenter is making his first pass over the Indian Ocean and then switches to a brief report of "other news" on the planet below him: President Kennedy will be making it easier for Red Chinese refugees, now in Hong Kong, to come to the United States; U Thant is trying to get the Netherlands and Indonesia to return to negotiations over New Guinea; the Brazilian cabinet has voted to nationalize foreign-owned utility companies; and the president of the Ivory Coast is continuing his state visit to Washington. Gregory thinks about which of these places he might go to someday, all of them ones that Scott will be visiting, or close by, within the next eighty-eight minutes.

00 43 15.5 P
> What in the world happened to the periscope?

00 43 25 P
> Oh, it's dark, that's what happened. It's facing a dark earth . . . Up north, coming south.

00 44 12.5 P
It's getting darker. Let me see . . . Oh, look at that sun.

Only 150,000 billion miles from the *Aurora 7*, and 86 miles farther than that from Gregory, a flash of light moves toward the earth. It is at the end of its journey, traveling the last 25 of the 170,000 years it has been on the road since the supergiant star in the Large Magellanic Cloud galaxy, from which it comes, exploded. It is as if Jim Noonan, having driven his family the 32 miles from Gregory's grandmother's house in Queens, were now pulling his Plymouth Valiant into the driveway at 111 Fillmore Terrace in Melwyn Park. Neither Gregory nor Scott Carpenter nor anyone else yet knows of this light. The first earthling who will see it is today only four years old, a Canadian boy named Ian Shelton, who at this hour is playing with toy trucks in his bedroom in Winnipeg. And he will not be aware of this supernova until 2:40 A.M. on February 24, 1987, when, just before bed, he will look into his ten-inch telescope at the Las Campanas Observatory, on a mountaintop in northern Chile, and see, coming toward him, a light.

Gregory closes his eyelids tighter, so that the speckled swirls on the backs of them will grow more brilliant. He imagines that he can feel the earth moving, rotating under his back. He imagines what is only the truth: that he is riding it. He feels wonderful and strange.

00 47 46.5 P
It's now nearly dark, and I can't believe I'm where I am.

The schoolyard bell, which is activated by a button in the principal's office, rings not at 9:30, as it is supposed to, but at 9:33. Mrs. Johnson, secretary to the principal, has been down in the Teachers' Lounge watching the flight on television and has forgotten the time.

But now it rings and Gregory hears it, and for the third time this morning he is up in a flash, smacking dirt off his trousers, scooping up his books, racing across the map of the United States painted on the schoolyard's asphalt, through a green fire door, down a peach-colored tiled hall and into the chair behind his desk in the fourth of six rows within the cheerful yellow walls of room 4.

00 48 08 P

Oh, dear, I've used too much fuel.

---

00 49 45.5 P

. . . Everything is normal with the exception of — the fact that I am a tad behind in the flight plan.

The 9:30 bell has rung but Mrs. Linley isn't in the room yet. She is still in the Teachers' Lounge, catching one last minute or two of the flight on the television there, with the handsome gym teacher, Charlie Danaher, and her best friend at the Melwyn Park School, Sylvia Meyerson, Gregory's fourth-grade teacher last year.

The students in room 4 wait for her. Gerald John and Mike Cooper are splashing each other with water from the drinking fountain in the back; Ellen Ianucci and Jeannie Martin are looking at Jeannie's vinyl Richard Chamberlain loose-leaf cover. Ellen makes politely admiring comments, although she prefers the more hairily handsome Vincent Edwards — Ben Casey to Chamberlain's Dr. Kildare — who bears a fulfilled resemblance to Joey Carbone, who is sitting in the next classroom, among the sixth graders in room 3, and whom Ellen will marry on May 18, 1970.

Almost everyone but Gregory is talking. He sits quietly, pressing one ear closed so he can hear the transistor wire in the other.

Joan Linley, who until last year was Joan Anderson, enters the room. All talk stops instantly. Gerald John and Mike Cooper race to see who can get back to his blond-wood desk first. The vinyl Dr. Kildare slides into the open drawer beneath Jeannie Martin's desktop. And Gregory slides his transistor wire out of his ear and into his shirt.

The students do not fear Mrs. Linley. In fact, they are all, in different ways, in love with her. A tall athletic blonde with a wide grin, Joan Anderson Linley (Manhattanville '57, a year ahead of Joan Kennedy) is, depending on the sex and maturity of the child in question, a fantasy mother, a wished-for big sister, a vaguely erotic totem. (An underpaid woman in a shirtwaist dress, ten years from now, after her divorce, she will give up elementary school teaching and go to law school.)

To Gregory she is a stunning demonstration of the American way of life, the sort of woman who will soon settle the stars and start marvelous Amer-Martian families. Some months ago, in a tentatively erotic dream, the two of them had been wearing down-filled space suits and riding in a sort of interplanetary schoolbus. But Gregory, emotionally and glandularly behind the rest of the boys in room 4, is mostly aware of her as a kind of Supermom, the woman who spotted him walking along Wilson Avenue after school on October 5, 1961, the day the Yankees lost the second game of the Series, 6–2, to the Cincinnati Reds, a day when things were starting to look bad, and slowed her car down to say hi. He said hi back, and she noticed he was on the verge of tears. She stopped the car, got out and asked him if he wanted to talk about it. Being who he was, Gregory immediately got a grip on himself and said, "No, ma'am." So she just cupped the back of his head and gave it a couple of comforting pats that started it on its way to her small athletic bosom, where it rested for the most thrillingly mortifying two seconds of Gregory's life.

Right after she enters the room, where silence now reigns, she says, "Okay, class, let's stand for the Pledge." Gregory and the rest of them are instantly on their feet, and before transferring his eyes to the flag, Gregory rests them for a second on Mrs. Joan Anderson Linley, twenty-seven years old, and realizes how much she looks like Rene Carpenter. His reverence thus increased, he feels a forgiving pang about the no-TV-till-splashdown edict.

"I pledge allegiance to the flag of the United States of America and to the republic for which it stands, one nation, under God, indivisible, with liberty and justice for all."

While he recites these words, his gaze moves from the flag to the row of "Current Events" pictures, clipped from *Life* magazine, which runs above the row of perfect-penmanship cards, *Aa Bb Cc* and so on, which runs above the blackboard. He sees Freedom Riders, the brand-new New York Mets, reserve soldiers called up for duty in Berlin, John and Annie Glenn, and then, off to the extreme right, a picture of Yuri Gagarin. This is the picture his patriotic eyeballs hate to look at, the one he wishes would come down (it's been over a *year*, hasn't it?), the one that forces him to acknowledge what he would rather not, that *they* had been first. On April 12, 1961, a man piloted a ship that escaped the pull of the earth's gravity, performing for the human species an event equal to what happened at the moment the first cell created by God had stood still, then quivered, and then divided itself in two. Gregory could never look at Gagarin, because to do so was to experience a mixture of awe and anger, to be racked by ambivalence, that torture to the conscience of childhood, which equates mixed feelings with impure ones.

"All right, now, please bow your heads." The students

have reflexively reseated themselves at the end of the Pledge, taking their right hands from the spot where they think their hearts are and folding them into their left. "Almighty God, we acknowledge our dependence upon Thee, and we beg Thy blessings upon us, our parents, our teachers and our country."

Thirty-two days from now this enforced recitation of the New York State Regents' prayer, which Gregory and the rest of the students know as well as they know the Pledge, will be declared unconstitutional by the United States Supreme Court. At his news conference on June 27 the nation's handsome, philandering President will suggest to those disappointed by *Engel v. Vitale* "a very easy remedy, and that is to pray ourselves . . . I would think that it would be a welcome reminder to every American family that we can pray a good deal more at home, we can attend our churches with a good deal more fidelity, and we can make the true meaning of prayer much more important in the lives of all of our children. That power is very much open to us."

When the prayer is over, Gregory lifts his eyes. Mrs. Linley is adjusting one of the penmanship cards above the blackboard. She fixes it so that once again the row of perfect letters stretches perfectly, high up and all along the front wall of room 4.

Fourteen summers after this one, during the bicentennial, a month after the forty-one-year-old once-again Joan Anderson graduates from New York University Law School, the National Air and Space Museum will open, on July 4, 1976, in Washington, D.C., near the Smithsonian. The words SHEPARD, GRISSOM, GLENN, CARPENTER, SCHIRRA and COOPER will be painted in a heavenly ring just beneath the museum's high ceiling, a pantheon of names stretching above the gallery filled with artifacts from the ten-year journey to the moon. One of the last names in the ring, far away from his Mercury comrades, is that of SLAYTON, Donald K. "Deke" Slayton, the man whose place Scott Carpenter has taken this morning, after Slayton was discovered to have a "slight heart irregularity." Thirteen years from now Slayton will get his chance — in a cooperative voyage made by the Americans and Russians, the *Apollo–Soyuz* docking, the erotic climax of the brief international flirtation called détente.

At this moment, though, Slayton is speaking into a transmitter on the ground in Muchea, Australia. He is talking to Scott Carpenter about the unexplained rise in the latter's space suit temperature.

00 50 17 CC

Okay. Blood pressure starting. We suggest that you do not exercise during the blood pressure since your temp is up.

00 50 23.5 P

Roger. This is the story on the suit temp. I have increased two 10-degree marks since lift-off. And now about — well, 15 degrees above launch mark. My steam vent temperatures read 69 and 80. I'll take one more stab at increasing or decreasing temperature by increasing flow rate. If this doesn't work, I'll turn them off and start lower. Over.

Twenty-five years from today, tourists filing past the generic Mercury space suit in a glass case in the Air and Space Museum won't see the faded letters on the name tag: CARPENTER.

00 52 25.5 CC

Aurora 7, Muchea Cap Com on UHF. How do you read?

00 52 28 P

Roger. Muchea Cap Com. Loud and clear. Tell Jerry
and Gus and Lewis and — everybody else there, that I
worked with "hello." John Whittler, if you see him, tell
him to saddle Butch up.

The bones of Lady, the fastest little pony around, the one
Scott rode up the hills outside Boulder, near the house
where he grew up, at the corner of Aurora and 7th, lie pul-
verized under the Colorado soil this morning as Scott rides,
at 17,500 miles per hour, above the Australian desert.

Twenty-five years from tonight, at the Crown Space Center of the Museum of Science and Industry in Chicago,
Charles Williams, custodian, will finish vacuuming the last
gallery on his rounds. He will miss a green M & M, dropped
by an eleven-year-old boy who was in the gallery with his
parents between 3:30 and 4:00. After Williams shuts the
lights, it will lie until morning, still and undisturbed, near
the heavy pedestal on which rests the *Aurora 7*.

---

00 58 12 P

Roger. Going to fly-by-wire. It doesn't cost so much.

Looking at the Medicare figures, the President is slightly
exasperated, and somewhat more bored. It costs so damned
much they'll never pass it. Not with the stock market as nervous as it is now, and not with these sons of bitches in the
AMA. He'd gotten a good one off against them at his press
conference yesterday afternoon. Asked to comment on their
hysterical reply to his proposal, he said, "Well, I read the
statement and I gathered they were opposed to it." But he's
going to get it passed anyway, if not this session then the

next, before he has to go up against Rockefeller or Gold-water. The whole thing, too, Social Security financing and all.

It *all* costs so damned much, he thinks, dropping the note-book of figures onto the carpet and rocking quietly for a min-ute. Like this show we're putting on today, the Mercury cap-sule not much bigger than this rocking chair. How many zeroes for it alone? But there's no turning back now. Forget the press conference bullshit about cooperation with the Russians ("I must say that we strongly support any coopera-tive effort we could make on weather, prediction of storms, and all of the rest, and I hope it will lead to other areas of cooperation in space") — he threw down the gauntlet last May and that's it. To the moon and back by the end of '69. Christ, he thinks, pushing back his hair. When we haven't done it they'll come looking for me with I-told-you-so's. Well, they won't find me in the District of Columbia; I'll be up on the Cape, editing some little weekly, popping off in my own editorials every Saturday afternoon. A nice enough early retirement, if the kidneys let me live to enjoy it.

The disappointment passes off, as well it might on this day when the House, however parsimonious it may be feeling about other things, will approve, by a vote of 342–0, NASA's $3.67 billion authorization for fiscal year 1963. A jolt of the President's natural competitiveness kicks in like an antidote, and he rocks forward, gets on his feet and goes to the outer office, where the television's on.

"How's the flight going, Mrs. Lincoln?"

---

01 03 55 P
I am in VOX record only now. The time is 01 04 00 elapsed. I'm searching the star charts.

01 04 19 P
   The finish on the star chart is so shiny that — it's impossible to read because of reflection.
01 04 44.5 P
   I've got to turn white lights on, that's all.

Twenty-one-year-old Dave Marsh looks uncomprehendingly at the bar graph displayed on the glossy right-hand page of his economics textbook. Bored, he leans back in his chair, shuts his eyes and presses his fingertips together. His ears are filled by the noise of TV and mass conversation here in the Glenn Miller Ballroom at the University of Colorado in Boulder — alma mater of Rene and Scott Carpenter, as well as of the astronaut's parents and grandfather.

It's "Dead Week" on campus, the one before finals, but most students are giving up the day to watch the flight, and to watch themselves being watched. All of the networks have crews in Boulder, and Mrs. Florence Carpenter, the astronaut's mother, is supposed to have a press conference right here after Scott is plucked from the ocean early this afternoon. It's not yet 8 A.M. in Boulder, just east of the Rockies, but the room is already pretty full. A jock in a yachting cap walks around barefoot, wearing a white T-shirt with "Go Aurora 7" Magic-Markered on the front and "Go Scott Go" on the back.

Dave Marsh, eyes still closed, doesn't see him. "Spacey" is not a 1962 word, and if it were, it would mean something other than what it will, but vague Dave Marsh would probably accept the coming neologism as a fair-enough definition of himself. He's not interested in the flight — in fact, a week or so ago he was in the new Boulder Public Library and didn't walk ten feet out of his way to inspect the life-size mock-up of a Mercury capsule they had on display.

He didn't even know that Carpenter was from Boulder or UC until a couple of minutes ago when they mentioned it on the TV. A music major struggling through his required economics course, Dave can't get absorbed by any of this. For that matter, he's not really interested in music, or his girlfriend, or much else. He tends to drift off (or, in the parlance of a dozen years from now, "space out"); he likes to lie back in the practice cubicles of the music building, staring, holding colored Life Savers up to the fluorescent lights' radiance before sucking on them during one plotless reverie or another.

When the noise in the ballroom thwarts his attempt at a morning nap, Dave picks up yesterday's *Boulder Daily Camera* from the chair next to him and gets through the first paragraph of the story about the Continental Airlines crash before he shuts his eyes again.

Dave Marsh will spend the next twenty years pretty much uninterested in anything. He will drop out of the university this coming fall; reenroll a few years later to avoid the draft; join the Navy, to avoid the Army, a couple of years after that; spend about ten years in California, allowing, without complaint, six jobs and two marriages to fold underneath him, before, two weeks after his fortieth birthday in 1982, quite uncharacteristically inspired by some New Age books and tapes given him by an ex-girlfriend, he returns to Boulder. For the next several years he will have an apartment near the corner of 30th Street and Arapahoe Avenue, and each day on his walk to the Pearl Street pedestrian mall, where he works in a shop selling crystals and giving out his card ("Specializing in Visualization Therapy, Energy Alignment, Planetary Ascension and Post-Life Regression"), he will pass what will have been for twenty years Scott Carpenter (formerly Valverdan) Park. When a tourist asks him who Scott Carpenter was, he will hazard the guess that he was the brother of the anorectic singer who died.

01 05 14.5 P

Attitudes are of no concern to me whatsoever. I know I'm drifting freely. The moon crossed the window not too long ago.

---

01 11 10 P

Roger. I've been reading you for some time. I've tried to contact you on HF with no success.

"Pssst," whispers Kenny Kessler from the desk diagonally behind Gregory's.

Gregory ignores him.

"Pssst."

Kenny is sort of a friend, but he's also sort of a jerk, and Gregory is opposed to talking in class. They're supposed to be "working quietly" now, doing half an hour of long division carried to two decimal places, while Mrs. Linley works at her desk. She won't tell them yet whether this will count as a test. Gregory realizes that she is using "psychology." Because he knows this, and because he's good at arithmetic, he feels no pressure. He enjoys working the problems, even as the transistor radio continues to report the flight through his earphone.

$$88\overline{)296.000} \qquad = 3.36$$
$$\underline{264}$$
$$320$$
$$\underline{264}$$
$$560$$
$$\underline{528}$$
$$320$$
$$\underline{264}$$
$$56$$

It comes out right and it comes out neat. He in fact finds it beautiful, without knowing that the word can apply to something like this. One more problem to do, and then he will take the page from the cloth-covered loose-leaf notebook, snap its silver rings shut and "put his head down" — standard pacification procedure, and the signal to the teacher that you're finished.

Kenny Kessler, who has succeeded in copying three of the five problems Gregory has executed, is bored with straining his neck and decides on another method of getting his friend's attention. He pokes him in the upper arm with the pink eraser on his number 2 Mongol pencil.

"Quit it," says Gregory.

Kenny knows better than to expect active collaboration from Gregory, but he's bad at arithmetic, and tortured by sitting still, so he persists. He tears off a small strip of loose-leaf paper and makes a pellet-size note that he flicks onto Gregory's desk. "HOW'S CARPINTER?"

He is also bad at spelling. Great, thinks Gregory: now that Kenny's seen the earphone, he'll start pulling the cord and get us both into trouble, and he'll think he's being neat.

"He's okay," Gregory whispers, deciding on appeasement.

"What's he doing?" Kenny continues.

"Leave me alone," Gregory whispers.

"Come on," Kenny says back.

01 13 13.5 CC

Did you — could you comment on whether you are comfortable or not — would you . . . a 102 on body temperature.

01 13 21 P

No, I don't believe that's correct. My visor was open; it is now closed. I can't imagine I'm that hot. I'm quite comfortable, but sweating some.

Gregory looks to see if Mrs. Linley's noticing them. He rubs his eyes, acting casual, before whispering in Kenny's direction, "He's supposed to be eating something. Testing space food."

Kenny is silent, as if to consider the historic event, Carpenter's having become the first American to eat solid food in space, his meal (now badly crumbled) referred to by the Cap Com as a "midnight snack," since it was consumed five minutes ago in darkness over Asia.

Gregory, happy to be left in peace, goes back to his last arithmetic problem, until Kenny bursts out in a laugh that can be heard in the next room, and shouts, *"Greg, you mean his mom gave him lunch money this morning?"*

Shithead. Bastard. These are the worst words Gregory knows, and if they had time to come to his mind, he would find both of them inadequate retaliation for the embarrassment he's feeling.

"Shoosh, boys," says Mrs. Linley, not looking up from her work.

Gregory finishes off the last problem and, his blush subsided, he cradles his head in his forearms and lays it down on the desk. He is the second person in the class to finish. This new position is good, because it puts the earphone completely out of sight; but it also puts Kenny Kessler into his peripheral vision, and Kenny, aware of this, gets his attention one last time.

"Greg," he whispers. And Gregory sees him lifting his thimble-size plastic pencil sharpener in a parody of flight, as he makes a low whistle and then a sound-effects crash, bringing the pencil sharpener smack down onto the desk. "Mayday! Mayday!" he whispers.

"Kenny, that's enough," says Mrs. Linley.
Gregory closes his eyes.

01 14 16.5 P
Roger. I cannot confirm that the flight plan is completely
on schedule.

Joan Anderson Linley looks at her watch and says to herself, "Damn it." (A dozen years from now, in analogous difficulty, she will say, out loud, "Shit.") The results of the standardized tests she's working on were due in the principal's
office yesterday, and she feels guilty to be marking them
now, giving the students busywork on a day they're also
going to be losing an hour to the pageant rehearsal. But she
somehow never keeps on top of her lesson plan. She figures
she can in good conscience keep them at their arithmetic for
another five minutes, and she goes back to marking the tests,
putting the cut-out key over the pencil marks, so that the
wrong answers come up as blanks.

She gets to Gregory's. He scores high and she drops his
test into the folder with the card that lists his IQ as 138, his
height as 56 inches, his weight as 70 pounds; which checks
off that he is neither "Unkempt and Neglected?" nor from a
"Broken Home?"; which "Comments" that he is "A lovely
boy, very bright. A bit of a worrier"; and which lists MUrray
Hill 3-0250, the number of Lowndes Brothers, as one of two
numbers that should be dialed in case of emergency.

————————

01 15 02.5 CC
. . . queries, you can continue on with your observations.
Over.
01 15 05.5 P
Roger. Thanks, George, see you next time around.

01 15 10 CC
Okay, Scott. Good luck.

Mary Noonan goes to put a card of thumbtacks into a kitchen drawer and comes upon the section of Monday's *Times* with Martin Tolchin's article about passive men and domineering mothers. The paper is folded so that an ad for Scott paper products is on top, an ad meant to speak directly to her. Without taking the paper from the drawer she reads it:

> . . . she is the Golden Goddess of the market and the super-market. She is the autocrat of the breakfast table and the bridge table, mistress of bedroom and bathroom, living room and dining room, manager of the garage, head gardener, sole owner of the washing machine and dishwasher, the superin-tendent of banks and schools, chairman of the ironing board, and four-star general of her own troops. She is the Supreme Treasurer and Head Bursar.

Mary does not play bridge, does not have a dishwasher, will not drive on highways or serve on PTA committees and feeds her small family on the $25 a week Jim gives her each Friday night. The ad is really addressed to the ones Jim calls eager beavers, the ones you can find taking the Brownies to the zoo while their husbands are running Little League prac-tice, the couples who sell chances for the volunteer fire de-partment and organize dances for the golf-courseless country club. Jim will make a Dads' Club meeting up at the school about once a year, and last fall, while Ellen Herlihy was hav-ing her latest daughter, Mary served for two meetings, to Gregory's acute embarrassment, as a substitute den mother.

Part of Mary envies the energy of the town's Ellen Her-lihys, who staff committees and organize picnics and produce babies with the tireless regularity of Ethel Kennedy. But from Jim she has picked up a suspicion of do-gooders and social climbers that she finds handy in justifying a guilty desire to just stay home.

Pondering the ad, she wonders where, if she did all the things it mentioned, she would get the time to "bolster" Jim and save Gregory from passivity. She is, she realizes, full of doubts about her child this morning, and to calm them she does what she sometimes does — recites, in her head, the first line of Dr. Spock: "You know more than you think you do."

The telephone rings. It's her half-brother's wife, Judy, in Bay Ridge.

"Mary, I'm calling about the seventeenth. Will you come with us to see Papa?"

The seventeenth of June will be Father's Day. Papa is Mary's father, John Frazzi, who died in 1949 and whom Judy never even met.

"Judy, you probably shouldn't figure on us. I think Jim and Gregory will probably do something that day, maybe go to a ball game." Jim refers to Mary's half-sisters-in-law, Judy and Irene, as the Morbid Twins, two women who view the vast Calvary Cemetery in Queens as a civic amusement, like a beach, as well as an opportunity for demonstrating noble feelings of family solidarity. Having missed the rush to the true suburbs, left behind in the dull precincts of Brooklyn, they view Mary, with her one child, as someone overprivileged and probably no longer quite "regular" — a term they prize.

"But Mary, you missed Mother's Day, too."

"Jim's not much on cemeteries, Judy." Neither, in fact, is she, but to both her and Judy Jim's name carries more weight.

"Why? It's so pretty. You haven't seen it in ages. You know, it's Perpetual Care, Mary."

This is Judy's way of reminding Mary that she and her husband, Frank, selflessly pay the $7 a year that keeps Papa and Mama's grass clipped. Mary gets the message, but the words "Perpetual Care" also remind her of a brand name of hair coloring, something she used for the first time last month.

"I'll ask Jim."

"Well, we'll hope to see you. It would make everybody happy. Remember, Mary, we're blood."

Actually they're not, and after this primal invocation, Mary is resolved that her child will not spend Father's Day in a graveyard when he can spend it at Yankee Stadium with his father. If, that is, they've made up by then.

"I'll call you."

"Okay, Mary. Remember, I'm hoping."

Hanging up, Mary knows that what Judy is hoping is that the Noonans won't show, so that Judy and Irene will have a chance to shake their heads over this sad lack of devotion to Mama and Papa. Why, Mary wonders, waste hope on something so petty? When there will be so many other things one will need it for. And what *is* hope? She recalls the gist of the answer to question 62 in the Baltimore Catechism: "Hope is the virtue by which we firmly trust that God will give us eternal happiness and the means to obtain it."

She sits down at the kitchen table and looks out into her back yard.

----

01 18 51.5 P

All right. My — I am at 01 19 02. Have been several times completely disoriented. There, I have Cassiopeia directly in the window and am yawing around for the sunrise . . . photographs. The sky is quite light in the east.

Gregory has turned his cradled head so that it now faces the window. The late morning light is a bright pink behind his eyelids. He has, of course, forgotten the earphone. It's been made quite visible by his change of position, and Joan Linley, whose eyes keep moving from the standardized tests to her watch to the children in front of her, notices it and smiles. *A lovely boy, very bright.*

Scott Carpenter, whose disorientation is with respect to the earth, keeps using his hydrogen peroxide fuel to maneuver his sealed little cone, pitching and yawing, seeing stars first one way and then another, flying forward and then backward, but always in the same direction and at the same speed, the marvelous Mercury capsule tumbling and flying, like a tossed jack, at the same time. Only his fuel supply, not his wonder, is dropping.

01 22 03 P
   I have the fireflies. Hello, Guaymas.
01 22 18 P
   I have the particles. I was facing away from the sun at sunrise — and I did not see the particles — just — just yawing about — 180 degrees, I was able to pick up — at this. Stand by, I think I see more.
01 23 00 P
   Yes, there was one, random motions — some even appeared to be going ahead. There's one outside. Almost like a light snowflake particle caught in an eddy. They are not glowing with their own light at this time.
01 23 32 P
   It could be frost from a thruster.

He is on to something. The "fireflies" that John Glenn claimed to see in space, the little glowing things he reported to good-natured skepticism and teasing, perhaps they're coming from the capsule itself. Carpenter wants to tell the Mexican tracking station, but he's still five minutes out of range. So he just keeps recording his observations.

Gregory tightens his eyelids so that the pink light shatters into bright speckles. He makes them dance like a kaleidoscope's, squeezing tighter and brighter, until it starts happening again, the feeling that sent him out to the back yard and up into the tree an hour and a half ago; not fear this time, but a surge, as if he's being taken up, carried off, rising. He feels the way he used to when as a little boy he'd fall asleep on the floor, in front of the TV, and his father would pick him up and carry him upstairs to bed. He'd know he was rising and who was taking him, but be too sleepy either to cooperate or resist. Now he feels the same way, only he's rising much, much higher and faster, and he doesn't know who's taking him. He's being drawn away, carried off, but to where? By whom? To float free? Or to be held captive? He is flying somewhere, as fast as one of the Darling children holding on to Mary Martin, but he is not on wires and where he is going is someplace real, somewhere never seen by anyone he knows, and he's on the verge of being there, of seeing where he's being taken, when he feels himself dropping back, descending fast in an arc, as if on a playground swing, until suddenly he's back here in room 4, at his desk, eyes open, as if he's done nothing more than emerge from the Queens–Midtown Tunnel, back into the normal light, while sitting in the back seat of the Valiant, as he and his parents made a detour through Manhattan on the way home from Grandma Noonan's.

He has no idea where he was taken, but he knows two things: he didn't quite get there, but he was closer to it than he had been in the tree.

He isn't frightened, just shaky, as if he's stepped off the

rocket ride in Rye and is finding his feet, glad to be landed, if only temporarily.

Ol 24 11 P
The weightless condition is a blessing, nothing more, nothing less.

Ol 28 19 P
Roger. My body comfort is good. I am tracking now a very small particle, one isolated particle, about — there is another, very small, could be a light snowflake.

Walter J. Hammill's long regard of a light brown mote swimming in the shaft of light to the right of his cot is threatened with disruption by the passing sound of the guard's radio, which reports that "Boulder's own" Scott Carpenter is now roughly eighty-eight miles above the Pacific Ocean, a little west of Mexico.

The guard turns the corner, leaving Hammill, who is roughly one hundred miles south of Boulder, in Cañon City, Colorado, on death row of the Colorado State Penitentiary, to concentrate fully on the speck of dust. His left hand plays with his red hair while the index finger on his right, raised like an artist's thumb, tries for a second to block the mote. By the time he's lowered his finger, Hammill has lost sight of the mote; it's disappeared into a swirl of them. Weird, weightless things, he thinks, as he has so often; why don't they drop, like everything else, with the pull of gravity?

Tomorrow night, May 25, 1962, barring any unlikely last-minute deference to his continuing insistence upon his own insanity, Walter J. Hammill, former circus roustabout, will die, several minutes after the pellets are dropped, in the gas chamber within the walls of this building.

Now, 2,500 miles and two hours to the east, in Melwyn Park, Gregory Noonan, his math lesson nearly over, flicks a pink eraser shaving off his blond-wood desk and onto the linoleum.

Walter Hammill, bored, raises his hand once again, grabbing an intangible fistful of motes and squeezing them, thinking for a moment, as his fingernails press into his palm, of the skin of Lester G. Brown II of Denver, who, in 1958, when he was strangled by Walter J. Hammill, was eleven years old.

---

01 29 36 P

Mark, coastal passage coming over the — Baja.

01 29 41 CC

Good.

01 29 43 CC

How does it look?

01 29 46 P

Half covered with clouds, and — and the other half is dry. Will you pass on — this message for me, Gordo, to all the troops at Guaymas?

01 30 05 P

Hola, amigos, felicitaciones a Mexico y especialmente a mi amigos de Guaymas. Desde el espacio exterior, su pais esta cubierto con numbes — and — es — also — se muy bello. Aqui el tiempo esta muy bueno. Buena suerte desde Auror Siete.

01 30 33.5 CC

Roger, muchas gracias, amigo.

01 30 35.5 P
Ha ha, okay.

A moment after Scott Carpenter finishes laughing, his wife Rene hears of the Spanish greeting on the television in the rented house in Cocoa Beach, and laughs too, thinking this must be one of the little surprises he told her he'd inserted into the flight plan. When the tape of this transmission is played over CBS fifteen minutes from now, Cronkite will remind his viewers that they've just "heard the third language spoken from outer space."

In room 4 of the Melwyn Park School, Joan Linley rises from her desk. She's got two standardized tests to go, but she doesn't dare keep the children at their arithmetic another minute; even Susan Nelson, the dumbest kid in the room, poor thing, has her head down.

"All right, class," Mrs. Linley says, rising as briskly as she can. "We've only got a few minutes before we go to the gym for rehearsal —"

"*Yay!*" shout five or six of them. Isolated patches of clapping.

"— and before we go I want to make sure you're all set with your South America reports —"

"*Boo!*" shout the same five or six. Isolated patches of hissing.

"That's enough," says Mrs. Linley, trying for the least credible effect in her pedagogical repertoire, sternness. "Those reports are due Monday, and if you're still having trouble, I want you to talk to Mrs. O'Hara in the library before you leave for home today. All right? Now how many Bolivians do we have?"

Three hands.

"Good. Paraguayans?"

Another three hands. "Good. Any —"

The small black wall phone, more like an apartment-house intercom with a little round receiver, buzzes. Mrs. Linley walks over to it. "Excuse me a minute."

The susurrus begins.

She talks to Mr. Merlino, the custodian, who wants to know if he's got to clear away some chairs that are backstage, and whether or not she needs the door to an equipment room unlocked.

The whispers grow.

Joan Linley decides she'd better trot down to the auditorium/gymnasium herself, since Paul Merlino is the fussy type, what her dad would call a ballbreaker. Get on his bad side and she'll have to grovel every time she needs a strong arm to open a new jar of white paste.

"I'll be right down to see, Mr. Merlino." She hangs up the phone. "Children, I have to check on something in the auditorium. I'll be *right* back, and in the meantime I want you to take out your Dittoed scripts and look them over so you'll be ready for rehearsal."

She exits room 4 and the whispers amplify into loud chatter that, after fifteen seconds, becomes an orgy of insults.

"Cootie head," among the most popular since an alarming outbreak of head lice in the splendidly hygienic school last spring, is the first to be launched, from Bobby Nolan to Billy Ronan.

Volume rises; utterance accelerates; targets blur; meaning disappears.

"Pirate's delight."

"So funny I forgot to laugh."

"Carpenter's dream."

"Did you have polio?" "No." "How come your third leg's so short?"

"Made you look, made you look . . ."

"Is."

"Not."

Gregory has not caught any fire but, as if on automatic, he finds himself saying, in response to no one and nothing in particular, just looking out the window, "I know you are, but what am I?"

---

01 32 02 P
No, I'll have to get in a better attitude for you first, Gus. It'll mean nothing this way, I mean Coop.

A real live one here, thinks Lucille Rosen, fingering the chain from which her harlequin eyeglasses hang.

Across her desk at the Good Deal Agency, 136 West 42nd Street, sits Waldy Munoz, tugging on his hair, wiggling his foot, feeling shy.

Lucille, misreading shyness for sullenness, asks, "So which is it, cookie?"

Waldy hands her the ad he clipped from the *Times*, the one for an elevator operator at $67 a week.

"We don't speak?" Lucille asks, sorry she's said it even before she sees Waldy's startled look. As usual, she thinks, I've got it wrong. This is a nice boy. Her inability to read the young is what a year ago drove Lucille out of high school teaching in the Bronx and persuaded her to accept her brother's offer of a job here.

"Okay," she says, filling out a slip. "It's right off Gramercy Park. Do you know where Gramercy Park is?"

"I can find it," Waldy says, relieved, since he does not know where Gramercy Park is, to see the hotel is on a numbered street.

"Of course you can," says Lucille, sounding sarcastic when she meant to sound encouraging. She wishes she could start over with this boy. She looks at him and tries to figure him out. "Honey, do you really want this job?" This comes out right. Sincere. Concerned.

"Sure," says Waldy.

"Okay," says Lucille, pushing back her dyed red hair. "Then do me a favor. Smile when you meet Mr. Mullins. He's the gentleman you're to ask for."

"Okay," says Waldy, actually smiling at Lucille.

"Tell him to call me, and you check back in person or by phone this afternoon."

"Thanks," says Waldy.

"Don't mention it," says Lucille, who after ten months here is still amazed to hear human beings say thank you after she's given them instructions — another reason she continues to be glad she left DeWitt Clinton High School.

Waldy crosses Fifth Avenue at 42nd Street, passing the sidewalk stand of Project Mercury sweatshirts and heading south, intent on saving fifteen cents by walking. In a moment or two he is passing under the showroom windows of the Lowndes Brothers Glove Co. He looks up at the Empire State Building and his heart sinks. He remembers what Ramón was saying this morning at breakfast and thinks he doesn't want this job after all. *You want to go up, up, up!* He wonders if he'd keep walking if his mother didn't have bills, and if he didn't have a girlfriend.

01 33 26.5 P
Roger. The gyros are caged.

The *Aurora 7*, flying eastward, ready to begin its second ring around the planet, comes into contact with the Cape Canaveral tracking station. A message from Gus Grissom comes over the capsule's radio:

01 33 41 CC
Aurora 7, this is Cape Cap Com on emergency voice.

ORBIT 2

No, no emergency. Just a test.

01 33 44 P
    Roger, Cape. Loud and clear. How me?
01 33 48 CC
    Loud and clear. I'm going back to HF/UHF.

A minute later Carpenter tells Gus Grissom his "status is good"; his only problem is being a "little ahead on fuel consumption."

---

01 35 13.5 CC
    And after the IOS voice has dropped, will use Zanzibar in that area.
01 35 20 P
    Roger. I heard IOS calling, but I couldn't raise him.

At 10:16 A.M., Tommy Shanahan, after wandering around a not-yet-very-drug-ridden Bryant Park, sits in the periodicals room of the New York Public Library, copying out a passage from the winter 1961–62 issue of *Worldvision*, the quarterly magazine of the Society for the Propagation of the Faith. It is not from Bishop Sheen's ferocious editorial — "There is little or no persecution of Buddhism, Moslemism or Holy Rollerism. These are not sufficiently Divine to evoke the prejudice and hatred of the forces of Satan" — but from a much gentler production, an article by Sister Pientia Selhorst, a teacher in South Africa, about "Art and the Spreading of the Gospel."

> We know of the beauty and strength of traditional African art, as it was produced most beautifully in Central Africa. But at present all Africa is affected by the impact of technical civilization. The African desires it, and we must not withhold it from him. Probably this civilizing process will destroy for the time being something of the spiritual strength that he possessed in his earlier history. But there is also reason to believe that the naïve, child-like trend of his genius will enable him to better withstand the dangerous impact. The unproblematical work of my students makes me believe this. Africa and Europe together seem to have a future. Maybe Africa will save Europe and all it stands for. European contemporary art with its love of the primitive illustrates this. Europe knows that it needs Africa.

Tommy rereads what he's copied down in his neat script, its slight effeminacy exaggerated by the Peacock Blue ink he uses in his cartridge pen. Sister Pientia's argument appeals to the pro–Third Worldish sentiments he's been feeling this morning. "Third World" is not a 1962 term, but he's got the spirit of the thing, and so, in a small way, does she: maybe the Africans can teach *us* a thing or two. Tommy has decided that this will be the ticket for his sermon. Of course, she makes it sound as if they'll teach us style after we've given them substance — that is, the Truth of Christianity. After we've excited them with tales of miracles, they'll start depicting them in their knowing primitive ways. It's still a bit arrogant, if you think about it. (And will the Africans really keep buying these worn-out tales of loaves and fishes and of Lazarus coming forth? Won't they really need to see some fresh miracles for their own eyes? Couldn't the convertible natives of Zanzibar do with a present-day Lazarus, someone they know, being raised from the dead, right in their midst, on May 24, 1962?) Never mind for now. Time is running short — his mass is in less than two hours — and Tommy has decided that Sister Pientia's article will be his text.

Before putting his Peacock Blue notes into his black briefcase, he notices a young man about his own age sitting farther down the table and reading *Business Week*. (On the front page of the May 26, 1962, issue: "How do you sell the Negro market?" — turn to page 76.) This guy is not exactly his idea of a stockbroker. He's got a square jaw and big shoulders that make his Brooks Brothers jacket a little tighter than it's supposed to be, but Tommy's not complaining, just staring at the handsome face (Irish and German?) under the dark brown Vitalisized hair.

Staring so hard that the guy looks up and catches him at it and flashes him back a brief, confident grin. Tommy dives back down to Sister Pientia. He tugs at his cardboard collar, under which he is slightly warm. The guy is probably used to being stared at, Tommy thinks, but *he's* not used to being caught doing the staring. It's time to get out of here.

His tightly laced black-leather shoes squeak down the marble corridor toward the Fifth Avenue exit. He really doesn't know what he's supposed to do with this free-floating, seems-to-land-anywhere lust. And there's no pretending it's anything else. As for just saying a couple of Hail Marys or making a furtive breast-beating or two, the hell with that; it won't solve the problem, and Tommy is getting sick of pretending it will.

He sits down for a minute on the sunshine-covered marble steps outside, the dried pigeon droppings gleaming beside his black shoes. He watches a bus go by; watches a man get up from his desk near a window on the sixth floor of the Rogers Peet Building; glances at the marble rumps of Patience and Fortitude, the two lions; gazes southward at the blocks leading toward the Empire State Building. The Fifth Avenue flux is taking his mind off the problem. It's more effective behavior than Hail Marys, which are, in any case, always embarrassing to say with half an erection.

"You don't want to work either?"

He turns to his right. It's a girl, a pretty one, in a straw hat and a blue skirt that spreads out beneath her like a cape. She makes him think of Audrey Hepburn in *Breakfast at Tiffany's*, which he went to see a few weeks ago. (Father Francis, upon hearing of this, had raised an eyebrow. Like a seminarian, Tommy had had to point out that the Legion of Decency rated it A-3: morally unobjectionable for adults.)

"I guess not," Tommy finally replies, "but I ought to be. I have to write a sermon."

"Oh." The girl laughs. "You're a priest. I didn't even notice the collar."

Tommy, at a loss for what to say next, looks at his black shoelaces.

"Do you really write a new one for every mass?" she asks. "I thought priests were like professors, that they just brought their old yellowed notes up to the lectern. Or, I guess I should say the pulpit. I'm a student."

"Oh," says Tommy, looking at her white teeth and the shiny hair under her hat.

"Art history," she says. "Up at Barnard. I'm a senior."

"That's funny," says Tommy, emboldened by a brainstorm.

"I was just reading about art. An article by a nun who uses it to teach Africans about Christianity. Although she really seems to think they have just as much to teach us." He quickly decides this is inane, and the last thing he wants to do is talk about his vocation, so before she can even say uh-huh, he changes the subject and asks, "It's a lovely day, isn't it?"

"It certainly is," she says. "My name's Maria. What's yours?"

"Tommy Shanahan."

"Well, it's nice to meet you, Father Tommy Shanahan." She reaches out to shake his hand and Tommy takes this completely unexpected offering.

But as soon as he does she withdraws it and stands up in a lively, elegant motion, her blue skirt contracting as if it were a set of wings. "I'll bet you that those Africans could teach us to stay outdoors on a day like today. But I've got to spend the whole thing working up in the reading room. I've got a big exam tomorrow morning. So goodbye, Father Tommy Shanahan, and give a good sermon." She's cantering up the steps, the blue skirt flouncing like a laugh, before he realizes that she's tousled his hair.

She's touched him, and he would like to touch her, and he's so ecstatic and crushed and confused that he forces himself to get up from the steps immediately and start back to St. Agnes's. He'll never see her again, he thinks. She'll probably run into the stockbroker later in the day. They'll make a date. A year from now he'll be marrying the two of them. An image of them both naked, making love, comes into his mind.

Has he ever felt such an exile? At the corner of Fifth and 42nd he does say a Hail Mary, hoping that the Blessed Mother will just get him through the lunchtime mass, after which he can go up to his room in the rectory and stay under the covers. "Holy Mary, Mother of God, Holy Mary, Mother of God." He repeats the phrase as he walks east, until it changes in his head and he's saying, then silently singing, something else. "Maria, I've just met a girl named Maria" (*West Side Story*, also rated A-3).

The afternoon! He won't spend it in the rectory, under the covers. He'll go back to the reading room. He'll find her. He'll hold her hand. Before the day is over he'll find out.

Say it soft and it's almost like praying.

Ol 36 58 CC
  Roger. I'm going to give you a Z cal.
Ol 37 00.5 P
  Roger.
Ol 37 07 CC
  Okay. I'm going to give you an R cal.
Ol 37 10 P
  Be my guest.

Just moving along up First Avenue, on the right side of the street, between 14th and 15th, at the southern tip of Stuy Town. Then bing, Eddie Rodwicki has her, way across First, in the corner of his eye. Tall, skinny, blond hair, long and straight, black sweater, black skirt: beatnikky. In a hurry. Thinking of making a dash for it in front of the cars moving north. Eddie shouts out his window. "Wait for the light. You'll live longer." He pulls to a stop at the eastern curb and waits for her, looking at the brick walls and green window trim of Stuy Town, square block after square block of it, not so different from stuff going up in his own part of Queens. Once, a couple of years ago, when he was settling his late mother's tax bill in a midtown skyscraper, he'd looked down through the window near the elevator bank and seen this adobe village, looking just like a model one of his kids had made for school, and wondered what the hell it was until he realized it was Stuy Town. Something a lot lower and flatter than most of what was then in his view. You'd never know that here, though, waiting at the curb, looking across and up at it. It's all a matter of perspective.

A song by Peter, Paul and Mary trails off the radio, WMCA, and the DJ comes back on just as Eddie's fare, who looks a little like Mary, gets in the cab: "Well, Good Guys, spaceman Scott Carpenter's gone a lot farther than 'Five Hundred Miles' this morning. He's already done about twenty thousand as he heads into his second orbit . . ."

"Eee, Eee, Eh," the girl says, ignoring the radio, sighing with relief to be in the cab.

"Eee say wha?" asks Eddie. Is she French or what?

"Sorry," she says in her foreign accent. "Eenternasyonol Eensteetute of Edoocation."

"Second Avenue. Up around Forty-third, right?"

"Right," she says, rolling the r and cracking a smile into Eddie's rearview.

And they're off up First Avenue, past the loonies in Bellevue, past the tunnel, up to Tudor City and then left, just below the UN, where the slaughterhouses used to be.

"Right *here*," says the girl, obviously pleased with Eddie's speed. She's smiling again as she delves into her purse. She's younger than Eddie would have guessed when he spotted her, probably a student living in a crummy walk-up across from all the families in their many rooms in Stuy Town.

"I hope I have the change," she says, and Eddie would like to remind her that exact change isn't exactly the idea, until he looks again at his meter and sees that the fare is an even dollar. "Slow down, doll," he says, when he notices she's trying to find a tip to go with the bill in her left hand. "What's the rush, anyway? What's a pretty girl on a nice spring morning got to be doing?"

She laughs and rolls her eyes in a way that's got some

oomph, some experience — not the way, kind of shy, an American girl the same age would do it. "Visa problems," she says. "I either get stamped the paper saying I am still a student or, what you say, bye-bye. Here. I've got." She hands him $1.35 and scoots. She waves at Eddie and he thinks, as he does with maybe one fare in two hundred, how peculiar it is he'll never see her again. There are eight million stories in the naked city, and she was his eleventh one today. And now she's gone to get her passport straight. Weird that you should need a passport at all in this day and age, when this guy over their heads is sailing over fifty different countries every hour.

Time for number twelve, he thinks, marking his time sheet and pushing down the stick shift in two quick motions. Where to? He decides to head up and over to Sutton, find some rich dame who wants to go shopping. He's actually got more freedom than Carpenter. His flight plan's his own, and who knows what he'll run into today?

———————

01 39 17 CC

Aurora 7, did the balloon inflate?

01 39 19 P

The balloon is partially inflated. It's not tight. I've lost it at this moment. Wait one, I'll give you a better reading shortly.

01 39 50 P

There is an oscillation beginning.

01 39 54.5 CC

There is an oscillation in the balloon?

01 39 56.5 P

Yes.

01 40 11 P

The line is still not taut. I have some pictures of the line just waving out in back. I would say we have about a one-

cycle-per-minute oscillation. It's both in pitch and yaw.
01 40 38.5 CC

How many cycles per minute?
01 40 40 P

One cycle per minute, or maybe 1 cycle in a minute and a
half.
01 41 01 P

The moon is just above the horizon at this time.
01 41 17 P

I have a picture of the balloon.
01 41 25 CC

Aurora 7, Cap Com. Repeat your last message.
01 41 28.5 P

Roger. I've got a washer to put away.

Gregory's communications are running about three minutes behind Scott's. He hears news of the balloon's deploy-
ment through the wire running up his shirt as Mrs. Linley
leads the class through the peach-colored tile corridor between room 4 and, just around the corner, the audi/gym.

Five months later she will lead another class of fifth graders into this corridor and tell them to keep very still, sit down
against the peach-colored tiles and put their coats over their
heads. She will keep them still until the principal calls "Un-
cover" and the drill is over.

At 10:27 A.M. on May 24, 1962, as she escorts Gregory and
this year's fifth graders, a young man with blond hair and fair
skin, a boy really, far away from his parents and sister in
Lvov, and unaware that the Americans have a man in space
this morning, lifts his arm and wipes the sweat from his sun-
reddened forehead before giving his wrench another turn,
thereby tightening a bolt on the frame of a metal hut he is
helping to assemble at San Cristóbal, on the northwest coast
of Cuba.

This summer San Cristóbal will be deemed a good place to

site Soviet MRBMs, whose range of 1,100 nautical miles can take them over and beyond Melwyn Park, New York.

Gregory knows nothing about the washer loose in Scott's capsule. The radio reporter is only making a confused explanation of the balloon's status.

The two lines of students, girl-boy-girl-boy, arrive at the audi/gym and mount the steps to the stage after being told by Mrs. Linley to watch out they don't scuff the thickly waxed floors, on which tomorrow they'll be playing dodgeball.

But for now the big room is a theater, because Mrs. Linley's class is going into a forty-five-minute rehearsal of "Dancing Through the Ages," the pageant they will present to the rest of the school and every cast member's mother a week from today.

01 47 18 P

I'm taping now the fuel quantity warning lights in preparation for the dark side. I think also excess cabin water I'll tape. It's not a satisfactory lighting arrangement to . . .

Gregory crouches in the dark wings off stage right as his friend Gary Jackson mimes the movements of a fiddler to a phonograph record of square-dance music. The first group of eight students are practicing what they'll do next week in front of friends and moms. Last spring Gregory had been particularly affecting as Kasim, when the fourth grade put on its version of *Ali Baba and the Forty Thieves*. But he can take little interest in this pageant idea Mrs. Linley has come up with: five very American performances, from this frontier square dance to the hula (newly popular since Hawaii came into the Union). Without his quite knowing it, Gregory's taste runs to neat, climactic stories. There's none of that here, and there's an almost communistic quality to the way this year, in marked distinction from *Ali Baba*, everyone will be onstage for almost exactly the same amount of time. Not much chance for anyone to shine in this thing.

As he sits in the dark, waiting for his number, he regards the lights above the dancers: hot, bright circles of red, yellow, blue — the primary colors. His friend Ricky, who is an audio-visual room captain, is getting to work the board, flipping switches on and off just like Scott must be doing in space.

What has gone wrong with the balloon? Gregory wonders. He is out of radio contact, having ditched his transistor behind Ricky's control panel. If Marlene Milligan, whom he's sitting next to, sees the cord running out of his shirt and into his ear, she will either tell or just torment him with threats to, and he hates Marlene Milligan, who is fat and nearly as smart as he is. In any case, he wouldn't be able to dance with the radio inside his shirt.

The square dancers are bad. Mrs. Linley has to keep stopping and correcting and starting them. He can't see why there has to be, of all dances, a stupid square dance in this stupid pageant (not even a play), when just about everyone in school from third grade on up has a couple of weeks of square dancing each year in gym.

A heavenly break: Mrs. Linley approaches.

"Gregory, will you take this note out to Mr. Danaher on the playground?"

"Yes ma'am."

He is up in a flash, freed by this small anointing that excites envy in the dozen unchosen childish hearts forced to witness it. He bounds down the steps from stage right, ostentatiously, and races across the waxed floor to the back of the audi/gym, liking the sound of his sneakers on the shiny strips of wood, and badly miming a lay-up before switching sports fantasies and running, literally, to daylight. In this case, out the fire door and onto the sunny playground.

Mr. Danaher is the handsome gym teacher, and if Mrs. Linley weren't married, Gregory would be wondering if this is a love note he is carrying, something to set up an assignation after the 3:30 bell rings. But Mrs. Linley is married, so that is impossible, and because Gregory is a nice (and prudent) boy, he doesn't open the note.

He hands it to Mr. Danaher, who is supervising a softball game on the field beyond the chain-link fence. "Thanks, Gregory," he says before blowing his whistle over something going on in right field. "Right," says Gregory, nodding as butchly as he can and trying to trot off with the insouciance of Mickey Mantle. Like Scott Carpenter, Mr. Danaher is another order of being, a titan, unchallengeable, something one hardly dare aspire toward. Gregory hopes he's done a good job delivering the note.

Back at the fire door he pauses and looks up into the golden-blue sky. The American flag, visible above the school roof, puts a patch of red and more blue into it. Primary colors. He imagines he can see Scott, a black metal speck, racing across, though he knows that isn't so. The capsule is somewhere between the Canary Islands and Nigeria now. He wonders again what's wrong with the balloon, and wonders what was in Mrs. Linley's note. Last fall the whole class had launched notes tucked in little plastic pill bottles and tied to the end of helium balloons. It was an experiment to help them learn about distances and weather, but what they really all wanted was the answers to their messages. No one in the class ever got an answer, even though each note contained the sender's address. All day long after the launching — thirty balloons in primary colors leaving the playground and soaring past the flag — Gregory continued to track what he calculated should be his balloon's progress. He pored over a map in his bedroom with a pencil and a protractor. In the middle of the evening his father came in to say hi, and Gregory reported that the balloon could reliably be estimated to be traveling over Newfoundland.

In fact, it went down, with the rest of them, over Long Island Sound, but Gregory never knew that.

---

01 49 40.5 P
> Roger, I did observe haze layers but not the ones that were separated from the horizon that we expected, and that John reported. I'll keep a sharp lookout next time and try to see them after sunset. On the light side there is nothing more than the bright, iridescent blue layer, which separates the actual horizon from the deep black of space. Over.

01 50 15.5 CC
> Aurora 7, you are fading rapidly. You are fading. Mercury Control Center is worried about your auto fuel and manual fuel consumption. They recommend that you try to conserve your fuel.

01 50 28.5 P
> Roger. Tell them I am concerned also. I will try and conserve fuel.

Sitting on the platform under the hot sun, the President checks the cards holding the brief speech he will get up to deliver in another minute, after the rabbi and the two other clergymen are through:

> No monument, no memorial, no statue would please him half so much, I believe, as to have his name preserved here in this fashion on Capitol Hill. The Congress was his life, the House was his home, and he not only served it far longer than any who preceded him but with distinction and wisdom as well.

This should really be Lyndon's show, the President thinks, as he looks over these remarks in his lap, ones with which he'll pay tribute to Sam Rayburn. When he's through speaking he'll take a silver trowel and apply mortar to the cornerstone of this office building they're naming for Lyndon's "other daddy."

This is pretty poor stuff, he thinks, wondering who in the White House churned out this speech for him and why they couldn't have done better. The white index card blazes in the sunlight, but the words are as dull as can be. How could the writer have failed to make some reference linking the capsule flying above them in space right now to the time capsule that's going into the cornerstone? If he'd written the speech himself, he'd have done something good with that.

Well, he thinks, looking down at the card again, the Congress *was* Rayburn's life, so I suppose this is all right. It could have been my life, too. But now that I've left the Hill there's probably no way I'll ever persuade myself to come back up here. He thinks, as he did earlier this morning, of the newspaper up on the Cape. If he ever does that, he'll bang out better stuff for it than what he's got here in his hand.

What, he wonders, will be *his* monument? If he leaves office in '69 he'll be just fifty-one. Suppose everything — back and kidneys — holds out for another thirty-five years? It'll be past the year 2000. They'll have forgotten all about him down here. He'll probably have to settle for some Kennedy Boulevard in Brookline.

Amused at this thought, he waits for his cue to take the lectern. Thoughts of prose and immortality give way to what's been most on his mind this morning: money. "John," he whispers to the Speaker of the House, just before he gets up from his chair. "How much is this building costing us?"

"Seventy million dollars, Mr. President," replies Speaker McCormack.

"When will they have it finished?"

"August of 'sixty-four. Or so they say."

---

01 51 56.5 CC
  Aurora 7, do you have anything to report on your balloon test? Over.
01 52 02.5 P
  Roger. The balloon is oscillating through an arc of about 100 degrees.

Carpenter looks out the capsule window and sees a bright blue band of color shining between the horizon and absolute blackness. The balloon drifts in and out of his sight.

"Gregory!" Mrs. Linley's voice travels down the audi/gym and through the fire door, which Gregory holds open, looking up at the sky. "Time for the minuet!"

One hundred years ago this morning, on Hospital Hill, just north of Richmond, a ten-year-old boy gazes upward at a huge balloon, which is fully inflated but covered with a lacy cord of strings. He can see the trees to which the balloon, hovering at three hundred feet, is tethered. The huge silken globe seems to breathe, puffing a bit in, a bit out. The man in the basket below it surveys what is below that; he can see as far as fifteen miles through his binoculars.

"Damn that aeronaut!" whispers the boy in disgust.

The boy has come, with a few other early arrivals, to watch whatever action the day may bring. In a few days, if General McClellan can ever get the Army of the Potomac to move, the final battle for the city will take place. Brigadier General Fitz John Porter's men are at Mechanicsville, just six miles to the northeast, and Major General Erasmus Keyes's IV Corps are no farther away, at Seven Pines. They're so close they're said to set their watches by the chimes coming from Richmond's church steeples.

His city thus threatened, the boy glares again, in patriotic anger, at the distant Yankee aeronaut so calmly surveying the Confederate positions. Why, the boy wonders, is there no Confederate balloon? Why is the South behind? Why doesn't she have a man like Thaddeus Lowe, whose horse-drawn gas generators follow the Union army and feed the balloons?

And why, the boy wonders, not for the first time, can't he join Stonewall Jackson's army down below? It just isn't true that he's too young. As he's told his mother repeatedly, that Yankee drummer boy at Shiloh last year, Johnny Clem — he was no more than nine. I ought to be down there, the boy thinks, doing what drummer boys do after the dawn breaks: carrying water, selling cakes. And being ready to pick up a gun if that suddenly needs doing.

He gives another frustrated look toward the Yankee aeronaut, who is beginning his descent, the morning's intelligence having been gathered. The balloon twists as it slowly drops, and in the dawn's light the boy, for the first time, can make out the letters of its name: INTREPID.

Gregory takes hold of Marlene Milligan's hand — God, she's fat enough to be Mary Todd Lincoln — and they form a steeple with their raised arms. Lucky Gary gets to do this with Susan Riordan, who's pretty and red-haired and very nice, too, but too tall to partner Gregory. Marlene's pudgy hand is unbearably clammy as he waits for the strains of the strings to come from the phonograph.

The record starts, and soon he and Gary and Marlene and Susan and the two other couples are bowing, pacing, cutting sharp corners, swishing and preening like antebellum pros. But when they do this next week, it will be in Civil War costumes, Gregory's a scarlet sash and smart blue Union tunic fashioned from his blue-serge First Communion suit, which, to his mortification, still more or less fits him three years later. Gary Jackson and Kenny Kessler will be in Confederate gray, and although this makes no sense (what would Yankees and rebels be doing dancing with one another when the Civil War is going on?), and although he has not failed to point this out to Mrs. Linley, the number has not been changed, Mrs. Linley pointing out something about historical license and how it's more colorful this way.

Gregory, who is still a great believer in right and wrong, is troubled by this notion of historical license, which Mrs. Linley, smelling faintly of lilacs, patiently explained to him one afternoon last week as he walked her to her car. "Oxymoronic" is not a word children at the Melwyn Park School will get around to for some years — and then only the "college-bound" ones studying for SATs — but without knowing the word, that's what Gregory thinks "historical license" is. History is history. If you play with it, it is no longer true. Any tampering could make the world veer off course, send it into the wrong solar orbit, keep it from getting where it's supposed to be going, which eventually, Gregory dimly supposes, is back into the palm of God — a small sphere returning, like a baseball, to the pitcher.

"All right. That was good. But let's try the first steps once again," Mrs. Linley calls up to the stage.

The other thing that bothers Gregory about this part of the pageant is the idea that the Confederates should be able to take any part in it at all. Here next week will be Gary and Kenny, bowing and cutting corners just like him and Alan Weinstein, the other Yankee, made somehow equal, almost just as *right*, by their presence. Does history, just because it goes on for so long, gradually make everyone just as right or wrong as everyone else? This is not something Gregory's Catholic mind (albeit instructed in the faith only on Wednesday afternoons) will willingly permit. The Confederates had been wrong; they had kept slaves. And the price for moral incorrectness, in Gregory's mind, is root-and-branch extirpation. The way it will probably, eventually, have to be with the Russians.

The question of what is lately, on the fifteen-minute evening news, being called civil rights bothers Gregory, infected as it is by ambiguity, the element that keeps life from being as clean as science, as peaceful as space. In this case the ambiguity comes from Gregory's own heart. He knows that civil rights are right — President Kennedy has more or less said so — but can Gregory really say he feels comfortable with the dozen or so Negroes who come to Melwyn Park School because of a districting anomaly? Can he imagine touching Bernice Williams's hair without wincing? Can he imagine James White becoming an astronaut the same way he can imagine himself or Gary or Ricky becoming one?

Can he, he wonders, as he cuts a corner and at last gets to release Marlene Milligan's fat, sweaty hand, imagine Scott Carpenter being . . . a Negro? He knows in his heart of hearts (a favorite phrase of his mother's) that he cannot.

And then there is the problem of his father, who doesn't seem to add up on this whole question. He says the most contemptuous things about the Freedom Riders — enough to make Gregory dread their watching together certain portions of the news. And yet when he caught Gregory, a year or so ago in the back yard, trying out the word "nigger" — saying it with Ricky, with the same thrilling giggle they experienced when first uttering the word "fuck," a gleeful flirtation with evil — he smacked him across the face and sent Ricky home.

Did his father love him?

01 52 40 P

It also oscillates in and out. Sometimes the line is tight and other times it is not.

They go through another repetition of the first part of the dance. Susan Riordan and Gary Jackson aren't quite getting it.

01 55 08.5 P

... I expended my extra fuel in trying to orient after the night side. I think this is due to conflicting requirements of the flight plan. I should have taken time to orient and then work with other items. I think that by remaining in automatic, I can keep — stop this excessive fuel consumption.

"Okay, better. Now switch partners and move to the right," orders Mrs. Linley. Gregory is beginning to sweat under the red, yellow and blue lights, and thinks about how hot it will be next week in his Communion suit/tunic.

01 57 38.5 CC

Are you perspiring any?

01 57 41.5 P

Slightly, on my forehead.

The record comes to a stop when Barbara Farlino trips over the cord and accidentally pulls the plug. Gregory uses this as an excuse once more to extricate his hand from Marlene Milligan's. During the delay his mind wanders back to the question of the likelihood that James White, who sits two desks in front of him, will get the chance to be an astronaut.

01 59 05 CC

Roger, Aurora 7. Would you care to send a greeting to the people of Nigeria?

01 59 09 P

Roger, please send my greetings and best wishes of me and my countrymen to all Africans. Over.

01 59 21 CC

Roger. Thank you very much. I'm sure it will be appreciated.

Gary Jackson, who is really sort of a spaz, just isn't getting it. He wheels around in the wrong direction and bangs into Gregory's pocket, crushing the chocolate-chip cookie wrapped in wax paper earlier that morning by Mary Noonan.

02 02 43.5 P

At this time, oh-oh, this doggone food bag is a problem.

02 03 00 P

Actually, the food bag is not a problem, the food inside it is. It's crumbled. I dare not open the bag for fear the crumbs will get all through the capsule.

"All right, that's enough. Charleston people, onstage."

Gregory, relieved, wanders away from Marlene Milligan, into the darkness of stage left, and sits down.

02 03 43 P

Things are very quiet.

––––––––

CBS cuts to Boulder, and reporter Murray Fromson comes on. "Walter, as we've been able to determine, Scott Carpenter's been having some heating problems up in orbit, and with us is a man who's taught him something about heat transfer, Professor Ben Spurlock of the University of Colorado. Professor, exactly what is heat transfer, and what did Scott learn from you?"

Professor Spurlock, a handsome, silver-haired man in a plaid blazer, answers shyly, "I don't know. He failed his course in heat transfer. Let's put it that way. So I couldn't tell you how much he learned."

An audience of boys wearing glasses, ties and pocket protectors starts laughing.

Fromson persists: "How is he applying the principles that you tried to teach him, at least, up there in orbit today?"

Professor Spurlock answers, "I'm sure he's right on the hot seat." Embarrassed, he attempts to clarify his previous remark: "But Scott never failed his course. He just didn't come — show up — for the final examination."

----

02 07 29.5 CC
   Roger, Aurora 7. That's a hard one to pronounce, anything that we can do for you . . .
02 07 38 P
   Negative. I think everything is going quite well.
02 07 41.5 CC
   Roger, we'll be waiting. Out.
02 07 43.5 P
   Roger. See you next time.

The young man lies contentedly on the hotel bed, falling into a nap, though he can still see his wife across the room, swaddling their baby, Russian style. "In a few weeks, you'll be able to use diapers," he tells her. "Safety pins aren't hard to come by in America." She smiles, he can see. She's been smiling all day, bug-eyed over the embassy secretaries with their bouffant hairdos and swanky American shoes. She's cheerful now, he thinks, closing his eyes, and he's glad of it, remembering how sad and confused she was the other night as they got on the train and said goodbye to Minsk.

He rolls over, pleased with himself and the comfort of the beds in the Hotel Ostankino, here on the edge of Moscow. He's done it; once again, he's made them give him what he wants. Back in '59 he'd gotten the Soviets to let him stay, and now that he wants to go home he's gotten permission to do that, too; made the Americans give him back the passport he flung at them two and a half years ago. And that's not all, he thinks, rolling over and adding up his victories: he's gotten a visa for his wife, too — something all their Russian friends said he'd never manage. Ten days from now they'll be on a train for Holland, and after that on a boat to the States. The American embassy wants to float him a loan, but he's pretty certain, if he pushes hard enough, that he'll get them to pay for it flat out. He'll just hold his ground. And if it means filling out more forms and waiting in more offices, like they did today, well, it's easier than being back in the radio factory in Minsk, whose dull exertions are now falling away from him. What made the Soviets stick him with a loser's job like that in the first place? He was a defector, after all, a prize catch. Trust the party bureaucrats not to make the most of him.

It doesn't matter. Not now that it's settled — now that those papers are signed and dated May 24, 1962, and sitting on the officer's desk back at the embassy on the Sadovoya Ring. When he's back in the United States, he'll give them all something to think about.

Right now he recollects his triumph late this afternoon, just before closing time, and the funny business he'd witnessed of a secretary coming into the office of her boss — the officer who was interviewing him — with a piece of teletype.

"Well, he's up and away," she'd said, before returning her eyes to the sheet in her hand and asking, "Which does he call himself? Malcolm or Scott?"

"Either one," the officer had replied. "So long as it's not Yuri."

They'd both laughed at that, and she left the room. The young man, whose fantasies run toward espionage, had wondered who this Malcolm aka Scott aka Yuri might be. Some CIA operative under embassy cover?

"Alka," his wife calls out in Russian, "take your shoes off before you fall asleep."

Alka. What *he's* called. Over here. Alka or Alik. But when they're home, he realizes, a bit annoyed, only Marina will be calling him that. With everyone else he'll be back to being just plain Lee Oswald.

----

02 15 11.5 P
   Well, I have — I am in record only, and I am getting warm now.
02 15 34 P
   Don't know what to do with the cabin.
02 15 45 P
   I'll turn it up and see what happens.

"My, what a lovely, delicate-lookin' thing," says Winifred Woodward, holding the lace shortie Jim Noonan has handed her across the main showroom table at Lowndes Brothers. She turns it discriminatingly, making it do a slow lazy-Susan turn on her palm. "And what're you callin' this color?" she asks in her North Carolina accent.

"Bone," says Jim.

"Oh, my," says Miss Woodward, "what a forbiddin' name for somethin' so lovely."

"It was either that or something plain and sensible," says Jim, "like ivory or off-white." He's hoping she'll take a truckload of them for the hundred or so Belk department stores she buys for. But he also knows she likes to take her time, so he's not surprised when she gently puts the glove back on the table.

"And how's that little boy of yours, Mr. Noonan?" she asks.

A great wail, dreadful and consuming, fills the air. A similar scream began uptown a few seconds ago. And after another few seconds the sound waves in every corner of the city carry nothing but this blind, sickening cry.

Miss Woodward covers her ears.

"What the hell *is* this?" Jim asks Sal Spano, the bald guy from accounting who's passing through the showroom.

"'This is only a test,'" says Sal, mimicking the familiar language of broadcasters. "'Were this an actual emergency . . .' They're just testing the sirens. Every one in the city," says Sal, pointing to Jim's folded *Herald Tribune*. "Jimmy-boy, do you just buy that thing, or do you read it, too?"

All 733 air-raid sirens in New York City are being sounded at once, as planned, at 11 A.M. Had this been an actual emergency, all eight million residents would have begun tuning their radios to CONELRAD for further instructions. The sirens are set to blast for three minutes; then they will fall silent for another three; and then, for a final three, they will warble unnervingly — *ooh-ahh-ooh-ahh-ooh-ahh* — the signal to take cover.

The steady blast continues, but Winifred Woodward uncovers her ears. "It's just a test, Miss Woodward," says Jim.

"I see," she says, nodding her hatted head and closing her eyes. "Why don't we just use this time to gather our thoughts," she suggests, "instead of shoutin' at each other over this table full o' gloves?"

Jim nods agreeably and walks over to the window by himself. He looks down the three stories to the Fifth Avenue sidewalk and watches the pedestrians walking faster than normal. Had this been an actual emergency, they'd be running like hell, he thinks. And what would he be doing? Heading for the stairwell? Trying to phone Mary? Finding the circuits too overloaded to take the call? (This is what will happen eighteen months from tomorrow afternoon, when Sal Spano runs into the showroom to announce that Jack Kennedy's been shot.)

Jim shuts one of the windows, trying to kill some of the sound. He looks at the taxis moving south. The last time he stopped and stood at this window was almost three months ago, when John Glenn's parade passed. He'd been waving with everyone else and thought he'd been getting into the spirit of the thing until Fran Belkin, a girl from the order department, handed him a fistful of shredded invoices, saying, "C'mon, Mr. Noonan. Live a little." He took the confetti and showered it onto the motorcade. Glenn's car was already half a block north of the window, but there were other astronauts and their wives in the cars behind, and the tiny right-hand corner of invoice number 114747, a copy of what was sent to the Chic Shoppe in Butte, Montana, on January 12, 1959, had caught for a second in Rene Carpenter's yellow hair.

Gregory had, of course, wanted to come with him into the city that day, but Jim had said no, or more exactly and for the fifth time, "N-O, Gregger, you can watch it on the news." Three months later, with the siren still going, still entering his ears, it seems foolish to have refused.

Jim shuts his eyes and recalls the sirens in Nuremberg in '45, the sirens that cried incessantly and without meaning, since fire was a normal, hour-after-hour condition, like sunlight or darkness, and since alarm was something you could take only anticlimactically, filled as you already were, civilian and soldier, with terror.

Are the sirens being tested in Melwyn Park? Is there a

drill at the school? Is Gregory in the hallway, huddled use-
lessly under his paper-thin Yankees jacket? (The only siren
that will sound today in Melwyn Park, an hour from now, is
the twelve-o'clock whistle. Now, at 11:02, the only noises
that can be heard in the empty school corridor are those of a
hula, coming from a record player in the audi/gym.)

Jim thinks of the coat — not Gregory's Yankees jacket but
the piece of coat he's always remembered — sticking out
from the collapsed wall, the brown coat: so poor, so indeter-
minately styled, just like the shoe that stuck out beneath it.
He had never known if the small body he and two buddies
hurried past, trying not to be killed, was that of a boy or a
girl.

The siren stops. (Tomorrow's paper will report that 7 out
of the 733 units failed to sound.)

"Now, Mr. Noonan," says Winifred Woodward. "Where
were we?"

---

02 26 26 P
Capsule stability, Deke, is very, very good . . .

Gregory's neatly hand-drawn stock market graph for
McDonnell Aircraft, its last penciled trajectory stopped at
42½, lies undisturbed in his desk back in room 4, which is
empty. He was right: Mrs. Linley won't get to the stock project today. The rehearsal is running over and all they will
time to do between it and the lunch bell is one quick spelling
drill.

The Mercury capsule, Max Faget and Caldwell C. Johnson's brilliant little cone, whose blunt end is designed to
ablate great quantities of fire during atmospheric reentry at
3,500 degrees F, now cruises with perfect regularity more

than a hundred miles above the earth. If Scott Carpenter moves the control stick, jets of hydrogen peroxide will make it pitch, roll or yaw like an amusement-park ride. The atmosphere inside the capsule's thin titanium shell is, if a little warm today, perfectly pressurized, cooperating with the space suit to keep Carpenter's blood from boiling — which is what human blood will otherwise do above sixty-three thousand feet. The Environmental Control System works as well as a green plant, delivering pure oxygen and filtering out carbon dioxide through lithium hydroxide:

$$2\text{LiOH} + \text{CO}_2 \rightarrow \text{Li}_2\text{CO}_3 + \text{H}_2\text{O}.$$

The nearest thing in size that man has found to a magic carpet — a kind of sealed club chair flung into the void — this capsule, product of McDonnell Aircraft, functions almost perfectly. (The serious errors today, in space and all over the earth, will be human ones.) Its hundreds of switches, gauges and dial faces; its periscope, two portholes, one window and two parachutes; its survival kit and its four-inch globe (showing the flight path and marking out the world's fifty largest cities and sixteen longest rivers and, inside a four-ring bull's-eye, the *Aurora 7*'s landing area) — all of it as cunningly packed as a type font and weighing no more than the Noonans' Plymouth Valiant loaded up for a trip to New Hampshire — moves at seventeen thousand miles per hour over the Indian Ocean.

In New York City the brokers of Merrill Lynch and Kidder Peabody and Scudder Stevens & Clark have all morning taken buy-and-sell orders over the phone lines stitching the liquid world beneath the capsule. It is a reasonably stable day on the Street, but the trend of the market this season is down, and this afternoon McDonnell Aircraft, two hours after its little masterpiece lands in the Atlantic, will close for the day off another half point.

---

02 44 50 CC

Do you plan on eating as called for by . . . Over.

Mary Noonan looks at the sunburst clock with its satellite numbers. It's 11:30. She crosses into the linoleumed kitchen and stands before the Bermuda Pink GE Frost-Guard refrigerator, wondering what to do about dinner, whether it's too late to thaw a chicken, whether it was only Tuesday that they'd had chicken last. It would all be easier if she could bring herself to throw Swanson TV dinners at Jim and Greg each night, the way Ellen Forte down the street does with her husband and kids, but she isn't about to start that. Not that it would matter much to Gregory, who has recently told her that he will be happy, and mankind better off, once food is replaced with pills: one capsule each morning, washed down with something horrible like Tang, and you'll be set for the day. He is a firm believer in progress, that one. When they last went shopping for school clothes he selected one of those clip-on ties — not a bow tie, but a regular long tie with a knot and nothing else; nothing to tie under the collar, just a plastic hook behind the knot: you hang it over the top shirt button. Gregory insisted that it made regular ties — "the old ones," he called them — obsolete.

Until the food pills come, he will have to put up with Shredded Wheat, she thinks, clearing off from the counter the box still out from breakfast and putting it into one of the pale yellow metal cupboards with boomerang handles.

Hamburger, she thinks, looking into the freezer compartment behind the top Bermuda Pink door. She will do something with it; just what, she doesn't know yet. Nothing fancy. Running the frozen Saran-Wrapped chunk of it under the faucet to start it melting, she rolls her eyes good-naturedly. Jim's ancient Irish mother has crippled his stomach against anything but boiled potatoes and dried-out beef and over-cooked vegetables. Forget the three or four Italian things her own mother taught her. She can remember Jim's rib cage in-voluntarily stiffening the one time she brought veal parmi-giana to the table; on the same occasion Gregory stared ner-vously at the pole lamp over near the window, probably wondering if they ate this kind of stuff on Mars.

So. Hamburger.

02 45 32.5 CC
. . . I take it, from what you said then, that you have con-firmed that your faceplate is closed for the decision on the third orbit.

What next? The small pile of clothes on the other counter. Mary scoops Jim's Sanforized shirts and Gregory's under-wear into the front-loading automatic. She drops in two Salvo tablets — nice, neat hockey pucks of soap, new on the mar-ket — and closes the circular glass door.

02 46 08 CC
. . . Could you hit that button again?

She starts the machine and sits down at the Formica-top table for a moment, thinking about the rest of the day, won-dering if Gregory will come home for lunch or eat at school, wondering if she and Jim will really get out to that movie, *Lover Come Back*, is it? Doris Day and Rock Hudson, any-way. (Mary does not know that it is rated B — "Morally objectionable in part for all" — one notch above "Condemned.") Or will they just call it a night after dinner and watch Gregger watch all the space stuff that's bound to be on television? Maybe they should get to Sears instead, she thinks, noticing the ad she tacked to the refrigerator last night: a sale on men's slacks, $12.95 a pair, the Saturdaddy kind of chinos Jim wears on the weekends. She reminds herself to remind him that he's got to do something about the gutter on the back of the house.

02 47 16.5 CC

> Do you have any specific comments on your balloon experiments; for example, the best color contrast with the —

02 47 36.5 P

> Yes, I would say the day-glow orange is the best.

Her eyes look past the threshold and into the living room, settling on the blond-wood RCA color television, which Jim won three years ago in a salesman's raffle in Philadelphia, and which made them the first family on Fillmore Terrace to have color TV. Mary doesn't like the thing: it's not perfected — forever turning Eddie Fisher some sickening shade of green, or the fire at the beginning of *Bonanza* some unintended purple. Gregory will obligingly jump up from his sprawled position on the colonial rug to fiddle with the Hue and Color and Contrast knobs with his little fingers, precise as a safecracker's, explaining what's happened and why, but all she knows is that the thing is always on the blink and the tubes are too expensive and that she's putting Jim's money in the pockets of Ellen Herlihy's husband. She thinks back fondly to the book-cover-size black-and-white they had in Brooklyn, just after Gregory was born — more like a radio really, her father's radio, on which she can remember hearing about Lindbergh when she was four, can remember because her father *told* her and her half-brothers to remember, gravely sat them down next to the shiny twill of the speaker's cloth and told them this was something important.

Unsettled by this memory, she gets up from the kitchen table and goes into the living room, picking up the copy of last week's *Life* from the top of the TV. Scott and Rene Carpenter, the astronaut and his wife, blaze up from the cover in color and health. She's certainly stunning, Mary thinks, realizing from TV this morning that she pronounces her name *Reen* and not *Ruh-nay*. The platinum hair can't be for real, of course; it's got to be Miss Clairol. But imagine being pretty enough to get away with it. Mary puts the magazine in the rack near the La-Z-Boy. She won't look at it again. She read the piece on the family last week, and she doesn't want to see them now.

Fidgety, she looks around for something to do, wonders if she should give the rug a once-over with the Hoover Lark electric broom that's at the foot of the stairs with a pile of stuff that includes Gregory's Bob Shaw third-baseman's mitt and Jim's canvas shoes, and which is all supposed to go upstairs.

02 47 50.5 CC

Everything continues to look very good here on the ground.

No, she decides against the electric broom — the rug is fine — and heads instead for the stairs, eager to move, to climb, scooping the shoes and mitt and towels into her arms and taking them up with her, fast, to the second-floor landing. She enters Gregory's room to put the mitt on his chair, which is by the window, and is so struck by the pink-and-gold sight of the apple tree coming through it that she puts the mitt on the bed instead and sits down in the chair to regard the tree and the yard below it.

02 48 39 CC

As I said before, everything looks very good here. Surgeon is after me here for you to try another blood pressure. Is this convenient?

02 48 47.5 P

Negative. I won't be able to hold still for it now. I've got the sunrise to worry about . . . I have a beautiful sunrise through the window. I'll record it so you can see it.

Mary looks at the tree and is astonished by the beauty and the bright light. She briefly wonders how Jackie Kennedy can wear sunglasses all the time and miss things like this. She can feel the warmth coming through the window, and she touches her hand to one of the panes of glass to be closer to it. She remembers the even warmth of her own skin when she was carrying Gregory, a little globe under her stomach, remembers the way she would touch the roundness and feel the tranquilizing heat. She opens the window to smell the apple blossoms; to hear the faint angelus of Jane Koenig's wash flapping against the metal clothesline tree in the next yard; the distant murmur of the littlest ones on tricycles in driveways.

She knows why the thought of her own stepbrothers unsettled her; why she didn't want to look again at pretty Rene Carpenter's four children; why she had the fidgets and came up here. It's because of what she realized — how long ago was it? six months? That she wants another child, a baby. And that it is really too late. She will be forty next winter, too old. Why did she put it off? Why didn't she have the good sense to want it during all the last eleven years, when they'd waited, or decided against it (some Catholics they were!), in favor of just doing better for the one they had?

First they'd bought the house, in '54, "more house than they needed," as her half-sisters-in-law in Brooklyn never stopped telling her; and now Jim, who was in his own way as long-range as Gregory, was beginning to talk about school bills. But that was so many years from now, and they would never be out from under the mortgage, not until July 31, 1984, she thinks, remembering the absurdly distant date they'd affixed their names and futures to.

For a minute she allows herself to picture Jim and herself still in Brooklyn, in a railroad apartment, bringing up four kids instead of one. What is so special about what they are giving Gregory, anyway? Aren't they just giving him solitude? Lord, here in Fertile Valley everyone has four or five. How barren she feels at Saint Anastasia's each Sunday, the rest of them coming in with trails of ducklings, and she and Jim with only Gregory ahead of them, in his blue-serge jacket, his pink ears still smelling of soap.

She pictures her son's ears and feels in herself a momentary protective resentment against three hypothetical children who will never be hers; she wants only Gregory, her solemn, skinny pride and joy. Foolish, wrong even, to wish for anyone else. No, she wants no other, she thinks, scanning his bedroomful of possessions, visually stroking them like the hairs on his head: the small wax Indian they'd brought home from Cape Cod; the already-yellowing picture of Roger Maris clipped from the *New York World-Telegram* of October 2, 1961; the Civil War centennial stickers neatly pasted, in the proper historical order, from Fort Sumter to Ford's Theater, on his closet door. Her gaze lingers over the small telescope from last Christmas, and she thinks that surely he deserves a better one. Love surges up in her, fiercely for a moment, and she decides that yes, it's better to put it all — love and money and hope — into one alone. She has her boy.

She closes the window, notices it can use a cleaning, goes into the bathroom for the Windex and, while she's wiping the spritz into a brilliantly clear apple tree, at 11:38, wonders if he'll be home for lunch, and hopes so, and realizes that everything, her life, is fine.

Descending the stairs, she sings softly to herself: "It's a lovely day today, / For whatever you've got to do . . ." What she can do now is set three places for dinner, make it fancier than usual, think about a whole new meal, in fact, not hamburger. She can play with place settings now because if Gregger makes it home for lunch he'll take it not at the table but on a stand-up tray in front of the television. He'll be watching the astronaut, she thinks, realizing that the flight will preempt the one soap opera she permits herself to watch, *As the World Turns.*

And just where, she wonders, is Rene Carpenter's husband right now? She takes out embroidered place mats and arranges them, one, two, three, on the square table before stopping to look at the mahogany spot where a fourth might, she thinks, giddy with sudden reversal, still go. What if it merely happened, if fate, not planning — if accident — gave them another child?

---

02 54 18.5 P
  There were some more of those — little particles. They definitely look like snowflakes this time.
02 54 26 CC
  Roger. Understand. Your particles look like definite snowflakes.
02 54 32 P
  However —

Gregory walks the peach-colored corridor, passing a stretch of it decorated with posters left over from the last

Fire Prevention Week contest. (The winning effort is a parody of the Chesterfield jingle: "Twenty-one great tobaccos
make twenty . . . terrible fires! Don't smoke in bed!") Mrs.
Linley has given him permission to go to the library while
the rest of the class is finishing the rehearsal.

Mrs. O'Hara nods to him when he shows her his pass. After taking down *The Sky Observer's Guide*, a tiny volume he
has looked at many times, he sits at a blond-wood table near
the sixth-grade class's bulletin board, BRASÍLIA — CITY
OF TOMORROW, an idea that, like space, appeals to him as
a clean, well-lighted place. Which is what the library, empty
of people except for himself and Mrs. O'Hara, is now too. He
turns the transistor to its lowest audible point and fishes the
earphone out of his sweater:

> . . . the astronaut's capsule, as we mentioned earlier, carries
> the number 7, as have all Mercury missions so far. The num-
> ber indicates Commander Carpenter's solidarity with his six
> extraterrestrial colleagues, but the 7 in *Aurora 7* has a special
> meaning for the Boulder, Colorado, native. He grew up in a
> house at the corner of Aurora and 7th streets in that town.

Gregory thinks for a moment about orbiting the earth in a
capsule named for the intersection nearest his house. Traveling in the *Fillmore Honeysuckle* is not an inspiring pros-
pect, so he opens up *The Sky Observer's Guide:*

> Many persons have seen auroras without recognizing them.
> Look twice at any foglike glow seen toward the pole. Real
> clouds hide stars; auroras do not. Watch for any change in a
> hazy glow near the horizon.

One never really sees the horizon in Melwyn Park. One
snug little street cuts off another before you can ever see the

end of it. There are only two places where Gregory thought he'd seen all the way to the edge of the earth: at the beach and in New York City, looking all the way down Sixth Avenue one day when he went in with his father. The street went on and on until the buildings vanished to a point, or into another dimension, as they said on *The Twilight Zone*. He imagines his father now, twenty-five miles to the south, below the horizon, which means he's walking slightly sideways on a tilt, meaning that he needs to be propped up. Gregory has the kind of thought he hates to have, an embarrassing one: he pictures himself extending his arm to his father, steadying him, retrieving him toward home, where things are level and steady, Melwyn Park.

But Melwyn Park is not at the top of the world's sphere. Its gravitation is no stronger than any other place's. And what Gregory would like most, he thinks again as the radio talks of orbits and balloons, is to escape gravity entirely, to be in weightless transit toward a new and perfect place.

"Pizza, Greg!"

He can't believe it's Kenny Kessler who's just come in and already been hushed by Mrs. O'Hara.

"Why did she let *you* out?" Gregory asks, disappointed in too-nice, standardless Mrs. Linley for giving loud, unstudious Kenny the same privilege she gave him.

"Because I'm so wonderful and mature," Kenny says in a mock goody-goody voice, batting his eyelids like Margaret in *Dennis the Menace*. "Seriously, Greg, they're having pizza, on a Thursday. I saw it with my own eyes on the way here. I'm gonna stay. My mom won't care. How about you?"

Gregory is distracted from the decision he has to make by the mystery of why the cafeteria is having pizza when it's not a Friday. (Fridays, in heavily Catholic Melwyn Park, pizza generally alternates with fish sticks, which are disgusting and unpopular.)

"I thought the menu said Salisbury steak for today," says Gregory, beginning a cautious conversational deduction of the reason for the change, an exercise he knows Kenny will not be able to sustain.

"Woof, woof," Kenny responds, earning a severe glance from Mrs. O'Hara. The peculiarly named Salisbury steak bears an agglutinous resemblance to canned dog food and is usually served with an ice cream scoop of instant mashed potatoes and gravy. "Nope, no Laddie Boy. We won't be able to play suction bomb, but pizza'll be worth it." (Suction bomb, a game Gregory does not play, involves creating a vacuum by placing an empty glass dessert cup upside down over the small dish of potatoes and gravy. If it's done well, any attempt to remove the former from the latter — by the cafeteria lady or whoever loses odds or evens — will reliably send a stream of potato shrapnel all over the remover's shirt or blouse.) "Maybe it's on account of Scott Carpenter, like a holiday or something," Kenny speculates.

"No," says Gregory, disgusted again at how dumb Kenny can be. He puts his earphone back in and returns to *The Sky Observer's Guide*, which reminds him that Neptune, about 2,700,000,000 miles away, takes nearly 165 years to go around the Sun. And yet its own rotation takes just twenty-three hours, almost the same as Earth's. Is it maybe a parallel universe? Is there a version of himself sitting in a school library almost three billion miles away? Does he have Neptunian parents? The chart shows that around 1990 Neptune will be positioned in the sky against Sagittarius, the astrological sign of both Jim and Mary Noonan, who will then, on Earth, be incredibly old. (In fact, Jim Noonan will have been dead for ten years, having decided in 1964 that the surgeon general was just one more government busybody who didn't know anything except how to cost money. Mary will have sold the house in Melwyn Park and gone to live with one of her half-sisters-in-law in a retirement condominium in New Jersey.)

Kenny (who will be driving a cookie company's truck when Neptune is traveling through Sagittarius) ponders an ad in *Look* magazine and feels a furtive, ambivalent interest in Kathy Kersh, Miss Rheingold 1962. Gregory looks once more at *The Sky Observer's Guide*, tracing his finger over the constellations — Cancer, Gemini, Taurus, Orion. Tapping the last, he realizes he is having trouble seeing the stellar specks through a smudge on his glasses, and so he takes them off and, in a gesture he's learned from his father, fogs them up with a short huff of breath and wipes them with his handkerchief. The dots representing the infinitely distant stars of Orion come into clearer focus, but the image that has swum into Gregory's ken is, to his surprise and confusion, that of his father.

---

03 02 12 CC
 Roger, 7. Do you — have you ... perspire or have you stopped perspiring at the moment?
03 02 20 P
 No, I'm still perspiring, Al. I think I'll open up the visor and take a drink of water.
03 02 27 CC
 Roger. Sounds like a good idea.

Jim Noonan, alone for a moment, pops a Pep-O-Mint Life Saver — the breath-conscious salesman's constant companion — and opens the single drawer of his showroom table. He takes out a small envelope with a four-cent Project Mercury stamp on it, canceled one week ago in Melwyn Park:

May 17, 1962

Dear Dad,

Please change your mind. I really want to go with you. I know we can't afford to go to Cape Canaveral, but I can go to Langley if you're going to be near it. Please, I may never have another chance.

Gregory

P.S. I am sorry that I am going to send this to you at work.

Jim rereads this and shakes his head. Weird kid. "Gregory" — just plain "Gregory." Would he even sign "Love" to his mother? Probably not. The day this arrived Jim came home from work good and mad. "How do you think I feel when the girl in the office who opens up the mail sees this and puts it on my desk? You don't *do* certain things, Gregory," he'd shouted, before adding, somewhat contradictorily and more softly, "Why did you do this, anyway?" Before the kid could shrug his shoulders Jim had grabbed them and asked his question again.

"Because when I talk to you, you act like I'm silly," Gregory answered, looking at his sneakers, "or like I'm not here."

And then of course he wasn't, having wriggled away and fled to that space station of a bedroom.

What thread attaches him to this little odd boy, so rigidly frail, unattracted to getting dirty, uninterested in getting a dog, unamused by *Mad* magazine? How had Jim offered him to the world? Gregory seems inconceivable, literally, at least by him. Jim recalls Clark Gable's newborn son, a son born after his father's death, a connection of biology and nothing else.

And Gregory doesn't even look like me, Jim thinks.

He puts the letter back into the drawer and wipes his forehead with the back of his hand as he walks to the water cooler, down a corridor in technological transition. Lowndes has a primitive new IBM room, full of punch cards, but the company still operates mostly with comptometers and carbon paper; half the typewriters are manuals.

Sweating once again this morning, Jim lights a filtered cigarette and thinks of Gregory as he looks through the mix of flame and smoke. The water cooler bloops nauseatingly; he has had bifocals for more than a year now, but sudden downward shifts of glance still make his stomach flip. The bubbles stop and he downs a paper cupful of water, which makes the peppermint on his tongue sting pleasantly. He closes his eyes for a second, trying to calm himself, hoping nobody notices him, realizing that he's never recovered from that siren an hour ago.

"Nooneleh?"

It's Rhea Adler, the head of the order department, tapping him on the arm. "You all right? I was looking for you. You got a message from Miss Woodward. The old southern biddie, no?"

"Yes."

"She wants to meet you at Longchamps at quarter to one if you can. She says she's going anyway, so just show up if you're able. She's between Arnold Constable and Saks at the moment and is 'therefore unreachable'? What kind of way is this to do business?"

"Her way. She always does this. We went through the catalogue a little while ago. She knows what she wants, but then she'll say, 'Mah, mah, I just cain't be sure. If you kin bear it, I think I've got to take one more walk through one of your fancy Fifth Avenue department stores and see the kind of stuff they've got out. Jest for a little reassurance, y'know. After all, I'm jest from a small southern town.'"

"I hate these corn pone barracudas," says Rhea, picking a flake of mentholated tobacco off her lips. "Why do you put up with her?"

"Because she eventually comes through. And I was no good with her this morning. That air-raid test fouled me all up."

"I paid it no mind," says Rhea, the legendary workhorse of the office, crude and bulldozing, prone to mistakes but never to their admission, someone who makes up for her own carelessness by the sheer amount of paper she pushes around. "How does Rhea do it?" Sal Spano jokes, like in a carpet commercial. "Volume!"

Rhea is fond of no one at Lowndes except Jim, who, she likes to point out, is "a gentleman." This is true, though Rhea appreciates Jim's gentlemanly qualities less than what she regards as her unique sensitivity in recognizing them.

Jim is the only person in the office who's fond of Rhea, because he's the only one unafraid of her bluster. He recognizes her for what she is, one more scared person having to make her way in the world, shooting her mouth off the way somebody else pushes a broom — making do with what God gave her.

"So," says Rhea, having finished her own cupful of water. "Why so jumpy? You got problems at home?"

"Nah," says Jim, snapping on a fake smile and tossing his paper cup into the wastebasket. "Just an Excedrin headache, dollink."

Rhea knows better, but is stopped by one of the qualities that links her and Jim, even with their totally different demeanors: shyness. She gives his tie a tug and starts to move away. "Have a belt at Longchamps. And squeeze Tallulah for a big order. You'll feel better."

Had it been the siren? The memory of the shoes and coat? Or had he been feeling bad all morning, ever since he'd gone out the back door and found that the milkman had left nothing in the metal box? He'd been edgy on the train, he remembers, but nothing like this, so jumpy he doesn't want to be around anybody. He's glad old man Newman is away for the day, flying off to the factory in Puerto Rico.

He'd like to be able to go to lunch early, just sit by himself on a stool at the Chock Full o' Nuts down the street, but now he's got to wait for a quarter to one and Winifred Woodward. Who, he suddenly thinks, might be sold on number 1356, a four-button with matching seed pearls in a semiquilted design. He can offer it to her in Coral Glow, Ash Rose, or simple pink. She didn't see it this morning, so he'll go get a sample he can take to her at lunch. He looks forward to the solitude of the stockroom, as he passes a transistor radio dangling from the porter's dolly: ". . . and so the word from Mercury Control is that Scott Carpenter has been given the A-OK to head into a third and final orbit . . ."

The flight has been the last thing on his mind since he got to the office, but this tinny annunciation from Louis's radio fills him with warmth from the only interest or significance he attaches to it: imagining his son hearing it, happily, at school. He feels his eyes glisten and is upset that his feelings should be so close to the surface, that there should be something wrong with this fragile day, something he can't divine.

He walks down an aisle formed by gunmetal gray shelves, scanning the neatly stacked boxes for number 1356, like looking for a library book. In the next aisle, he can now hear Louis's dolly rolling by, the news bulletin on his transistor having given way to something from a couple of years back: "Stay," by Maurice Williams and the Zodiacs.

He opens an Ash Rose box of number 1356. It is inexplicably empty.

The wheels of the nearby dolly stop. "You all right, Mr. Noonan?"

"Fine, Louis. Just hay fever. Ash Rose seems to give it to me."

Louis laughs and rolls on. In the next aisle Jim muffles his sobs into the sleeve of his Bond's suit.

ORBIT 3

03 08 35 P
. . . its behavior is strictly random as far as I can tell. The balloon is not inflated well either. It's an oblong shape out there, rather than a round figure; and I believe when the sun is on it, the day-glow orange is the most brilliant, and the silver. That's about all I can tell you, Gus.

Elizabeth Wheatley stands before Bellini's *Saint Francis in Ecstasy* and wishes her vision could reduce it to Cezannian blocks, oblongs of color without content. What *had* been her thought about Bellini before the Venetian altarpiece a couple of weeks ago? Whatever it was it now seems gone forever. Her reactions to the picture in front of her seem no more profound than the ones being had by the midwestern ladies, a couple of canvases down, with guidebooks in their hands. The hills in the painting's background make her think only of the Tuscan villa she was staying in two weeks ago. The figure of Saint Francis himself seems slightly ridiculous: with his chest out, arms spread, palms turned up, he looks like a popular singer, Morton Downey hitting a big note.

And yet Saint Francis was an appealing saint, someone harmless, perhaps even good. She'd left him off her Index of proscribed religious nonsense when she was raising her daughter; she'd even read her the tale of the wolf of Gubbio's conversion as a bedtime story.

She keeps scanning the canvas, hoping not for a reaction — let the midwestern ladies have them — but for an *idea*. She looks at the latticed saplings, the book, the *memento mori* skull. Nothing makes her think, until she notices the treetop in the upper left corner. It's being bent and blown as if by a hurricane's gale, though everything else in the picture is calm enough. Saint Francis himself, *pace* the title, hardly seems ecstatic; just expectant.

And then Elizabeth has not a reaction and not an idea but a sort of absurd imagining. She looks at the saint's breast — extended to the world as if he's just inhaled; vulnerable, unprotected by anything but the rough brown cloth of his cassock — and she imagines a fusillade of gunfire, or a whole quiverful of arrows, rushing toward it. It seems as if something terrible must be about to happen, even though Saint Francis received only the stigmata, not martyrdom.

It's the movies, she realizes. Whenever you see someone quietly walking forward, all alone, moving peacefully from couch to icebox, you know something horrible is going to happen. The man with the hammer or the piano wire is going to spring. (Elizabeth sees movies quite often, usually sneaking off to them alone in the afternoon, a little guiltily.) This thought — really just the analysis of a foolish reflex created by her only popular vice — is the best she's going to get today.

She leaves the gallery and walks to the Frick's indoor courtyard, sitting down for a moment to listen to the cool slurp of the fountains, where the midwestern ladies are wondering whether it would be all right to take a flash picture.

Elizabeth is glad to be off her feet. It's been a long walk from the dock at West 44th; across town and up Fifth Avenue; into Saint Patrick's (why, she doesn't know, immaculate as it is of any beauty). Even that came after a walk through Scribner's, where she purchased Peter Medawar's *Future of Man*. It is not a subject that much interests Elizabeth, who finds man's present quite wickedly absorbing, and she has even less interest in Medawar's approach (scientific); but she'd met him once at a party in London, and liked him, and in these ever less literate times that was more than enough reason to buy someone's book. She's about to open it when —

"Elizabeth!"

It's Connie Funt, dear old

"C-o-o-o-nnie!" Elizabeth says, enjoying the vowel, prolonging it the way she will when pleased, an extra half second, as if in song. She *is* happy to see her old college classmate, who's a good soul and citizen — was always trying to get her and Robbie to work for Stevenson — a warm lover of children and pets who's probably just come from seeing the Fragonards and thinking them pretty instead of sick-making.

"Elizabeth, this is perfect. I was just thinking: who can I find to have lunch with? Can I persuade you? I don't want to take you away from your writing" — Connie has always been properly awed by Elizabeth — "but it looks as if you've given yourself the morning off."

"In a way," says Elizabeth, her mouth spreading into an immense smile, her blue eyes crinkling closed. "I've just gotten off the *Leonardo*. I walked here."

"You mean you haven't even been home?" Connie says, so loudly in fact that her civic conscience looks around to make sure she hasn't bothered the other patrons. "Where's Robbie?"

"Still in Italy."

Connie decides it's impolite to ask why. She really doesn't know them well enough, only sees them once or twice a year, didn't even know they'd been away.

"You mean you came to the Frick before you even picked up your mail?" Connie asks, marveling. "Oh, Elizabeth, you are something."

The corners of Elizabeth's exceptionally attractive smile lose no altitude; her beaming face is an uncanny feat of simultaneous animation and fixity. But then, realizing poor Connie will soon be out of things to say, she responds.

"The *mail*. Connie, *what* a good idea. Let's collect it and then go out for lunch."

---

03 16 41 CC

Aurora 7, Cap Com. Can you give us a comment on the zero g experiment?

03 16 53.5 P

Roger. At this moment, the fluid is all gathered around the standpipe; the standpipe appears to be full and the fluid outside the standpipe is about halfway up. There is a rather large meniscus. I'd say about 60° meniscus.

The clear liquid drips through the tubing and into the left arm of the twelve-year-old boy. He is awake now, and he looks at the small bandage into which the tube, like the tail of a glass mouse, disappears. The sight of this left arm doesn't bother him. It's the right one that he doesn't want to look at, even though it's raised comfortably and completely covered in gauze now.

The arm is his again. The neck bone's connected to the shoulder bone. The shoulder bone's connected to the humerus. And on that shaft hang, and live, his biceps, the brachii connecting beneath, just as they should, to the brachio-radialis. Blood flows in the arm from top to bottom, through the right axillary, down the right brachial and, after diverging through the right radial and right ulnar, down into the hand, which the boy, Everett Knowles, Jr., lying in Massachusetts General Hospital, still cannot move.

But the arm is his once more, sewn back on by Dr. Malt and the other surgeons. For a few minutes yesterday it was not his. It was a thing, separate, cut off from him when the freight train roared past and slammed him into the bridge abutment. Like a drawing that someone had started to erase, one of his lines gone, he'd been brought here in the fire department ambulance, with the arm. It almost seemed as if they'd been waiting for him.

In a way, they had been. Waiting for someone, someone nearby, to whom it would happen — so they might try the operation and make that person what Everett "Red" Knowles now is: the first person ever to have his arm successfully sewn back on.

The painkillers, which have replaced yesterday's anesthetic in his blood, float through the right brachial, through the right ulnar, up and down and back through all the circuitry of life. As he drifts in and out of sleep he tries not to think of the train, and not about whether the new connections will hold, and whether the arm will stay his. He tries not to wonder if he will pitch again for the Somerville Stride-Rites. He tries instead to think of the spaceman the nurses mentioned this morning, the spaceman who has drifted into his third orbit and will soon be wondering if his fuel supply will hold, if there will be enough, an hour and a half from now, to push him through the correct column of the atmosphere and back down to the ocean.

———————————

03 25 01 P

> Hello, Canary Cap Com, Aurora 7. Reading you loud and clear. How me?

03 25 08 CC

> Aurora 7, this is Canary Cap Com. Do you read? Over.

03 25 12.5 P

> Go ahead, Canary. Reading you loud and clear.

03 25 18.5 P

> I am going — I am in the record only position now. I think the best answer to the autokinesis — is that there is none . . . I don't get autokinesis. I don't get — now wait a minute, maybe I'm beginning to.

When does the next train come by? If you piss on the third rail, do you really get electrocuted and die?

Gregory looks through the diamond spaces in the chain-link fence separating the schoolyard from the railroad tracks. He thinks of how his father will come home along these rails at the end of the day, and about how Scott Carpenter, who is in his third orbit, will about an hour from now be making preparations to come home.

He does not imagine himself going home at the end of the day. No picture of that comes into his mind. In fact, right now, at 12:10 P.M., he needs to decide, right away, if he's going to go home for lunch. Lunch/recess began ten minutes ago, and will be over at 12:50, and he still hasn't made up his mind. The ones who are staying to eat the unexpected pizza are already in the cafeteria, and the ones who are going home have long since sprayed away from the bicycle rack. But he hasn't been able to do anything except wander to the edge of the schoolyard, as if he's waiting for some sign telling him what to do. If there were some emergency, like a nuclear war, and the need to evacuate the entire school "in an orderly fashion," this is where he would be: with the Blue group, familiar with his station from the "go-home" drills they have once or twice a year, less frequently than drills for air raids and fires.

But no one's here but him now, and he walks back toward the building, still undecided, across a lawn, over a baseball diamond, where fifteen minutes from now one will hear the rubbery blunking sound of kickball; he walks across the United States, from California to the New York island, on the map painted on the asphalt, where, as the kickball game goes on, the smaller and spazzier kids will be playing map tag. "Nevada!" someone will shout, and if you don't make it to the Sierras before being tagged, you're it.

He runs his fingers along the window sill of the cafeteria until he hears two sharp taps on the glass. It's Kenny Kessler holding up two mozzarellaed English muffins — that is, pizza — and licking his lips like one of the Campbell's Soup kids. Gregory just shakes his head and Kenny, in one last-ditch effort to sell the product, holds the two halves of the English muffin in front of his flat boyish chest: pizza breasts. He flutters his eyes like a girl. He's such a jerk.

No, Gregory isn't going in there. But will he go home? Arrive late? Hear his mother humming "Sugartime," like one of the McGuire Sisters, until she breaks into a vocal when he gets near and she kisses him on the cheek? "Be my little sugar, and love me all the time."

He looks into the window of Mrs. Kelly's third-grade class and sees a bulletin board: COLUMBUS DISCOVERS AMER-ICA. He recalls last fall's class trip to the planetarium in New York City, with the side trip to Columbus Circle, where a Redstone rocket was set up near the monument to Columbus. Standing atop his obelisk, Columbus was just about the size of the Mercury capsule and its escape tower. The two pillars, metal rocket and concrete pediment, were almost exactly the same height. When stupid Marlene Milligan asked why the two things had been stood up together, Mrs. Linley explained that it was a matter of "continuity," and asked if anyone could spell that word. Gregory was pretty sure he could, but he wasn't talking. Now he hears the radio:

"Scott Carpenter, now up over the Atlantic Ocean at the start of his third and final orbit, will soon be seeing his third sunset of the day. Can you believe that? I tell you, if you're like me, you're pretty pooped by the time that first sunset of the day rolls in, especially if you're riding home through it on the Belt Parkway or the L.I.E. Well, at least our man Scott won't have any traffic to worry about when he starts for home about an hour from now. He'll have a clear path on that old exit ramp above Florida. Unless, of course, a little red sports capsule launched by Mother Russia is unexpectedly on his tail" — oleaginous DJ chuckles — "but from all reports Commander Scott and Uncle Sam have this day all to themselves. The only company our astronaut has is the millions of Americans praying for his safe and successful return. And here's one from a few years back that seems appropriate right about now, from our English buddy Laurie London, right up to Scott Carpenter and the *Aurora 7* —"

> He's got the whole world in His hands,
> He's got the whole . . .

Gregory frowns, banishing Laurie London's pious castrato in favor of a frequency that will give him some real news about the flight.

He reaches the window of the Teachers' Lounge and sees a television going. It shows a crowd watching the television screens, and he's confused. He is also afraid that he'll be spotted by godlike Mr. Danaher, so he allows himself to get just close enough to hear the announcer say the word "terminal" and to see a board marked "Departures" before ducking and darting away to the brick space beneath the next set of windows, those of his own empty classroom.

Except it isn't empty. A voice comes through the window: "Can't decide whether to stay or go?"

It's Mrs. Linley, who is eating a tuna-fish sandwich at her desk and was looking forward to sneaking a smoke before she noticed him — *A lovely boy, very bright. A bit of a worrier* — outside her window.

Gregory jumps up, brushing some gravel from his hands and trousers, and says, "I'm going." As soon as he says it his embarrassment evaporates: he has decided at last, and not just to have an answer for Mrs. Linley, who, far from being annoyed with him, is smiling as kindly as Miss Crabtree does in *The Little Rascals*, on television every morning at 8:30 ("Gee, Miss Crabtree, you're pretty. You're even prettier than Miss McGillicuddy"). He gives her a soldierly wave as he starts for the bike rack. Her smile turns into a laugh and she says, "Goodbye, Gregory."

Yes, he's going. He knew it the minute he said it, knew at last where he was supposed to go, supposed to end up. He knows where he's been drawn, pulled, all morning, ever since the apple tree. He's got to get to the Melwyn Park railroad station so he can get the train, so he can get to where the people on the television are, under the huge vaulted ceiling, near where it says "Departures." As the spokes of his bicycle quicken and whirl into two racing clouds, he's heading for the train, heading for the city, heading for the terminal, because that's where it's going to happen to him.

---

03 26 40 P

... I haven't operated the thruster, not for some time ...
I am unable to see any stars in the black sky at this time.
However, these little snowflakes are clearly visible.

Weekday masses speed right along at Saint Agnes's. Keep it short and sweet and convenient for them. Assure their continuing patronage, as old Father McInerney likes to put it.

So sixteen minutes after the ringing of the entrance bell, Tommy Shanahan is winding up his four-and-a-half-minute sermon: "So, just as Sister Pientia is using her talent to bring souls to Christ, we must each use our own. We may not be special. We may not be artists. We may not be spacemen, but each of us has something to give, whether it be a lifetime of work or a small donation. I have it easy. I preach to the converted, as the saying goes. But I hope you will give as generously as you can so that through the good priests and nuns supported by the Society for the Propagation of the Faith, the unconverted of our world will be able to hear the words of our Lord."

It's a professional job, and Tommy's vanity knows it. His vanity is also disappointed, because his audience consists of about twenty-five people, some of them snoozing. Old men with time, women with troubles. And certainly no Fulton J. Sheen.

Consecrating the hosts, Tommy is depressed. He thinks he's losing his nerve. He will probably wind up napping in the rectory instead of looking for Maria at the library. Our Lady of the Reading Room. Tommy stares into the chalice of white wafers — as Scott Carpenter looks at the frost particles swirling around outside his spacecraft — and says the Latin words that turn them into the body of Christ. Now he wonders if Maria has run into the stockbroker. What art book does she have opened up in front of her? Scary Rubens nudes? Heroic history paintings? Tommy hopes it's something else, something soft and pretty, Impressionist women with bonnets and parasols.

If he naps upstairs this afternoon, will he masturbate? This is one thing he is, rather resentfully, supposed to be "working on," and although he hasn't done it in several days, he can't help believing that the real solution to the problem isn't finding another person with the same problem so they can work on it together. He dreads the future, dreads being, thirty years from now, a good guy who pals around with the kids in the CYO, and cheers for them at basketball games and takes his memory of them in their uniforms back with him under the covers at the rectory.

"A complete penilectomy, Tommy me boy. The only solution." That's what his fellow seminarian Bobby Gleason — husky, sensible and probably experienced with girls — used to say to him, which made Tommy, who never enunciated his confused feelings on the subject, wonder: Did it show in his face? Was there something guilty and obsessive there, a telltale wanness like a hairy palm?

For obsessed he was, which made him dread what was coming next: placing the hosts directly onto the tongues of the communicants walking up to the rail. Just a few geezers and grannies today, but no matter. There was something so intimate and even gross about it that Tommy had once or twice, quicker than you could say *dominus vobiscum*, felt an erection starting under his cassock.

Time to turn and face the music. Tommy looks over at the altar boy, a new kid whose name he forgets, who's very scared, and gives him a small, still reasonably reverent smile of encouragement. And then, just before turning around to the parishioners, he really notices the flowers in front of him, these great gorgeous lilies, and he thinks, They shouldn't be here. It's as if they're trapped in a hospital. He wants to liberate them, and in a flash he settles on a solution, at least for a few of them. He's going to bring them to her.

03 28 53 P
> Hello, hello, Kano Cap Com, Aurora 7. Reading you loud and clear. How me?

03 29 24 P
> I've noticed that every time I turn over to the right everything seems vertical, but I am upside down.

The stapled mimeographed sheets lie in a pile rising several inches, but the men in their drip-dry suits and the women in their short white gloves let them go begging. Having returned from the dedication of the Rayburn Building, the members of the White House press corps, at 12:14 P.M., are too occupied with thoughts of lunch to display any interest in the "Joint Statement Following Discussions with the President of the Ivory Coast." None of their editors is going to be interested in that on a day like this. Kennedy will wind up on page 3, either laying the cornerstone or on the phone to Carpenter, making the call he's sure to make whenever the astronaut comes down and they pick him out of the ocean. And since they've given him the go-ahead for a third orbit, there's plenty of time for lunch. He'll be up there for another hour and a half.

Actually, Mrs. Ivory Coast — Madame Félix Houphouët-Boigny — has made for some nice pictures. She's sort of an African Jackie, only thirty-one, and the two of them can chat together in finishing-school French. But forget another snoring Joint Statement.

So it lies neglected, reporting in its third paragraph that "President Kennedy commended President Houphouët-Boigny on his unique record of devoted service to the interests of the people of the Ivory Coast and of other nations of West and Equatorial Africa," and continuing with soothing grandiosity into its fourth: "President Kennedy noted with satisfaction the energetic efforts toward economic and social development being carried forward by the Republic of Ivory

Coast and of the favorable climate established by the Ivory Coast Government to welcome foreign private capital investment and give appropriate guarantees."

Today the savannah outside the small town of Yamoussoukro, Ivory Coast, lies undisturbed. But a quarter century from now, in September 1986, just before the price of cocoa drops by half, President Houphouët-Boigny, still in office, will, like President Kennedy today, be laying a cornerstone — for the Our Lady of Peace basilica, which will hold 300,000 people on its 7.4-acre esplanade, and whose 310-ton cupola will be higher than that of Saint Peter's. There will be 100,000 people in Yamoussoukro soon after that, and 1,500 artisans performing their work above the savannah, readying the golden cross for the cupola, inserting the French stained glass into the window frames. President Houphouët-Boigny will not argue along the lines of Sister Pientia; he will merely say that it is his land, and his money, and that the cathedral is his present to the Vatican. "In what way would my meager 40 billion francs — if it is 40 billion — change the crisis which has hit my country?" He will have suspended payments on the $10 billion foreign debt.

The *Aurora 7*, at 12:15, is flying just below the southwestern coast of Africa, as close as it will get on this third orbit to the pinkish sandy soil just beyond the Ivorian savannahs. Billions of its grains lie flat and undisturbed for now, two decades before they will be stirred into the basilica's cement, giving the eighty-four-foot-high Doric columns their pink cast.

---

03 30 03 P

> I could very easily come in from another planet, and feel that I am on my — on my back, and that earth is up above me . . .

"You're late!" shouts Mrs. Burke, the crossing guard, giving Gregory a big wave as the Rollfast rattles across the tracks.

"I know," he replies politely, though he's pedaling for all he's worth and can't actually turn his head to look at her without losing momentum. His knees are pumping up and down like crazy, and the baseball cards are buzzing against the spokes like an electric saw that's set on high. He knows there's a train at about 12:20, five minutes from now, because he can hear it go by each day during lunch, from the cafeteria. He tries to remember the numbers he once memorized from his father's timetable. But even if he knew the exact moment, it wouldn't help: he doesn't own a watch yet. (His first one, a Timex, is wrapped up inside his mother's top bureau drawer, already bought for his birthday present next fall.)

"Climb, climb," Gregory whispers as he exhales each breath, pushing the bicycle toward its rendezvous with the top of Tulip Street's hill. "Climb, climb," he wheezes, making the last effort, harder, until he can almost give no more and then stops, triumphantly, the bike having reached and gone over the crest. It is falling fast down the other side now, of its own will, so fast he must lightly apply the back brakes as he exults in his release from effort. "The booster has dropped away, I'm weightless, I'm in orbit," he says as he leans his head back, so far back that he sees nothing but the blue sky and fluffy clouds of this lovely day. He knows clouds lie in different planes — Scott Carpenter, whose depth perception today is one hundred miles, can spot four separate levels — but Gregory can only see clouds riding the same polished sheet of sky, see them until he suddenly remembers to be frightened, of oncoming cars, of losing his balance. (He is terrified of the trampoline in gym, is always afraid he will bounce over the hands and heads of the spotters and smash his spine on the hardwood floor — a fear made more embarrassing by his knowledge that Scott Carpenter is the most proficient trampolinist in the astronaut corps.)

With his eyes on the road again, he pedals past the bank. Its clock says 12:16, and even as he calculates distance to go versus time remaining, he makes a mental note that he has now earned the first half penny of the two cents of compounded interest his $91 bank account accrues each day.

The next block brings him past the Village Hall, its flag flapping in the direction of Arthur Avenue, onto which he turns, pedaling hard through the part of town named for the obscure presidents of the late nineteenth century.

One more hill before McKinley, the last hill before the train station, and he pedals hard and fast enough to hear his own heart, *dub, dub, dub,* fast and regular. He has periodically checked the sound with his hand since the other month, when Deke Slayton was grounded by the discovery of that slight irregularity in his heartbeat, the reason for Scott Carpenter's getting today's mission.

"Hi, Billy!" shouts a man in black. Realizing that the man means him, Gregory turns his head. It's that corny visiting priest, the one who ran the retreat for Saint Anastasia's confirmation classes last week, Father Bonfiore, the one who compared the indulgences you earn from corporal works of mercy to kicking for the extra point in football — and became the first adult Gregory ever felt embarrassed *for.*

The Rollfast goes past the steeple and Gregory crosses himself — *Look, Ma, no hands!* — before making one last turn with the handlebars, onto Taft Avenue, at the end of which lies the train station. Remembering the bank clock and calculating his speed, he is sure he will make the train — it *is* the 12:20 that he hears dieseling down a little to the north — and as he pedals the last block he is humming what the radio said this morning was Scott Carpenter's favorite song, "Yellow Bird."

———————

03 40 52.5 CC
   . . . Understand also you are drifting for a while.
03 41 10 P
   That is Roger. I am.

She shouldn't have bothered setting up the metal tray-table in front of the TV. She'd just been hoping. But if he'd decided in favor of lunch at home, he'd have come through the door ten minutes ago.

As Mary Noonan folds up the table she remembers thinking, an hour ago, about a fourth place setting at the dinner table, and realizes that even with another child there would rarely be more than two people in the dining room: the children — *children*, she likes the sound of the plural — the children would be eating in front of the TV.

It's a slow period in the coverage. A scientist from a university in Indiana is talking with a network correspondent about the industrial and medical benefits to be derived, sometime in the future, from experiments to be performed in space. Some of them involve crystals, the scientist says, and Mary, carrying the tray-table back to the kitchen, looks at the little dog bone on the knickknack shelf. It's actually something to rest your knife on during dinner, but she and her half-brothers had always called it a dog bone when it sat for years on Mama's bedroom bureau in Brooklyn. It had been a wedding present from the lady in Gramercy Park whom her mother had worked for, when she was really just a girl from northern Italy with long golden braids, during the First World War. Growing up in the thirties, Mary and her brothers had thought of this little piece of useless cut glass as something almost ancient, associated as it was with the world of off-the-boat servitude, something her parents and people like them had passed in and out of in a single generation.

She picks up the knife holder and wonders why men

would think of spinning crystal in the brand-new world of space. The scientist from Indiana has moved on to another topic while she was daydreaming about her mother's bedroom bureau, so she's lost her chance to find out why. She'll ask Gregory tonight; he'll know.

She puts the knife holder back but keeps looking at it, thinking about Mama, remembering the afternoon she was taken away by the medics, who tied her up in white canvas straps, the afternoon Mary had come home from P.S. 112 and heard the din and been stopped on the stairs by big Mrs. Anastopoulos and told not to go into the kitchen. But she'd broken free and gone in anyway, and found her father crying as the medics finished the job and took her mother down the stairs, "only for a little while, Maria, until she's better, only for a little while." Her mother's braids, which had long since gone gray, were falling from their circle around her head, as if trying to release her from the pressures of all the children — her widower husband's and then her own, in too quick succession — from all the strangeness that had taken her from one world and put her in another, surrounded by children with no connection to her own memories, land and language, little creatures of America, little creatures of school, even the ones who were her own somehow not her own.

She did come back, though after a long while and never really the same. Mary, nervous with memory, moves toward the kitchen and puts her mind on the future — this afternoon, tonight. Are she and Jim going to this movie or not? She'd really like to know. And so she calls Lowndes Brothers, MU3-0250, knowing he won't like the interruption, but too jittery in this quiet house to stop herself.

"I'm sorry, Mrs. Noonan, he's just gone out to lunch with a buyer. Shall I have him call you back?"

"Oh, no, that's all right," says Mary, with the flustered

politeness that never quite lets her relax, that on vacation makes her whisper in motel rooms, as if being a guest really meant that. "Sorry to have bothered you."

She puts the receiver down just as the washer audibly changes cycles. The box! She thinks, Maybe? and walks quickly through the back screen door and around to the garage.

"Gregger?" she asks, lightly tapping the huge cardboard cube with MAYTAG printed on the side. But no sound emerges. Disappointed, she runs her hand over the box painted up to be a Mercury capsule. Inside Gregory has even put in knobs and tinfoil lights. Saran Wrap makes the little hatch window on the other side. He'd made the capsule last summer and plays in it every so often, most of all last month, when over Mary's better judgment but with Jim's reluctant approval he spent five hours in it, by himself, in an attempt to duplicate John Glenn's cramped sensory deprivation. His only stimulation came from his father's watch, a flashlight, a star chart and a toy walkie-talkie, which linked him to his Cap Com, Georgie Herlihy, who lives diagonally in back of the Noonans and who after a couple of hours forgot all about his plans to check in with Gregory every fifteen minutes and went bowling with another boy instead. Mary was furious with Georgie; Gregory, upon emerging from the box, refused to complain or show he was hurt. "I lost contact over Nigeria" was all he would say, shrugging, when Jim went into his room that night.

Coming out into the back yard and looking over the hedge, Mary sees that Georgie Herlihy — at whom she's still annoyed — *has* come home for lunch. He's in the back yard with his mother, having Kool-Aid and a grilled-cheese sandwich off a paper plate.

Ellen Herlihy, in her peppy, Ethel Kennedy way, spots Mary, gets up, waves, says "Hi, kid!" with food still in her mouth and makes for the four-way intersection of waist-high hedges. Mary smiles and reluctantly joins her, afraid she'll be asked to contribute to a Girl Scout Bake Sale or sell tickets for the PTA dance before she can get away.

"Whatcha doing?" asks Ellen.

"Oh, I was just looking for Gregory. I was hoping he'd come home for lunch."

"Ah." Ellen laughs and pops a last corner of grilled cheese into her mouth. "He's probably a stowaway with Scott Carpenter." Pleased with her remark, she shakes her head and laughs again. "Yeah, he's a deep one, yours is."

Mary flushes, hurt by the implication that her Gregger is somehow less of a prize than husky Georgie Herlihy, a Little League star. Mary looks at him gulping the last of his Kool-Aid and feels faintly disgusted and once again angry. Flat-leaver, she thinks.

"Well, I guess I'll just see him later," she says. "I'd better take care of the wash now."

Ellen says "See ya," and Mary starts back for the house, passing the apple tree and remembering this morning's strange episode. She goes through the screen door and into the kitchen, aware of how nervous she is. She shuts off the washer even though it isn't through. She just can't stand the noise. But she can't stand the quiet either. She wishes someone, even Avon or the Fuller Brush man, would ring the front bell and break the silence.

Ashamed of her own nervousness, aware that she will never be the stolid rock that is Grandma Noonan, she considers hopping into the car and needlessly going somewhere, even though she hates anything busier than Melwyn Road. I am not resourceful, she thinks. I'm not like his mother. I'm like my mother. She's the one I'm like and she's the one I want to be like. Except for the hospital.

"Hey, Mary!"

It's Ellen Herlihy at the screen door. "There's a sale on air conditioners at Monkey Ward. Do you want to come look around with me? I just got rid of my kid and came through the hedge."

Mary is flooded with gratitude. There's really nothing wrong with Ellen. "Sure," says Mary, opening the door, and pleased at what constitutes, for her, impulsiveness. "Let's go." Ellen is a *superb* driver, and if she never stops talking, and if as a result of this trip Mary winds up having to canvass for the Cancer Society, then fine. At least she's being taken out of this house.

She gets her purse and with Ellen she starts out the back door, stopping only for a second to turn around and look at the knobs on the gas stove. "Off, off, off, off, off," she whispers to herself.

---

03 44 14.5 CC
Aurora 7, I did not hear your whole sentence. Will you repeat, please? Over.

"Where *to*. What *station*."

Gregory isn't exactly sure what to say when the conductor asks where he's going. "New York City," he manages to get out. "Grand Central Terminal." Now that he's said something, the conductor eyes him less suspiciously, but still with a look that's more disapproving than protective. "One dollar and five cents," he says, snapping off a bought-on-the-train ticket from his pad.

Money was something Gregory hadn't even considered on his headlong ride to the station, but he's got it. He pulls out a nickel from his right pants pocket and then goes for his Roy Rogers wallet, a little embarrassed that the conductor should see something he's had since he was eight. But the same thriftiness that's kept it unlost and in good condition is what accounts for the dollar — two weeks' allowance — that's in it. Birthday money from his grandmother and uncles lasts him for months. His father once laughed and said, "It really sews a hole in your pocket, doesn't it, Gregger?" when he'd found out that Mary had borrowed two bucks from him.

The conductor punches the slip of paper marked NEW YORK CENTRAL–ONE-WAY and hands it to him. He steps away but has an afterthought. "Are you under twelve, kid?"

"No."

"Good," says the conductor, happy not to have to bother to do it over and give the kid back fifty cents.

Gregory is, of course, eleven, but not thinking fast enough to realize the conductor was talking about a discount, he worried that maybe there was a rule against riding alone under twelve. *I just lied.*

A man sitting across the aisle shakes his head over the mean spectacle of a man pleased to see a kid not come into an extra fifty cents.

Gregory looks out the window of the train and sees his Rollfast, which he's left unlocked — there was no time to do otherwise — leaning against the little station bungalow. He's never left it unprotected before, but he's never done anything like this before. What will he be missing after lunch? Probably world geography — "Lebanon's capital, Beirut, is sometimes called the Paris of the Middle East, and since 1960 its government embodies religious toleration, with a ratio of six Christians to five Moslems in the national legislature" — if Mrs. Linley doesn't get backed up on her schedule. But he won't be there for whatever comes out of the textbook or is shown on the filmstrip. This railroad car, which reminds him of the shoebox dioramas they sometimes have to make — he and Kenny Kessler recently teamed up to do a mountain pass in Nepal — will be his home for a while.

The train pulls out, starting southward down the track like an iron filing toward the magnet of Manhattan. Passing beside the trackside phone poles and wires, his transistor radio crackles in and out, just like Scott's. The last item Gregory hears before turning it off concerns Karel Kynel of Radio Prague, who is "the first reporter from a communist-bloc country to cover an American lift-off." Kynel says he is happy to be at Cape Canaveral, but expresses irritation that so many American reporters are interviewing him he can't get on with his own work. He also reminds Americans that *Aurora* was the name of the boat that fired on the tsar's Winter Palace and started the Russian revolution. Gregory thinks of Boris and Natasha on *Bullwinkle:* "Come on, Boris, dollink, ve veel shoot down astronaut and geev comeuppance to squirrel and moose."

Two women, two seats in front of him, are on their way to an afternoon of shopping in the city. A branch of Korvette's (which will last at Fifth Avenue and 47th Street for less than twenty years) is opening today, and one of the women asks the other if "E. J. Korvette" really stands for "eight Jewish Korean War veterans."

"I think that's a myth," her friend replies, and then adds, after a pause and a sigh, "God. Korea. That seems like ages ago."

"What a weird little war that was," says the other. "Did we win it or lose it?"

"A little of both, I think," says her friend. "Next time they'll just drop the bomb and get it over with."

The man across the aisle from Gregory turns the pages of the first section of the *New York Times*, folding the item at the bottom of the front page — "Son of General Clay Wounded During Battle in South Vietnam" — out of sight. To Gregory, the man looks to be about his father's age (actually he is ten years older). He watches him break off a piece of Bit-O-Honey and start softening it in his mouth. He thinks of the peanut-butter-and-jelly sandwich his mother might be giving him now, and he thinks of how his father, in six hours, will be traveling home in the opposite direction, on the track just beyond the window.

Impatient with the hard Bit-O-Honey, the man cracks it with his teeth. He and Gregory wince simultaneously, the man at the shock to his nerves and gums, and Gregory with the memory of a fiasco at the dinner table one night three years ago, when he was eight and excitedly explaining to his mother that he'd come up with an idea that he was going to get patented: electric teeth. "You wouldn't have to chew. They'd do all the chewing for you. You'd just connect a wire from one of the ones at the back of your mouth to a dry cell in the middle of the table, near the salt and pepper shakers, and when you were ready to start eating you'd just turn on a switch." His mother, not sure what a dry cell was, nodded appreciatively at her darling's precocity, and then Gregory turned to see the reaction of his father, who was laughing, and who, just beginning manual mastication of a forkful of canned carrots, said, "Well, they'd keep you from talking, Gregger."

It was meant affectionately, but Gregory still doesn't know that.

He pushes this bad memory from his mind, which he sometimes pictures as an erasable Winky Dink screen, and looks down at his ticket, which shows six stops between Melwyn Park and Grand Central. He thinks of the planets: if Melwyn Park is home, Earth, then Grand Central must be Pluto, the outermost planet, the place from which you leave the known world, the solar system. And the terminal is the place he's going, riding backwards, his seat facing away from the train's direction, just as it is with Scott when the capsule's

Automatic Stabilization Control System is on. He's going to the terminal, where all the people are waiting for Scott's return, to hear that he's come through, come home.

Why are they waiting for him? Don't they know what he's just realized? That something is about to go wrong; that Scott isn't coming home, and he isn't either.

Full of this new awareness, he looks out the window as the train passes Mrs. Burke. He waves goodbye but she doesn't see him, and a minute later he's looking out at the southernmost fringe of Melwyn Park, ahead of him but behind the train, all of it — the Village Hall and the fire department, the huge Montgomery Ward on the other side of the highway, his own house between the two hills — receding like the blue-and-white earth from an outbound spaceship.

He leans forward to see what he's leaving, pushing up to the glass to take in as much as he can, his thin shoulder blades hunched, pressing against his shirt, like angel's wings.

———

At T plus 03 45 00 Cronkite says what is already evident about Scott Carpenter's day: "His flight has not been the same sort of smashing success as was Glenn's." But the last thing he wants to do is knock the heroic virtues of the pilot. This seems a good moment to point out that the astronaut is "a noble man by heredity," as well as by the courage he's showing today. Cronkite holds up the coat of arms of an Englishman, supposedly Carpenter's ancestor, who was knighted in 1622 for carrying messages for the king through bands of highwaymen. The greyhound shown on the seal signifies the knight's special favor with the king; only those who were close to the monarch could display the royal animal. The crest, says Cronkite, is now with Carpenter's uncle in Colorado.

At 03 46 21, as the medical monitor reads the astronaut's respiration rate ("I guarantee I'm breathing," Carpenter jokes), Mrs. O'Hara picks up the copy of *Men of Iron* that Gregory returned an hour ago, and reshelves it in its proper place in the Melwyn Park School library.

––––––––––

03 48 50 P

I'm taking a good swig of water. It's pretty cool this time. Stretching my legs a tad. It's quite dark. I'm in drifting flight. Oh, boy! It feels good to get that leg stretched out. That one and the right one too.

Sally Rodwell draws the dotted swiss curtains in the upstairs bedroom of her attached house in Audley End, England. She pulls the heavy plastic shade behind them and the room becomes quite dark, even though it's only 5:33 P.M. and the sun won't set at this 52-degree latitude until past 9. Her husband, Brian, will soon come in, off the London-to-Cambridge train, but he will find no dinner preparations under way, since Sally has spent the afternoon doing what she has done most afternoons for the past several months, sitting and thinking and waiting for the moment when she knows she'll be tired enough to fall asleep. It was the arrival of that moment which sent her upstairs to draw the shade and curtains and lie down without bothering to lift the bedspread.

Sally used to be different, used to have "quite a bit too much energy for her own good," by her own cheerful reckoning, which casual assessment, made last October to Dr. Nicholas Fletcher in his surgery down the road, led him to prescribe Distaval tablets, something that would let her sleep, or just relax her enough that the baby she and Brian were trying perhaps a little too hard to have wouldn't preoccupy her quite so much. "It can be a bit like love," Dr. Fletcher had said. "Sometimes you find just what you want the minute you stop looking for it."

A month later she found out she was pregnant, a piece of news that from the instant she heard it has left her alternating between moments of near terror and longer stretches of a kind of sick despair, since it was on November 10, three days before this news came to her, that Distaval, which is now in Britain better known by its generic name, thalidomide, was removed from the market.

Sally Rodwell's baby will arrive thirty days from today, on the same day a daughter will be born to Bill and Penny Hatfield in Omaha, Nebraska. As Sally lies on her bedspread in Audley End, Penny Hatfield, at 11:34 A.M., Omaha time, is already finishing her lunch and thinking about making a second sandwich. She's growing bored with the flight and has been eating like it's going out of style these past couple of months. She's glad Bill is back on the day shift at Swift and can't see her putting it away all day. Her appetite and size are the chief comic themes of her conversations, conducted on the Princess telephone near the living room couch, with her girlfriend Sherry. "I guess I'm already 'nesting,'" she said the other day, playing with a term she'd picked up from one of the baby books she's reading. It's hard for her now to believe how jumpy she was just a few months ago — worried about money and her mother and problems with Bill. All those things, plus Bill's months on the night shift, which left her unable to sleep half the time, had made her go to Dr. Carver for something to calm her down. But she's been so naturally relaxed the last several weeks that she's stopped taking what he prescribed. "Sherry, being fat is a great calmer-downer," she joked the other day.

What Dr. Carver prescribed for Penny Hatfield was familiar old Miltown, though, had Dr. Frances Kelsey of the Food and Drug Administration not had "a hunch" about it and refused approval of its sale in the United States, Penny might have gotten a new tranquilizer that the William S. Merrell Company of Cincinnati had been planning to bring out under the name Kevadon — another trade name less cumbersome than thalidomide.

Thinking that calling Sherry may keep her from making a second sandwich, Penny pushes away the TV tray-table and reaches for the Princess phone.

In Audley End, Brian Rodwell has arrived home and gone upstairs and gotten close to the end of the brief, pointless conversation he and Sally have most days about this time.

"But you *don't* know. Everything may be fine. We just have to wait, awful as that is."

"But I do know."

"How can you?"

"Because I never feel it kicking. It's got no legs."

---

03 51 13.5 P

... you just adapt to this environment, like — like you were born in it. It's a great, great freedom.

Cathleen McLinden Noonan sits across from a small black-and-white television set that is not on. A present made by her son Jim and daughter-in-law Mary after they acquired their color one, it is never on during the daytime in this dining room in Jackson Heights, Queens, where Cathleen sits each afternoon, more or less contentedly, and then sleepily, by herself. The set will come on tonight when her bachelor son, Jim's fifty-year-old brother, Danny, comes home from his job selling men's suits at Saks, several blocks up Fifth Avenue from Jim. The two brothers meet once every couple of weeks for lunch, and that, to use Cathleen's strongest term of approbation, is "nice." "That's nice, don't fight" is what she would say to them with her stern weariness when, forty years ago, they played in this same room and shouted for her attention.

Played next to this radio, which, except during spring cleaning and one change of tubes in 1946, has never moved, and through which Cathleen's husband, Joseph, heard McAdoo battle Al Smith and Tunney beat Dempsey before the morning in June 1929 when he left the house for the subway and fell dead of a stroke before reaching Roosevelt Avenue.

A widow for thirty-three years, she sits as she is most accustomed to, alone, her ear cupped, the better to hear the radio. The increasing deafness might make her miss the ring of the telephone, if there were a telephone in the house. She won't have one, has never seen the need, though born just four years after its invention. If she has some emergency (and she never does) to communicate to Jim and Mary, Danny can always phone them up from Rinaldo's candy store down the street.

"Fool of a boy," she whispers, shaking her head — not about Danny but about Scott Carpenter, who is rounding the earth for a third time and who is the subject of the radio reporter's confident-as-can-be ad libbing. "He'll be getting himself killed," she adds.

That is what it will amount to, for no one made him take this ride. Her oldest, Mike, who would be fifty-two now, never came home from Guadalcanal, but he hadn't gone and volunteered. She'd made him wait until they came for him, as she did with Jim, her youngest, her darling. Her philosophies are few but definite: among them is the certainty that one should neither seek nor fight death. A good life consists of a series of dignified encounters with the unavoidable. She respects life but does not love it. And life, like outer space, will not bear much looking into.

Having lost patience with the Carpenter boy, she turns the radio off and looks out through the window on her left, into the small garden behind the house. A squirrel is peering tentatively across the border of seashells circling her carefully tended tulips. With no more time for his nonsense than the astronaut's, she taps the screen loudly and he scurries into the next Irish-American yard. Foolishness has always earned her scorn. Her own father, an immigrant child of the famine, had been in New York for more than thirty years when her mother became pregnant with her; but he got it into his head that at least one of his children would be born in a country he could barely remember, and so he packed himself and his wife onto a clipper ship bound for Galway. Less than a month after Cathleen's birth, the three of them were on their way back to Hell's Kitchen. Eighty years later, during the most recent census, Cathleen did as she has here in Jackson Heights every ten years since Wilson was in the White House: opened the door and told the census taker "New York City" was her place of birth. America had treated the McLindens and Noonans reasonably, and she saw no point in honoring her father's thickheaded gesture decade after decade — as if she were supposed to remember some little place called Creagh, having spent all of a month there, and in her cradle, too. She is still called Cat-leen — a hard *t* in an Irish dactyl — but that's it.

As she drifts, sitting up, into a nap, one detail from the radio this morning reenters her mind: the boy's mother had had TB, been too weak to raise him for a while, had gone east and left him — with his uncle, was it? — in Colorado. Cathleen, just barely awake now, shakes her head once more, thinking of the woman, whose name already escapes her, and who must be waiting for her son — hopelessly, if she's wise. TB: worse than cancer to Cathleen's mind, still, sixty years after leaving Hell's Kitchen. She remembers her friend Nelly, carried off with it a month after they'd gone to work in the same row of the mattress factory in the winter of '93.

Her lips purse and she moves closer to sleep. It's at least one mercy that such things have changed. An image of her only grandchild forms behind her eyes. He is healthy. A dreamer, that one, edgy when he comes on Sunday afternoons to this old house, musty with linen and wax fruit and dishes of old hard candy; he's used to the clean edges and gleaming surfaces of the suburbs. A dreamer too shy to meet her eyes (though she's learned to kiss him hello and goodbye, a concession, really, to her pretty Italian daughter-in-law); he's always off, five minutes after arriving, into the basement or onto the catwalk in the attic.

And yet he's somehow like her, this boy. There is something about the wariness of his negotiation with the world that she recognizes as her own. And so what if he's a bit solemn? A few months ago, at the table a few feet away from the chair she now sits in, Danny made a joke about the boy, who was even quieter than usual and not wanting any dessert. He said, "You're the oldest one in the room, Gregger," and Cathleen told him, with enough of a bark to surprise the rest, to leave the boy alone.

He will do things his own way, she suspects, and that will be fine, just as she has done things, unchangingly, hers. She is still well enough to get out to the A & P each morning, and that's just how often she goes, too, every morning at ten, coming home with no more than she needs for the day. This morning, with her black straw hat pinned to her hair, she'd made two trips; what she required couldn't be put in a single bag, so she came back a second time. She wasn't about to trail a metal cart behind her, "like a donkey," she'd say, whenever Jim laughed at this stubbornness. If she wants no telephone, and chooses not to be one of the sixty-five million souls in front of television sets watching this flight today, it is — like all else — the business of no neighbor, priest or relation. Freedom is privacy, and it is to privacy that she will spot threats before spotting them to anything else. On her second trip to the A & P this morning she'd had a queer, unsettling feeling, one of being looked at, spied on, a feeling she could attribute to nothing until she put the grocery bag down on the dining room table, unpinned her hat and once more turned on the radio. It was that boy up there, riding around on top of the world, staring down on them all.

She is pulled back from the border of a light sleep by a sound coming through the window screen: a soft, hollow plop. She looks out to see a pink Spalding rubber ball taking a last bounce before rolling toward her tulips. It has been in the rain gutter since 7:49:53 A.M. on April 26, when Tom Hannon, a neighborhood boy, hit it with a stick bat on the next street. It had looked like a perfect launch, but as soon as it was airborne its telemetry was off, and it remained deaf to his commands of "No! No! Left!," impacting Cathleen Noonan's roof and rolling into its gutter at the same moment the unmanned *Ranger IV*, after a troubled journey of sixty-four hours, crashed into the moon at 12.9 degrees south latitude/ 129.1 degrees west longitude. The *Ranger* lies forever without a breeze to disturb one speck of the imprint it has sculpted into the moon's dust, but Tom Hannon's Spalding ball, with the help of a nudge by the squirrel Cathleen had chased from her tulips, has, twenty-eight days later, at 2:06 P.M., returned to earth.

Deciding she is too tired to go out and pick it up now, Cathleen, falling asleep once more, makes a mental note to get it later and put it on the shelf near her wicker sewing basket, so that on Sunday she can give it to Jim. (She means Gregory.)

---

03 58 20 CC

I'll give you retro time for end of mission and would like to have you set the clock to this at this time.

03 58 26.5 P

Roger.

03 58 28.5 CC

32 34

03 58 31 P

Understand, 04 32 34.

03 58 35 CC

Good.

03 58 35.5 P

Okay. It's going into the clock now — whoop.

03 58 46.5 CC

We indicate 35.

03 58 49 P

I do, too. I overshot. Stand by.

03 59 00.5 CC

That's probably close enough for government work.

03 59 07.5 P

For you, to the second.

"Sir, the phone hookup to the *Intrepid* will be ready any-time after two — that's a little more than an hour after the splashdown's expected."

"Oh, fine, good," says the President in his rapid way. "Maybe I'll go take a look at things for a moment."

He goes from the Oval Office into the outer one and looks at the television, which reports that Carpenter's capsule is making its third pass over Australia. A couple of young naval aides stiffen into respectful smiles at his entry.

"Well, I guess you're all finding this more absorbing than the visit by the president of the Ivory Coast."

"Yes, sir," the aides say simultaneously, laughing.

"Well, we'll be talking to Commander Carpenter as soon as they fish him out of the Caribbean," says the President, accenting the second syllable instead of the still more usually emphasized third. "And you fellows can look forward to getting a look at Mrs. Carpenter whenever we get them up here. They were here with the Shepards and the Glenns, and I don't know if you noticed, but she's quite an eyeful. If I'm any judge."

"Sir," says the bolder of the two aides, the Irish one that Kennedy likes, "I'm told that even the Republicans trust your judgment on such matters."

The President laughs and goes back into the Oval Office.

---

04 09 52.5 P

  . . . I have 22 minutes and 20 seconds left for retrofire. I think that I will try to get some of this equipment stowed at this time.

04 11 07.5 P

  There is the moon.

04 11 31.5 P

  Looks no different — here than it does on the ground.

"And I think forty-eight dozen of number four-oh-six ought to about do it, Mr. Noonan. Thirty-six white, twelve black." Winifred Woodward points to the sketch of a "four-button with scalloped top and side; wing effect stitching around matching pearl buttons" in the Lowndes catalogue, and Jim nods as he fills in the sizing breakdown on his order pad.

As they sit across from each other at Longchamps, waiting for their lunch to come, Jim's worry is momentarily dispelled. It's a good order she's given him, worth the wait. He's sure that sharp old Miss Woodward stopped in at Lowndes's competitor, Van Salter, between Saks and Arnold Constable, and he's glad to have won what must be the lion's share of her business. Still, he doesn't know how long the company can keep going with frilly dinosaurs like number 406, or for that matter half of what's in the catalogue. This stuff is going the way of the corset, and he knows it.

Miss Woodward has caught him staring at the sketch of his own merchandise, and she breaks into a smile under her flowered hat. "You look worried, Mr. Noonan," she says. "But I've got a lot of faith in old number four-oh-six. I can see lots of hands wrapped up in 'em draped over lots of young men's shoulder blades at lots of next year's senior proms. And when those girls are through with those gloves their mamas will always have one fancy *shmatte* they can accessorize with 'em the followin' fall."

Jim laughs at the Yiddish coming out of Miss Woodward's southern Presbyterian mouth. He's picked up the same expressions himself after fifteen years on "the digital fringes of the rag trade," as Manny Spear, the courtly old children's-wear man at Lowndes, likes to put it. About a month ago, while Jim was on a ladder at home, Gregory came over to show him some nautical knots he was doing for his Lion badge in Cub Scouts. "Better they should teach you how to fix storm windows," he told his son, who understood neither the syntax nor that it was a joke.

Oh, Gregger.

The dull roar of lunch at Longchamps is cut into by a sharp treble burst from the next table. "Another orbit, men?" asks one ad executive of a table heading into a second round of martinis.

The noise reminds Winifred Woodward of something. "You never did tell me about your boy this mornin'. Those sirens started blastin' just as I asked you."

"Oh, Gregger," says Jim, shaking his head and smiling. "He's fine. A little space-crazy. He's all wrapped up in the flight today. He'd like to go to the moon eventually."

Miss Woodward frowns and rather brusquely swizzles her ginger ale. "I don't hold with this at all. I don't see why they keep pressin' their luck. They almost didn't get the last one back, did they?" she asks, referring to the supposed loosening of John Glenn's heat shield — what remains, though for only another three quarters of an hour, the most harrowing episode of the American space program.

"Oh," Miss Woodward continues, after a pause, somewhat apologetically, "don't pay me much mind, Mr. Noonan. I'm just too old and opinionated for my own good. The fact is, I don't like travel itself, the whole notion and practice of it; people always goin' off, makin' pledges to return and then not keepin' them."

Jim is embarrassed by this little rhetorical burst. Miss Woodward, who has been reading him all morning, just as she has each spring since 1947, turns coquettish and confidential. Her face smiles and softens and drops a dozen years. "Oh, just *listen* to me," she says, laughing. "I'm still gettin' angry over what at home we call a romantic disappointment. I suppose the fact that Jamie Shackleford left Raleigh for Los Angeles, looking for work in 1933, and decided, probably quite sensibly, not to return to Raleigh and, incidentally, me, is no reason for us to cease exploration of the heavens."

Jim does not know how he's supposed to respond to this. She's laughing, but that doesn't mean she wants *him* to. He opts for changing the immediate subject while pursuing the general theme of travel.

"Actually, I'm not much for travel either," he says. "I've always been glad they took me off the road. I don't make more than a trip or two a year now. I've got one coming up soon, down to Virginia. But it's the source of some tension between me and this son of mine. He wants to come with me, and . . ."

Miss Woodward puts down her ginger ale and gives a mock shudder. "I'm sure you couldn't be more correct, Mr. Noonan. That side of life is lost to me — children, that is; because of Jamie Shackleford's failure to return from Los Angeles — and I'm sure it's just as well. I loathe the ones I know. There are some young boys down the street from me that I'd just as soon see strangled as fed. I'm sure your boy is different, of course."

Jim laughs uneasily as the waiter brings their plates.

Miss Woodward, newly content, spreads her napkin on her lap and sighs. "I just hope those boys give me a little peace tonight. I intend to be sittin' out on my front porch by eight P.M."

"Tonight?" asks Jim.

"Yes, Mr. Noonan, tonight," says Miss Woodward. "Being crotchety does not mean being entirely nonadaptive. I'm flying home from La Guardia airport at three-thirty. If my brother manages to remember to come to Raleigh and get me, I'll be sitting on that porch by eight and looking up at the moon. I'll keep an eye out for him."

"For who?"

"Why, your little boy. Isn't that where you say he wants to go?"

---

04 19 22.5 P

Sunrise. Ahhhhh! Beautiful lighted fireflies that time. It was luminous that time. But it's only, okay, they — all right, I have — if anybody reads, I have the fireflies. They are very bright. They are capsule emanating. I can rap the hatch and stir off hundreds of them. Rap the side of

the capsule; huge streams come out. They — some appear to glow. Let me yaw around the other way.

The "Glenn effect" is solved. Scott Carpenter bangs on the window of his capsule and its frost particles go dancing off like the mysterious lightning bugs his American predecessor in space thought he was seeing. There's no one but his tape recorder to hear of his discovery, though. He's two and a half minutes from radio contact with Hawaii, and when the Cap Com there starts talking to him it will be with instructions for preparing to fire the retro-rockets that will take him home — provided he punches the button some fourteen minutes from now, at just the right second, with the capsule at just the right angle. By the time he makes his third pass over Cape Canaveral and talks to Gus Grissom, in twenty minutes, he will already be on his way down.

Another sprinkle of fireflies goes off into the dawn one hundred miles above the Pacific.

Three miles under the Atlantic, the spicules of a glass sponge shiver near the natural coral cement that has begun to form over the *Liberty Bell*, Gus Grissom's capsule, which sank to this spot on the ocean floor last summer after he managed to escape it, and which will never be recovered. Glenn's *Friendship 7*, which ninety-three mornings ago was generating frosty fireflies in space, is at the moment sitting on a pedestal in Belgrade, Yugoslavia, one of twenty stops on its USIA-sponsored world tour.

Gregory Noonan looks out past some dots of mud on the window of the New York Central Railroad car he is riding in. After an unaccountable delay in southern Westchester, the train once again got moving toward New York City. Now Alicia Munoz's pink curtains and red geranium catch Gregory's glance as the elevated train passes her fire escape, traveling down through East Harlem. Gregory notices some Negro girls playing jump rope near a flagpole in the Carver Houses project. He thinks, as he did this morning, of Bernice Williams's kinky beribboned hair, and realizes that all the people beyond the window are colored, that he is in a territory harder for him to imagine than space. With shyness he returns his gaze to the interior of the car, looking straight ahead at the advertisements on each side of the door: "I Can't Save a Nickel . . . Let Alone Buy Life Insurance." Will Scott Carpenter survive reentry? Does he himself have a nickel left to buy M & M's, which he likes to crunch when he is anxious, and which he will surely need when he gets to the city, before whatever it is that's going to happen to him happens? His hand feels for the change in his right pocket. He has forty-five cents left.

The other ad is for a mattress. He reads: "Beautyrest . . . The Happiness Money Can . . ." before the inside of the car goes suddenly dark and the transistor goes completely dead.

---

04 22 26 P
   Roger, reading you loud and clear Hawaii. How me?
04 22 31.5 CC
   Aurora 7, Hawaii Cap Com. How do you read me?
04 22 35 P
   Roger. Do you read me or do you not, James?
04 22 39.5 CC
   Gee, you are weak; but I read you.

Christine Lombardo, thirty-seven years old, sits in a hotel room in Honolulu and carefully replaces the tissue paper wrapping the small wreath made of dried marigolds and wildflowers from her back yard in Vestal, New York. She made the wreath weeks ago, with flowers she'd saved from last summer, and she carried it with her on the plane. Next Wednesday she will drop it into the ocean over the 184-foot-long memorial that's been raised above the USS *Arizona* on pilings driven into the coral rock beneath the water. The officials dedicating the memorial will drop larger wreaths of blood-red anthuriums and Vanda orchids into the harbor, and after they've made their speeches she will go below, into what they're calling the shrine room, to search the white marble wall for the name of Billy McDermott.

Frank Lombardo, her husband, is a good man; he said he'd be happy to make the trip with her. They could make it a vacation, if that didn't seem out of keeping with the situation. No, Christine said, that would be fine. Frank is lying on the hotel beach now, listening to the spaceflight on a portable radio, while she's up here thinking about Billy, her first husband, the boy she married when she was seventeen, the boy who lies beneath the calm waters of Pearl Harbor, inside the *Arizona,* with 1,100 others.

As the thirty-seven-year-old naval lieutenant commander, Scott Carpenter, tries, above the Hawaiian islands, to make himself heard on the correct radio frequency, Mr. William Thorpe, sixty-two years old, a onetime ensign in the Royal Navy, stands behind the altar of Coventry Cathedral and picks a piece of lint off the largest tapestry in the world. Weighing literally a ton, it is a brilliant thing of yellow and green made, Mr. Thorpe knows, by the Frogs, but at least designed by an Englishman, named Sutherland. It's early evening in Warwickshire, and Mr. Thorpe is being as polite as he can to all these television people, trailing their cables everywhere and being anything but what one might call properly reverent.

But everything must be ready for tomorrow, when the Queen herself will be here for the consecration of the new cathedral. Two thousand people will be inside to see the

Archbishop of Canterbury go about his business, and some millions more, here and on the Continent, will be watching on telly.

Mr. Thorpe straightens a cloth on the altar, which, like the new cathedral's cross, is made from the charred rubble of the old one, destroyed by German bombs on November 14, 1940. He looks at the words FATHER FORGIVE engraved behind the altar, words that tomorrow, May 25, 1962, will perhaps be pondered (if what historians will later say is true) by the handful of Englishmen who allowed the Germans to go ahead with their plans to destroy Coventry rather than let them know — which an evacuation of the city surely would have — that the English had broken the Germans' code. A matter of the fewest deaths in the long run, of using God's gift of mathematics to do His work for Him.

And now, as Mr. William Thorpe, caretaker, avoids tripping over a wire belonging to the French national television service, the pilot of the *Aurora 7* gets ready to try to come home, to fire the retro-rockets that will make his spacecraft dive — not with bombs, just its solitary human rider — for the surface of the earth.

---

04 24 36 P

I'm aligning my attitudes. Everything is fine. I have part of the stowage checklist taken care of at this time.

At 1:14 P.M. Elizabeth Wheatley finishes smoothing the powder on her nose. She snaps shut the mirrored compact from Harry Winston that her agent bought her upon publication of *The Committee*.

"Honestly, Elizabeth, I don't know where you get the self-control," says Connie, who cannot believe Elizabeth has managed to sit through a nice long lunch, from a martini through coffee, without opening either of the two telegrams they found pinned to her apartment door before heading back out to this restaurant on Madison. Elizabeth, who likes impressing Connie, smiles one of her grand-piano smiles.

"All right, Connie. While you're in the ladies' room I'll read the telegrams."

Actually, Connie hadn't said anything about going to the ladies' room, but as soon as Elizabeth mentions it she is on her feet.

Elizabeth opens both telegrams at once, setting the little yellow envelopes near the ashtray and arranging the messages side by side.

She is pleased to discover that neither of them is from Robbie, or his lawyer, or his mother. "News travels fast," the first one begins. "Get back in cab. Meet me office for drink dinner night. Mac."

It is from Warren MacLeod, a rich, good-looking, nononsense lawyer for a lot of uranium and mining interests. Elizabeth met him in the summer of 1955 at her sister's beach house in California, and they had an affair in New York the following fall. Warren liked her intellect, and had enjoyed subduing it with his simple physical authority. Which, after what were already too many years with Robbie, was just what Elizabeth wanted: his opposite. The only thing Warren had in common with Robbie was an unfortunate determination to stay married — in Warren's case, to a pretty wife in Locust Valley. Questions of morality raised by the affair bothered Elizabeth not at all, but questions of convenience (Robbie's strongest suit) concerned her immensely. And since Warren wasn't going to give up his wife — something that, at bottom, neither he nor Elizabeth wanted him to do, since Warren's ceding any ground to Elizabeth would entirely disrupt the sexual dynamics of the affair — that was that. Given these circumstances, she didn't know why her departure from Robbie (which was, she assumed, the fast-traveling news) should make any difference.

Would she go down to 500 Fifth Avenue, at the corner of 42nd, and up to the twentieth floor, to find out? She turns over the yellow patch of paper and tries to summon up Warren's image, as if on a screen, the way she does when she's getting characters ready for a blank page, where she will one day no doubt fix Warren. She remembers a night in the Carlyle, which could stand for the dozen or so others, when she was pulling down on his broad American shoulders and looking at his white American teeth, even whiter than her own, as through them, he said, with perfect assurance and to her own perfect satisfaction, "Elizabeth, I don't give a fuck about your opinions."

Which is not something Fred Foy, her editor at *The New Yorker,* and the author of the second telegram — "Don't unpack. Want you in Mexico end of month with JFK. Call immediately" — would ever say. Elizabeth isn't quite sure what this means, but presumably Kennedy is planning a trip there and Fred wants her to cover it in soft-reporting, "Letter from Mexico City" style. It isn't really her subject, and she is at a loss to figure out why he's thought of her for it. She does, of course, know Mexico and her Spanish is excellent — she'd lived there for two years with her first husband after the war — but it hardly seems enough to suggest her for this assignment. She'd thought they were soon going to send her to Seattle, anyway. It is a city to which she has no connection, but some sharp observations on the vulgarities of the World's Fair there would be right in her, and the magazine's, line. But Kennedy? She has little interest in him — a pretty boy with (unlike Warren) no rough edges to grab on to. And that family! The men a loud bunch of Knights of Columbus, with just more than the usual amounts of money; the women a string of plastic rosary beads.

And yet little eldritch Fred often sees things she doesn't. He'd pushed her into doing that rather good piece she'd done on the Saint Lawrence Seaway, and who else on earth would have seen any possibilities in *that* for —

"He was approved for the third orbit," Connie says, resettling herself excitedly. "In fact, he's almost through it. The matron in the ladies' room had the radio on."

"Oh, *Connie*," says Elizabeth, smiling with indulgent savagery, as if her companion were telling her she'd just bought a hula hoop.

"Oh, I know," says Connie, recalling Elizabeth's reaction when the subject of the flight came up at Elizabeth's televisionless apartment, "you don't approve. But really, can you think of a better way to compete with the Russians? It's better than trying to build bigger bombs than they can. No wonder Goldwater sometimes seems so lukewarm about space," she says, reaching an unaccustomed level of self-assertion in Elizabeth's presence.

Sensing her friend's discomfort at such heights, Elizabeth gaily changes the subject. She hands both telegrams across the table. "Now, Connie, help me. Where am I to go this afternoon? To my current editor or my former lover?"

"Goodness," says Connie. "I can't imagine!"

With only three minutes before retrofire, Walter Cronkite says that "everything seems to be a normal situation in the capsule." The astronaut "has plenty of fuel; that fuel problem has been solved quite nicely."

---

04 29 15.5 CC
  Transmitting in the blind. We have LOS [loss of signal].

Ground elapsed time is on my mark, 4 hours 29 minutes and 30 seconds. Transmitting in the blind to Aurora 7. Make sure all your tone switches are on; your warning lights are bright; the retro manual fuse switch is on; the retrojettison fuse switch is off. Check your faceplate and make sure that it is closed.

04 29 59 CC

Aurora 7. Did you copy?

04 30 00.5 P

Roger. Copied all; I think we're in good shape. I'm not sure just what the status of the ASCS is at this time.

Having traveled the length of the Park Avenue tunnel, the train stops. The conductor announces to the almost empty car: "Grand Central Terminal. This is the final stop on this train. Please check the seats around you and the overhead rack to make sure you have all your personal belongings, and have a pleasant afternoon."

Gregory looks out the window, thinking it peculiar that his father, between daily crossings of their sunny green lawn, walks into and out of this sooty darkness. He lingers in his seat, wondering if he himself will ever walk back up this platform, or if his steps southward and into the main concourse will be his last in any direction.

The heels of the two ladies heading for the Korvette's opening click across the car's metal apron and out the door, leaving Gregory all alone, until the conductor says, "Everybody out. Last stop."

He gets up.

(In room 4 of the Melwyn Park School at this moment, 1:15 P.M., Joan Linley first notices that Gregory Noonan's chair, diagonally in front of Kenny Kessler's, is empty.)

Gregory walks down the platform of track 34 toward the light of the waiting room, passing posters for *No Strings* and

Come Blow Your Horn. He tries to tune in his transistor radio, but he is still too far underground to get anything more than static.

The *Aurora 7* flies between Hawaii and California, briefly out of range of both tracking stations. For the past three minutes a yellow light has been on in the capsule, the signal to Scott Carpenter to stow his equipment and be ready for retrofire and the return to earth. The instructions and countdown will be given by Alan Shepard, with whom Carpenter makes voice contact at T plus 04 31 36, or 1:16, the same time Gregory enters the main concourse and his own transistor flares into clear, receptive life.

04 33 00 CC

  4, 3, 2, 1, 0.

04 33 14.5 P

  Okay. Fire 1, fire 2, and fire 3. I had to punch off manually. I have a little bit of smoke in the capsule.

Gregory emerges in front of the brilliantly lit needles of the New York City skyline and under the northern constellations. He is standing under the stars painted on the main concourse's ceiling, across from the Kodak Colorama slide taking up the top of the eastern wall.

He cannot move. The room is filled with people, thousands of them, but the cat's got their tongue. There is none of the noise this many people would make in the crowded places he's been before — Yankee Stadium, the Connecticut shore. Everyone is looking at the CBS-TV screen set up over the ticket counters; over his now superfluous radio Gregory hears the announcement that Scott Carpenter should have just punched the button to fire his retro-rockets, "beginning the dangerous period of reentry into the earth's atmosphere."

From its outer edge Gregory looks through the slivers of light and space in the crowd. He can spot, at various points, a policeman with a nightstick; a Negro man wheeling a dolly; a lady with two suitcases; a funny-looking woman tossing an orange up and down in her right hand.

There are no children here — again unlike Yankee Stadium or the Connecticut shore. *I'm not supposed to be here.* The usual laws aren't operating. *You are traveling in another dimension.*

He moves to his right, inching sideways in as quick and quiet a way as he can, trying to detach himself from the crowd's rim the way he knows Scott Carpenter is now trying to break his own orbital stride. But Carpenter is trying to come home. Where is *he* supposed to be going? He doesn't know, but his sideways steps have brought him to one of the station's newsstands. His eyes immediately find the M & M's.

"Five cents," the lady behind the counter says, and he pays. She gives him a funny what-are-you-doing-here look. He turns quickly away from her and looks down into the little brown bag of yellow, green, brown and (pre-red-dye-number-two-scare) red disks, little candy planets that seem familiar, universal, just the same as they'd look if he bought them at Pop's in Melwyn Park.

He looks down the long corridor stretching away from the newsstand. He sees it break up in the distance, one ramp leading toward the street and daylight, he imagines, and another leading down into someplace else. The subway? A tunnel? He feels that he is supposed to walk down one of them; something is urging him to. He looks again into the M & M's bag, as if the candies might be pressed into service as a breadcrumb trail that could help him find his way back.

He wishes he had taken the Saint Christopher medal off his Rollfast before leaving the schoolyard. There is no Cath-

olic astronaut, but if there were, he wonders, would NASA
let him put a Saint Christopher medal in his capsule, someplace where it wouldn't get in the way, like above the seat
back?

He knows what is happening in space now. The capsule is
beginning to fall, not straight down like a stone, but like
something you've flung from a window, still moving outward
but losing momentum, beginning to drop, drop, drop.

And where she stops, nobody knows. They only think they
do, thinks Gregory. They'll all be waiting at 21 degrees
north, 68 degrees west. That's where it's supposed to land.
It's all planned. But he's sure they're not going to find it
there.

He looks again down the dark stone corridor and feels that
he's not going to walk down it now, that it's not time to yet.

He will go back instead to the grand vaulted waiting room,
where he will find a spot and wait to hear the fate of the
Aurora 7. He eats a green M & M and takes a small step back
toward the crowd, seven thousand souls standing under the
painted zodiac.

----

04 33 51.5 CC

Roger. We should have retrojettison in about 10 seconds.

04 33 55 P

Roger.

04 33 56.5 P

That was a nice gentle bump. All three have fired.
Retroattitude was red.

04 34 05.5 CC

Roger. Should have retrojettison now.

04 34 10 P

Ah, right then at 34 10, on time.

04 34 15 CC

Roger. How much fuel do you have left both tanks?

04 34 19 P

I have 20 and 5 percent.

04 34 23.5 CC

Roger. I guess we'd better use —

04 34 26 P

I'll use manual.

04 34 27.5 CC

— on reentry, unless ASCS holds you in reentry attitude.

04 34 31 P

Yes, it can. I'll have to do it with manual.

04 34 39 CC

Roger. Recommend you try Aux Damp first; if it's not working, then go to fly-by-wire.

04 34 45 P

Okay, I'll have to do that.

But as Scott Carpenter makes the switch to fly-by-wire to stop the capsule's tumbling, he forgets to shut off the manual system. And now, each time he moves the stick, trying to get the descending capsule in the proper alignment for coming home, he is spending the last of both his automatic and manual fuel supplies.

REENTRY

Eleven minutes before he is scheduled to impact on the ocean, Scott Carpenter is having trouble keeping the *Aurora 7* in the proper attitude. And he is unaware of the mistake he made with the switches, a mistake that could cost him his life.

Beneath him the landscape of earth is starting to define itself. Lakes, fields, rivers — even roads, he thinks — are now in view. But the capsule's alignment still isn't right, and from California, just before losing contact, Shepard has told him to get the spacecraft into the proper attitude and use as little fuel as he possibly can.

CBS has televised the "tense crowd" gathered at Grand Central, and Cronkite reminds everyone that as Carpenter's g forces build up during reentry, he will weigh as much as half a ton. "His capsule becomes, in effect, a meteor, smashing to earth in a flaming ball."

As he comes in range of the Cape Canaveral tracking station, the first question the astronaut hears from Cap Com Gus Grissom is whether or not he's got his faceplate closed. The answer is no. Carpenter closes it and says thanks. The horizon comes into view, and he reports, "It's going to be real tight on fuel, Gus." He now realizes how perilously short he is. His manual supply gauge indicates 7 percent, but he knows the truth: it's empty. And there's only 15 percent in the other tank.

At 04 44, or 1:29 P.M., the capsule reaches its maximum heat and enters the ionization blackout, a ten-minute period when all radio communication with the spacecraft is impossible. Unable to hear or speak with Grissom, Carpenter will have only his tape recorder to tell what's happening to himself and his ship.

He feels some encouraging oscillations — at least the capsule has reached the atmosphere. He rolls it at a rate of 10 degrees per second, trying to keep it on the right course. At 04 47 02 he looks out the window and sees an orange ring of burning particles. Are they coming off the heat shield? "Oh, I hope not," he records, not in plaintive panic but in imitation of Bill Dana's José Jimenez — the frightened-astronaut routine that cracks up the Mercury Seven whenever they see it on *Ed Sullivan*. The orange glow disappears, and now a green haze is visible at the capsule's point, the screw-in part of its light-bulb shape.

At 100,000 feet it begins to sway violently, and Carpenter tries to control the oscillations with whatever may be left of his fuel.

At 1:33 P.M. the giant TV screen in Grand Central shows a peaceful still picture of the *Intrepid,* the aircraft carrier charged with retrieving the spacecraft, which is expected to come down within several miles of it. Everything is ready. The recovery ships are even carrying men with rifles — to fight off sharks if they have to.

Closing his eyes, Gregory pictures himself in a metal cone surrounded by flames. He tries to imagine himself and his little ship speeding, falling toward the ocean. But he has never been in a plane. His only vivid experiences of height have come on class trips to city skyscrapers. And so, try as he will to picture the ocean getting closer and closer, the only thing he can feel rising up at him is not water but pavement.

"You want a lift, boy?" Herbert Johnson, smiling, pauses behind his dolly under Ras Algethi, brightest star in the constellation of Hercules the Strongman. Gregory, who is highly responsible about not talking to strangers, freezes in surprise in front of this large Negro man with friendly yellow teeth. He shakes his head no and darts into the next hole in the crowd.

Spooky little fella, thinks Herbert, a porter with Terminal Operations, now carrying five boxes of rolled tickets, each weighing twenty pounds, to the ticket windows of the New Haven lines. What he's got on his dolly will keep several thousand men shuttling in place between city towers and suburban frame houses for the next several weeks.

Tonight Herbert Johnson will take the IRT number 6 back up to the Carver Houses project in Harlem, getting there a little before most of the white men are home in Stamford. Once inside their dwellings they will be equalized by TV, the white fantasy world into which most nights Herbert automatically slips.

Last night he'd made a regular four-course meal of it, outlasting his wife and daughter. (His boy, who Herbert is sure is going to come to no good, was out who knows where.) At 7:30 Howard K. Smith had done a special — talking in his soft southern accent, which Herbert likes, since it reminds him of home — about "Guerrilla Warfare: The Challenge of Southeast Asia" (the place where a few years from now his son will die). Later in the evening it had been Perry Como, "with his special guest Anne Bancroft," whom Herbert and the white men up in Stamford, each one no more attentive than the others, watched singing at what was supposed to be a beach picnic, before joining "the rest of the gang" for "a salute to the state of Michigan." And then came Dick Van Dyke, up in New Rochelle, not Stamford, who dreamed he was caught in a world where the women, Laura and Millie, ran the show. By the middle of *Naked City* ("David Wayne as a man who assumes five different identities and lives separate lives for each in 'The Multiplicity of Herbert Komish'") Herbert had fallen asleep, to waken only when his wife, Helen, cried out for him to "turn that thing off and get into this bedroom."

Right now, tired of nearly slicing people's ankles off with his dolly, Herbert takes time out under Ras Algethi and looks up at the screen, so much bigger than the thirteen-inch Philco back in the Carver Houses:

> Cronkite: Crowds at Grand Central in New York and around the United States wait prayerfully for this moment. Here's Powers.
>
> Powers: Our data at this time indicate that it is distinctly possible that the *Aurora 7* spacecraft may land considerably longer downrange than it was planned. Our present estimate of his landing point may go as far as two hundred miles downrange.

Herbert Johnson doesn't know; he just doesn't know whether a man was meant to do these things. The rest of these fellas have come down on a dime, and now this one may be lost out there in the ocean with the fishes. What a man can do one week, he can't do the next. This time last week Herbert himself was down in New York State Supreme Court, serving on a six-man jury that awarded $60,000 in damages to one taxi driver whose cab had been hit by another. And Herbert had been the foreman, saying "one at a time" in the thick of the debate, counting ballots and announcing fate. Even though the panel included a white guy in a suit, just like all the ones who will get their tickets punched for Stamford tonight, the other jurors made Herbert the foreman. Maybe it was the ladies on the panel who liked him.

But that was last week and this is this week, and one thing you can bet Herbert Johnson will never figure out is the United States of America. Ask him what's the worst place in it, and he'll tell you without a moment's hesitation: Georgia, where he was born. Some of the meanest people on earth. But home is home, and nothing's made him feel so good today as the sound of that Georgia lady's voice a minute or two ago when she asked him if he could tell her where the baggage claim was. Cheered him up and sort of got him down all at once. Twenty-four years ago he escaped to this place, arrived in this very building, whose 275-foot-long waiting room he's once more inching his dolly along. Arrived: that's what he supposes, anyway. Came here to a place of his own choosing. But carrying his load of tickets for other men's journeys, Herbert Johnson takes another look up at the screen, and he can't help thinking that he, too, twenty-four years after setting out from Macon, has landed long.

At twenty-six thousand feet, Carpenter is tumbling violently and out of fuel. He can wait no longer for the drogue chute, and so, five thousand feet before it's supposed to come out on its own, he pulls the ring.

"Hey, peewee, how come you ain't in school?" As soon as Officer Robert Cancese asks the little guy the question he regrets it; the kid goes white and darts into a thicker part of the crowd. Poor shrimp, Bobby tells himself; he probably thinks I'm gonna turn him over to the truant officer.

Bobby is determined to do nothing much of anything to-day. He's a little pissed off, in fact, since this was going to be his day off, until Lundigan pulled him for this detail. As details go it isn't bad — watching over thousands of respectable people standing and praying — but Bobby wonders why they needed extra cops for this at all. God, not like that show down here the other Sunday night, when Officer Lawrence Whelan caught three men trying to pick the lock of a storage room near the General Electric display set up near Vanderbilt Avenue. After one of them cut Whelan over the eye with an ice pick, he chased them down to the lower level. But they disappeared into the tunnel. Soon a hundred policemen were looking for them, and a huge crowd gathered at the terminal to watch. Today if there are two pickpockets in this whole place, they've probably got their eyes glued to Cronkite like everybody else.

> Powers: . . . we feel that his ionization period now is over, that he has exceeded the range of our transmission equipment here at Cape Canaveral. We are diverting aircraft into the area both for the purpose of reestablishing communications and effecting the rescue operation.
> Cronkite: Well, that's the announcement. And that's a rather serious one to hear.

Shit, Bobby thinks, just when everything was goin' so good. All morning and all spring. Catchin' up with the fuckin' Russians.

Playing with his nightstick, Bobby shifts position a little under the star of Aldebaran in the constellation of Taurus the Bull. A big twenty-four-year-old kid, he hasn't got much patience, and as nothing happens up on the screen, just waiting, his mind keeps wandering up to the Bronx, to Yankee Stadium, half a mile away from where he lives. That's where he'd be now if it wasn't for Lundigan.

Before you know it it'll be 2:00, and Bobby has the impractical and unpatriotic wish that whoever runs the terminal would switch the TV from Channel 2 to Channel 11, WPIX, which will start to broadcast the Yankees–Athletics game at 1:55 P.M. Really restless now, Bobby chokes up on his nightstick, wrist over wrist, though he's not so uncool as to take a few imaginary cuts with it, not with seven thousand people watching him and thinking he's a dope.

He probably won't be missing much, he thinks. Mantle's out with a leg injury, and Boyer's got a bum wrist. It won't be much of a game. Better than the fuckin' Mets, though. What a joke; what are they, twelve games out now? At least. But, Jesus, who can follow it with ten teams in each league?

Bobby would have loved to play ball. Dream on. Not that he was so bad back in high school or knocking around in Van Cortlandt Park. Always a little too heavy and a little too slow, though. So he's a cop instead of being Pepitone. He joined up right after leaving the Army two years ago, and it's not a bad living. His father, if he were still alive, would be pleased as hell to see it. In fact, he'd be fuckin' amazed — him haulin' crates for thirty years and his kid givin' out summonses. *Amerrrrriga*, he can hear the old man saying.

Come on, Scottie. So maybe you didn't come down where you should have. But all you got to have done is survive. If they pick you up a couple of hundred miles from where you're supposed to be, we'll call it a ground-rule double, and we'll give you the medal anyway. So come on and win this one.

(Increasingly patriotic over the next twenty years, Bobby will express more than one man's share of opinions that editorial writers and academic pollsters will find deplorable. But even with a gut that gets too big and a pension that comes too early — retiring from the cops in 1982, at forty-four, to join his brother's soda distributorship — Bobby will also be capable of his share of surprises: a lingering liberal faith in *Amerrrrriga,* expressed on occasions like the summer night in 1980 when Herbert Johnson's daughter and her husband become the first black family on Wyman Street in Garden City Park and Bobby tells his aggrieved neighbor Eddie Russo, "Hey, Eddie, why dontcha shut your fuckin' mouth? The guy probably makes more than you do.")

Under Aldebaran, Bobby scuffs his feet on the marble floor and lets his mind drift back to the Stadium. (Actually, he'll be missing a good deal. Pepitone will hit a home run and a triple this afternoon and be driven in once by Maris. Jim Coates will relieve Bud Daley on the mound, and Tresh will make two errors in the sixth inning. A pretty eventful game all in all, which the Yankees will win, 9–4.)

Maybe, Bobby thinks, I can get to the Stadium tomorrow night. See Stafford pitch against Detroit. Maybe take my kid brother along.

The thought of his kid brother gives Bobby another thought: that little peewee who ran away from him a couple of minutes ago. Maybe he's really lost, just like Scottie-boy? Bobby wonders if he should go looking for him.

Looking west, from Al Rischa to Betelgeuse, Gregory's eyes widen. That man turning around: it couldn't be his father, could it? No. His father never wears his straw hat until after Memorial Day. It must be another speck of a man, already out of sight in the crowd, whose look and movements are making Gregory remember the early evening of February

20, 1962, when Jim Noonan came into the living room, where his son was still watching the TV coverage, and handed him the afternoon's *New York World-Telegram*: "Glenn Does Three Orbits of Earth; Returns OK." Gregory looked up from the headline, pointlessly amazed at this confirmation of what he'd been watching all day at school and in the hours since. "Not so bad, no?" his father said, making Gregory do what he almost never did, burst out laughing. Gregory didn't understand that he was experiencing the pleasures of understatement, or that he was laughing at the same quiet, wry side that had first attracted Mary Frazzi to Jim Noonan, which had three years later resulted in his own life. All he'd known at that moment three months ago, without being able to say why, was that he loved his father.

But that was three months ago. Right now the minute hand of the Westclox Big Ben is moving from 1:34 to 1:35.

---

04 50 51 P

Drogue out manually at 25 [thousand feet]. It's holding and it was just in time . . . Emergency main fuse switch at 15, standing by for the main chute at 10.

After walking three times up and down a long corridor — the one under the ceiling mural with its painted biplanes — one of the two corridors that lie between the great hall and Lexington Avenue, Joanne Kalkowski finds the wherewithal to burrow her way through the crowd and arrive at the distant point under Al Tarf in the crab of Cancer, not far from the staircase to Vanderbilt Avenue. One hundred and twenty-five feet below the ten-watt bulb representing Praesepe's clustered magnitude, Joanne achieves a brief, though twitchy, stasis. She picks at her knit headband, pulls at her cardigan. Her gaze darts, lands and departs in odd trajectories, though her eyes are good. All the way across the room she can make out the word "Barricini," and she smiles, thinking of the heart-shaped box her father brings her on Valentine's Day, the rectangular one he brings for her birthday.

Paul Kalkowski is a widower, and twenty-two-year-old Joanne is his slightly cracked pride and joy. A 1958 graduate of the secretarial course at Sewanhaka High School, she commutes each morning from their house in Elmont, Long Island, to her job as a file clerk, right down the street at Pfizer Chemical. About forty-five minutes ago she put a dime in a pay phone in the Chrysler Building lobby and called up her supervisor to tell her she won't be coming back from lunch. "I don't feel so good," she'd said, with the inflection that came naturally to her — that of a child just out of bed, testing the waters of excused absence from school.

Actually Joanne feels fine, if no less fearful and no more focused than on other afternoons. After lunch at Chock Full o' Nuts the sight of this crowd dared her into the phone call and the chance to play pretend with the afternoon. She finds the idea of a man riding around the globe by himself to be funny and not very interesting; but the great mass of people, no matter what they are here for, make it seem as if the rules are suspended, that the end-of-recess bell from school, or the office, won't ring today.

Her eyes lock on the floor for a second, and she spots a discarded *Daily News*. She skitters over to it, picking it up like it's a prize she's the first to notice. She flips backwards through its pages, feeling less like herself than her father after dinner. She notices the baseball scores, ignores the fashion illustrations, flips past the Inquiring Photographer ("Harry Truman thinks it's disrespectful to refer to the President's wife as Jackie. Is it?") and settles on the theater ads. *"Fantasticks"* is a word that makes her smile, and she thinks that's something she'd like to see, though she has no idea where Sullivan Street is and can't really imagine going to a play, by herself or with anyone else. She does know where the theaters are, though; if you keep walking along 42nd Street in a straight line, all the way in the opposite direction from Pfizer, you start to run into them. That's maybe what she'll do this afternoon — walk around there, and then, around 5:00, come back here and get, first, the F train for Jamaica, then the bus to Elmont.

> Cronkite: We still don't know that he is safely through the atmospheric layer. We haven't had a transmission from him. There — perhaps there have been radar indications — and there must be radar indications that at least the capsule is all right, if they have a predicted landing point at this point. So apparently the capsule did come through the atmosphere and the flame area all right. No communications, however. You heard Colonel Powers explain their theory as to why, that the impact point is two hundred miles over the mark, beyond the *Intrepid* and its two destroyers. They have sent aircraft out now to begin to contact the astronaut. As soon as that drogue parachute is released, as Bernie Eismann reported to you a little while ago, there is chaff released and a radar pickup of that would indicate that the drogue chute has — has ejected and give a fix as to what the line of fall is into the Atlantic.

Joanne hears Cronkite's voice no differently from the way, on any other day passing through the terminal, she hears the stationmaster's announcing a track or a delay. It is the voice of authority, the voice of the grown-up, from a remote realm in which she never imagines herself participating.

She reaches the front of the newspaper and sees a picture of Scott Carpenter, lingering over it not at all, without any response that might be classified as curious, rational or romantic. Joanne has never had a date.

She spots a little boy threading and bouncing his way

through one cluster in the immense pegboard of people. She breaks into a smile of affinity, connecting with him, another fraidycat. She thinks she'd like to play with him. The way he's moving around, he looks as if he's already playing skin the cat or dodgeball. Involuntarily she rubs the orange that's distending her sweater pocket to a foolish size, imagines tossing it at him. But she doesn't let herself.

Joanne is more or less normal — "a little odd," people still say in 1962, when "paranoid" and "schizoid" haven't become Everyman's diction for nervous and confused. But seventeen years from now, after her father's death and after living a few years alone, she will be quite definitely paranoid schizophrenic, by the clinical standards of either 1962 or 1991, though perhaps not those of 1979, when she will be released from a brief period of hospitalization upstate, when it is decided that she, with the help of drugs containing compounds manufactured by Pfizer Chemical, can "maintain herself" on her own, with the assistance of a psychiatric social worker. For a while she will do more or less that, until one afternoon she wanders permanently away from her single-room-occupancy hotel on the West Side and into Grand Central Terminal and the bit of ground beneath the Praesepe cluster in the constellation of Cancer — "A small dull constellation," according to McKready's *Beginner's Star-Book*, "but of importance because lying in the Zodiac or pathway of the planets" — the bit of ground she will hold amidst the commuters making their paths through the terminal, the portion of earth that, except for the hours from 1:30 A.M. to 5:30 A.M., when the terminal is closed, will be her home.

The only real energy crisis of May 24, 1962, is the one inside the *Aurora 7*. Down on the ground people are being even more profligate with fuel than Scott Carpenter has been, and so Ellen Herlihy, comparing air conditioners in the White Plains Montgomery Ward at 1:35 P.M., is looking for something big and arctic and blasting. Status-enhancing, too. (This is a second air conditioner, for the master bedroom.) Mary Noonan walks a respectful half-step behind her as she searches the tags for higher BTUs and higher prices. Mary is not surprised that Ellen, who can fix her son's bicycle and talk knowledgeably to the Texaco man on Arthur Avenue, knows all about air conditioners, too. Or that she wants the coldest, noisiest one available. Ted Herlihy has his own TV repair business, and he and Ellen trade in their Buick every two years for a new one. Mary — unaware that tubeless research and development being carried out half an orbit away in Japan will fifteen years from now have made Ted Herlihy's trade largely obsolete — wonders if Ellen and Ted will even stay in Melwyn Park much longer, or move onward and upward to someplace like Ardsley.

"You almost can't afford not to have two," says Ellen, not looking up, just moving on to the next tag. Mary, in her cotton dress, follows behind Ellen's grass-stained khaki slacks and wonders if this is a "dig," since Jim is more than cautious, practically tight, when it comes to keeping up with what he calls "the latest necessities."

Mary recognizes her usual cycle of feelings — ineptness, embarrassment, resentment, self-reproach, relief at blessings counted — like a quick automatic wash she's running in her mind. At the moment Ellen is giving her a swift pain in the neck; Mary also knows that if she can only get away from her for half a minute, she'll find Ellen likable, herself tolerable.

So it is a relief when Ellen, after an aggressive discussion with the salesman, decides on a model and starts filling out the charge-account forms as the appropriate Fedders is gotten from the stockroom. "This is gonna take five or ten minutes," she says, which Mary takes as permission to wander off on her own. Ellen is probably tired of being hovered over, anyway. "I'll meet you back here then," says Mary, who, liberated, heads off to the distant edges of the housewares department, hoping to come upon her favorite part of any department store, the cool seasonal land of Scotch coolers and lawn furniture, the aluminum outdoor hearth of the modern family — her little family — the gleaming safe haven of her adult life, far removed from sudden bad surprises being called down through city stairwells.

But she takes a wrong turn and ends up instead in a province of gadgetry — cameras, typewriters, electric organs and telescopes. She goes up to a gleaming red tube on a tripod, afraid to look at the price tag, wishing she had the impulsiveness to buy the floor sample and go back to Ellen Herlihy, saying, "I decided to get this for my son."

What was it that he once showed her in his science book, when they were doing the catechism questions about the creation of the world? That since distance was really time — light-years — eventually someone would build a telescope powerful enough to see back to the instant the world began, the moment God snapped his fingers and whatever was between them exploded and began traveling outward, making itself into the universe. Without daring to look at the price tag, Mary puts her eye to the thin end of the telescope and looks through it — into blackness.

"There's a lens cap on it, madam," says the approaching salesman, a throwback with a boutonniere.

"Oh. I'm just looking."

She moves toward the wall of televisions, all of them soundlessly on, half of them tuned to one network showing a graphic "simulation" of how the capsule is supposed to tip back into the atmosphere at the proper angle for coming home, the other dozen of them tuned to an agitated Walter Cronkite, who appears to be sweating above his ascot.

She looks politely from one silent bank of sets to another, and is startled when all of this televised attention to the future gives way to a sight from her past: the inside of Grand Central Terminal, where she would have been fifteen years ago today, coming up out of the subway on her way to Lowndes Brothers. She wonders what this is doing on, wonders if half the silent televisions haven't had their channels switched by remote control to an old movie. But then she sees the television monitors above the crowd and realizes that they are watching the flight, that she is watching them watching. A camera pans down and over them and she sees hundreds of black-and-white men dressed the way Jim was when he left the house this morning, hundreds of women in suits and dresses and occasionally a hat. The camera moves lower and closer to them, and Mary begins to notice faces: a heavy man chewing gum; another adjusting his glasses and squinting to get a better look at the big screen; a young policeman who looks a little like her half-brother Joe did at his age; more men in hats; an attractive girl in a headband; and to her right a small boy, standing stiller than anyone else, his eyes wide and his shoulders rigid.

Ellen Herlihy comes up behind her. "Found you. It's on its way out to the car. The stock kid will meet us out in the lot."

Mary doesn't look at her. She walks up to the nearest television and turns the volume knob up loud, causing a saleswoman to turn around and look at her.

"There is nothing to do now but wait," Cronkite is saying.

The boy has disappeared from the screen.

And this, I thought, was going to save me time? thinks Al Rosenzweig, who is trying to pass through the great waiting

room, on his way to the Bowery Savings Bank out on 42nd
Street, to deposit a week's worth of receipts for Better Sweat-
ers, his shop on Sixth Avenue. That's his custom: do it on
Thursday, beat the Friday crowds.

But this, here, on Thursday, this is a crowd. Al hadn't fig-
ured on it, but he knew what it was the minute he saw it, and
now he's blocked, stopped cold under the ten-watt bulb serving as Hamal, brightest star in Aries the Ram, a little way
from the information kiosk.

He isn't happy about this. He hates crowds, hates being
bumped — and now there's this frisky little kid in sneakers
trying to squeeze past him. He's hated crowds since before
the camps, from when he was a kid. You couldn't convince
him it was being stacked up in the barracks, everyone's infected rib cage lying next to everyone else's, that had left him
less than thrilled with the touch of his fellow man. Hail-
fellow-get-lost. And what's with "fellow," anyway? Fellow
Americans? Who's kidding and fellowing whom? Al has been
here nearly seventeen years now, since the British rescued
him at Auschwitz and he came over to Brooklyn, taken in by
his brother Abe, who'd had the good sense to get there in
'38. For Abe, by now, it may be home. But for Al, no thank
you. He's a polite guest.

He looks up and around but not at the screen, in which he
refuses to take an interest. His eyes notice the great chande-
liers, appreciate the marble and stone from Tennessee and
Normandy, without knowing that's where they're from; and
his gaze lingers on the huge Kodak Colorama slide projection, this month showing — without much imagination, he
thinks — the Manhattan skyline. But he won't look at the
screen.

Al sucks on a Tums and supposes that Elsie, the American
girl he married in '49, when they were both forty-four, second marriages for both, has still got the set on in the apart-

ment in Borough Park. She'd had it on half an hour before the thing even went up, watching the idiot box like an idiot.

He cracks the Tums with his teeth. He and Elsie aren't happy, never have been, have never really stopped being widowed through thirteen years of marriage. Her Joe killed in the Pacific, his Rose on her way to another camp — to this day he doesn't know which. But it's worse for him, because of Wlady, who when he perished was no older than this cockamamie kid who's bumping up against him once again (what's with the ants in the pants?). In his and Elsie's contest of grief this is the trump card, never openly played, but known to be held, by him.

She and Joe had never had one to lose.

An aircraft of a type aboard the *Intrepid* could reach an area two hundred miles away within perhaps thirty minutes, perhaps a little bit less than that, twenty-five minutes. It may be that long before we get any kind of a report on it. Here comes Colonel Powers again.

The coverage cuts away from Cronkite's voice to Shorty Powers's at Mercury Control.

. . . Pilot Scott Carpenter. We feel at this time, however, that it is out of our range of broadcast, and are in the process of diverting aircraft into the area.

Al, all of a sudden vastly, explosively impatient, starts walking northwest, determined to fight his way out of here, to get away from this nonsense. "'Scuse, please, thank you. 'Scuse, please, thank you." Over and over until he's cleared most of it.

He reaches the smaller waiting room, all that lies between him and 42nd Street, and he keeps going, looking up at one of the four skylights, still blacked out against the air raids that never came in World War II. (The blacking won't be removed until February 2, 1988, just in time for the seventy-fifth anniversary of the terminal, the morning Al will die in Elsie's dutiful, obligated arms.)

At this moment, on this afternoon in May, the war is over for neither the windows nor Al. As he crosses the waiting room Powers's words about "diverting aircraft" play over in his head, and he thinks about the "aviation doctors" sent to do their experiments in the camps, thinks about Elsie ignorantly looking upon the fat, smiling face of Wernher von Braun as she ate her corn flakes in front of the TV this morning.

Good, thinks Al, pounding the Tennessee marble with his soles. Divert your aircraft. Go find your boy bobbing in the ocean. Let your Nazis pluck him out of it; send the same ones who held us under in the water tanks until the bubbles stopped.

———————

The main parachute fails to open. It's supposed to come out automatically at 10,000 feet, but the *Aurora 7* is falling through the clouds with only its drogue out. So at 9,500 feet Scott Carpenter pulls the ring and sees "a glorious orange-and-white canopy" fan out above him. Beneath him he can see the water.

He can hear Gus Grissom radioing from the Cape, though Grissom can't hear him. No one has heard anything from him since the blackout period began ten minutes ago. He's never come back on their radios, and he never will, but as the capsule spends its last few thousand feet in the air, Grissom keeps sending instructions and Carpenter keeps responding as if Grissom can hear him.

04 54 27 CC

Aurora 7, Cape Cap Com. Over.

04 54 29 P

Roger. Loud and clear. Aurora 7 reading the Cape. Loud
and clear. How me, Gus?

04 54 41.5 P

Gus, how do you read . . .

04 54 56.5 CC

Aurora 7 . . . 95. Your landing point is 200 miles long. We
will jump the air rescue people to you.

04 55 06 P

Roger. Understand. I'm reading.

04 55 27 CC

Aurora 7, Aurora 7, Cape Cap Com. Be advised your
landing point is long. We will jump air rescue people to
you in about 1 hour.

04 55 36 P

Roger. Understand 1 hour.

During the final moments of scheduled descent by the in-
communicado astronaut, CBS' cameras continue to pan the
crowd at Grand Central, showing the nation what is still supposed by some to be its crossroads. The camera looks down
on a woman in a small hat, her hands continually pressed together into a steeple of petition. As she prays, she watches
the screen that watches her. A policeman walks through
the huge, silent crowd. "Scott Carpenter had difficulties
throughout this three-orbit flight," says Cronkite.

But those difficulties are over. At 04 55 57 the *Aurora 7*
hits the ocean's surface, almost gently, though it goes completely underwater before bobbing up and listing to one
side. The astronaut notices a little bit of water in the cockpit
and decides he ought to get out. He squeezes himself beyond the instrument panel and opens the hatch at the narrow

end of the bulb-shaped capsule. After putting his camera out of the water's way, he drops his life raft onto the ocean, gets in and realizes it's upside down. He gets back in it right side up and tethers his new rubber vessel to his old titanium one.

With its cameras still on Grand Central, CBS broadcasts an announcement from Colonel Powers at Mercury Control. "We are still working at establishing contact with the *Aurora 7* spacecraft. We estimate the spacecraft has already landed, and we estimate that it has landed two hundred miles long." But, he says, NASA won't be able to confirm that until they get some data. Meanwhile an SC-54 Air Force rescue team, with paramedics that can be jumped to the astronaut, is on its way.

Cronkite says that this plan to jump paramedics seems to indicate they don't expect to reestablish communication, something that should have happened by now.

Safely tied to the floating *Aurora 7*, Carpenter turns on his SARAH beacon, a signal to the aircraft that will be looking for him. Relaxed, nearly home, he says, "Thank you, Lord." He has never felt better.

"So you're saying he liked you," says Lucille Rosen with some confusion. Waldy Munoz is sitting in front of her desk at the Good Deal Employment Agency, three blocks from Grand Central, at 136 West 42nd.

"I liked him, too," says Waldy. "He was a nice man."

And you're a nice boy, thinks Lucille, looking down at the form and the oddball name on it; it's just that "You don't know what you want, right, Waldemar?"

"Right," says Waldy. "But not that job."

He remembers little Mr. DiCicco, the retiring elevator operator Mr. Mullins introduced him to, and the little hands that seemed to want to burst out of the white gloves but couldn't break through. "May 1, 1925. May 1, 1925," Mr. DiCicco told him four or five times. "That's the first day I ride in this car."

Lucille's brother, Steve, who's been listening to the radio, passes through her office. Ignoring Waldy, he stops to say, "This guy is in trouble. His spaceship is supposed to be down, but they can't get him on the radio. That is, they *think* his spaceship came down. If it didn't, he'll go on whirling around and around forever up there, till he suffocates."

Waldy thinks of the Japanese soldiers he hears about every once in a while on the news, the ones who never heard about the surrender and stayed hidden in the jungle for twelve, fifteen, seventeen years, until somebody found them accidentally.

Steve Rosen has gone into the office's third room, and Lucille hears him repeating his story about the astronaut with the satisfaction that only passing on bad news can bring. "You can't go back to school, can you?" she asks Waldy.

"No," he says. "I need the money."

Lucille, remembering her own years at DeWitt Clinton, thinks she can hardly blame him.

"Honey," she says. "You need time. A *little* time. Go home and think?"

"Okay," says Waldy, rising, too shy to shake her hand. She shakes her head, like the mother she once wanted to be, as he heads for the automatic elevator.

Out on the street he starts for home. The Lexington Avenue line, which leaves from Grand Central, will take him there.

––––––––––

As Waldy Munoz stands on the southwest corner of 42nd and Fifth, waiting to cross, Father Tommy Shanahan sits on one of the nearby library steps, looking up at a small gray-and-white square shining near an open ninth-floor window in the office building above Rogers Peet. TVs in offices are not commonplace in 1962, and the odd sight — complete with rabbit-ears antenna sticking out the window — catches Tommy's eye. If he could make out what the TV is telling the man in his office and the seven thousand people in Grand Central two blocks away, he'd hear correspondent Bill Evenson offering a manically happy radio report from the USS *Pierce* in the South Atlantic. Evenson is thrilled to be steaming toward what he still thinks will be a quick recovery of Scott Carpenter at the planned point of impact: "This bucket of bolts is really rolling right now, and what a happy crew we've got . . . We're on our way. Of course, we hear some rumored reports of the possibility the Air Force *may* possibly get there ahead of us, *maybe so,* but there isn't a man jack aboard that will go along with it."

Gazing up at the little sun-glazed screen, Tommy is nearly as slaphappy as Evenson. *She's on her way.* Maria will be floating down the stairs any moment now, her hair and skirt cutting a graceful wake for her beautiful face, her blessing smile.

He'd run up these steps just three minutes ago, carrying the lilies dripping water through their wax-paper handle. He sailed right past the guard who checks book bags, leaving drops of water every few feet — it's amazing what things you can get away with when you're wearing your collar — bounding up to the reading room, where he found her immediately, not near the handsome stockbroker, who was nowhere to be seen, but by herself, exquisitely contemplative over an open book of Renaissance paintings.

"For you," he'd whispered, handing them to her and splashing the nose of Titian's *Woman at the Mirror.*

She'd looked at him in alarm, though her beautiful skin was too olive to blush. She'd just said, "Meet me on the steps. I'll be there in a minute." He'd smiled and turned and flown off like a sprite with orders from the princess. And now she's — here! She's coming down the steps, but slowly, still carrying the flowers — and not smiling.

Across the street and nine floors above them, now at 1:49 P.M., the voice of Cronkite sounds slightly disgusted with reporter Bill Evenson. He says he hopes there's room for the reporter's optimism, and he reminds listeners that attempts are being made on all radio channels to communicate with the *Aurora 7.* Joe Campbell, aboard the USS *Intrepid,* eight hundred miles southeast of Cape Canaveral, files his own report by radio, and it's much closer to Cronkite's mood than Evenson's. "Every face wears a frown. There's a great deal of concern for astronaut Carpenter." If he's come down at all, he hasn't come down where the flight plan called for him to, which is right nearby. Navy photographers are folding their gear; the *Intrepid*'s jet helicopters and some other marine helicopters are returning; people are stowing their equipment and going below deck. Entirely lacking Evenson's competitive spirit, Campbell says, "If other rescuers get there first, wonderful."

His mood might as well be showering down on Tommy. She's not smiling. He should have known. It was all crazy.

She sits down beside him in the sunlight.

"Don't," he says, rushing to get an abandoned newspaper for her to sit on. "The pigeons." She accepts the offer — smiling! His hope flares and he tries to keep it lit with a billow of words: "I really just wanted to see you again. Really, that's all. I know it must seem funny to you, but I just wanted to see you again. Honest, I . . ."

"Do you think that's right?" she asks, grave once more.

"Just to see you again? Yes, of course. Don't y—"

He's stopped for a second by her frown. But then he plunges once more. "Really, I just thought we might spend an hour together, go for a cup of coffee, have a talk. I loved talking to you this morning."

He waits.

"I have my work," she responds, looking down.

"I have mine," he instantly offers. She laughs, her white teeth blazing. He laughs much more loudly.

"I have one more essay to write, after this exam I'm studying for."

"What's the essay about?"

"Bellini's *Saint Francis in Ecstasy.*"

"That's right up my alley!" says Tommy, and they laugh, together, again.

"It's in the Frick Collection, actually."

"We could go look at it. Tomorrow, after your test." He hasn't stopped smiling at her. She smiles back.

As the huge Westclox in the main concourse nears 2:00, CBS cuts back to St. Louis and the handsome McDonnell employee who throughout the day has been sitting in a Mercury capsule and telling CBS' Bernard Eismann how the various instruments work. The arrangement has prompted some good-humored sign-offs from Cronkite — good wishes for the rest of the "flight" and so forth — but things are more strained now. Eismann is being given a demonstration of "egress technique," what Carpenter might now be practicing if he's made it back through the atmosphere and feels he can't stay sealed up in the *Aurora 7* while waiting for the distant ships.

"We are simply standing by with unfortunately nothing to report," says Cronkite, when the transmission from St. Louis is over.

Under the constellation of Pisces, not far from Al Rischa,

Gregory remembers the Maytag box in the garage, and his own egress from the end he narrowed to be like the small one on the capsule.

When Georgie Herlihy abandoned him that day several weeks ago, he hadn't really minded. In some ways he was glad. It was peaceful watching his tempera-painted instrument panel and the garage light through the Saran Wrap window. As an only child Gregory is used to quiet, used to talking to objects, conversing with the spirit of his globe, the faces on his Civil War commemorative stickers. He closes his eyes now, just for a minute, before darting to another spot on the terminal floor, and tries to feel himself inside the real *Aurora 7*, tries to make himself be just where Scott Carpenter is now, because if he can feel himself inside the capsule, then it means that the capsule must still exist, and if the capsule still exists, then Scott has to be alive inside it.

Cronkite's voice says that the captain of the *Farragut*, a guided-missile destroyer, has been told to go to the new predicted impact point of the capsule, even though the *Farragut* was not supposed to be part of the recovery team.

At 2:02, Scott Carpenter sits in his life raft and thinks of the tremendous five hours he's been through. He is proud. He knows he has made mistakes, but he is sure his flight was a success. He wants to tell others about it, though not quite yet. Like Gregory Noonan an only child, he is enjoying his solitude, out at last into the fresh air of this lovely day, looking at the sky and the sea, at a patch of sargasso weed floating by. He spots an eighteen-inch-long fish, black and tame, and smiles: it's his only company here. He waits calmly for what he knows he will soon hear — the sound of airplane engines. When he does he will signal them by flashing the small mirror in his hand.

Under Al Rischa, the brightest star in the constellation of Pisces, Marjorie Carson, sixty-two, born with the century, stands without her luggage. She will claim it in a few minutes, she tells herself, but right now she's not even looking in her purse for the check. She has been immobilized by the great crowd in the main concourse, something she never expected to see when she stepped off track 24 a little while ago.

She was on the train all last night and this morning, coming up from the South, and so, having passed up the newspaper the dining-car waiter offered her with breakfast, she has been unaware of the flight. But now she knows what's going on, and she too is waiting, has joined the vigil, wondering if and when this Carpenter will come back to earth.

Like the man on the immense black-and-white screen, Marjorie is perspiring. Her blue traveling clothes are too warm, and she is tired. She did not sleep well last night, not because of the train, but from worry, a sense of her own unworthiness, irrelevance.

Afraid to fly, she is riding the train from child to child, visiting a son, a daughter and another son in the space of two weeks. The first visit, concluded last evening when she was seen off to New York, was not a success: her son and his wife are preparing to divorce, and for the four days she was with them she felt as pointlessly present as the child her daughter-in-law is carrying. She expects this visit ahead will be no better. As soon as she leaves the terminal she will have a taxicab take her to the East 79th Street apartment of her daughter and son-in-law, an advertising executive. And a half hour after that she and Lynn will be having a spat, which Marjorie, unable to stop herself, will provoke with something as small as the suggestion that Lynn consider changing that pretty barrette from the right side of her head to the left, a suggestion to which Lynn will react with alarming ferocity and volume, squeezing it like a trigger, setting off another oral barrage of recollected wrongs, all of them committed by Marjorie against Lynn during the latter's botched upbringing. Lynn is a school psychologist.

So Marjorie, a well-intentioned Methodist lady, who in her life has done precious little wrong to anyone, including Lynn, stands dispirited under this vast dome and false sky, beset by "strange indifference, dullness and coldness," the very conditions John Wesley himself shook off 234 years ago today, almost to the hour, when he walked along Aldersgate Street in London, after a church meeting of Moravians, and felt his heart "strangely warmed."

Good Methodist that she may be, Marjorie does not realize the anniversary, and is in no danger of enthusiasm, the condition of which Wesley and his disciples, after May 24, 1738, would find themselves so often suspected. Marjorie is not strangely warmed, just too warm, and even a little dizzy. She looks up at the two faded golden fishes swimming on the green ceiling mural, and she feels no inspiration, no expectation of miracles.

And would she even want these fishes to multiply, to come down like manna on this crowd of hats tilting upward to the false idol of the screen? The humanity here — except for the little boy not far from her, darting peculiarly from one spot to another between rapt concentrations upon the screen — seems a poor, undifferentiated thing.

Cronkite's voice, fighting for calm, pours down onto the gathering:

> We have a very — even more disturbing report, it seems to this reporter here, from NASA space authorities. They say they did not pick up any radar blips from the descending spacecraft. It almost beggars description as to what that could mean. Whether they should have picked up radar blips of the spacecraft as far as two hundred miles away is something that

experts will have to answer, and we're trying to get that answer for you. It seems to this reporter that they should have. If the *Aurora 7* spacecraft came safely through its atmospheric reentry, it would seem that even two hundred miles would not be too far to pick up a radar signal . . .

No, surely not too far, thinks Marjorie, not for a young man so singular and blessed. Suddenly there is no crowd, there is only this one man, hurtling down from the heavens, who matters, and who matters completely. Faith, she reminds herself, is not the same as certainty, and faith alone, not works, will bring salvation. No, thinks Marjorie Carson, all the buttons and wires and radar in the world won't bring that young man back. Only faith will. Ashamed of her discouragement, she closes her eyes and offers him her heart.

———————

So there's not even been radar contact with the *Aurora 7* since the last contact with Scott Carpenter by voice, which was that when he announced his g forces building for the reentry into the atmosphere.

At the bottom of the Caribbean, still waters surround the instruments once used by the captain of the *Aurora*. Having sunk to the ocean floor after the catastrophe, she lies undisturbed, lifeless. Near her lie the *Jenny and Sally*, the *Rose*, the *Good Intent* and the *David and Susanna*, all five of them sent to the bottom of Carlisle Bay, off Barbados, by a hurricane on August 23, 1758.

Scott Carpenter, about five hundred miles to the northwest, sits in a rubber raft beside his capsule, guarding his camera and waiting for his rescuers. He watches the bobbing *Aurora 7* a bit warily, hoping it won't go under like Gus's *Liberty Bell*.

Gus was the last man he heard, thirty seconds before the capsule hit the water. "Be advised your landing point is long. We will jump air rescue people to you in about 1 hour." But no one heard Carpenter reply "Roger," and none of them on the ground had heard him for twelve minutes before that, when the blackout period began. So they knew where he would come down — if, that is, he made it down. Did they know he'd gotten through the atmosphere? They must be on their way, looking for him, but are they expecting to find him?

The dye marker stretches for ten miles behind the capsule. When helicopters or P2Vs — the plane he flew during Korea — approach, he'll begin signaling them with his mirror. For now it's just pleasant to be out here — and so cool! The capsule temperature read 105 degrees upon landing, so he is content to sit, his helmet off at last, part of a vastness instead of a sealed container. He looks at the sky, unable to see the hundred-mile-high arc he was riding just half an hour ago; and he looks down into the water, unable to see to the depth of 205 feet, where three summers from now he will spend thirty days in *Sealab II*, becoming the only man to travel so far in both directions from the surface of the earth.

The order could hardly be better. She's gone for forty dozen more than he'd ever expected. Jim Noonan stands at the northeast corner of Madison and 44th, waiting for the light to change and exhaling deeply, trying to drain the day's unaccountable dreads and tensions from his body. He looks west, down the sun-brightened length of 44th all the way to the Hudson. He can almost see the small shape of the *Leonardo*, docked one block south of the spot where, years from now, after her years of fighting the Japanese and recovering astronauts and sending bombers over North Vietnam, the *Intrepid* will be docked, for the rest of her days, as a floating museum. Beyond the river Jim can see the cliffs of New Jersey before reeling in his gaze and noticing Brooks Brothers, just across the street. The light changes, and he wonders if, on his way back to Fifth Avenue, he should stop in there and compare what they've got set out with Lowndes's small, struggling men's line.

Stepping across 44th, he decides against it. He's felt a sudden shadow falling, like a cape, over his left side. He looks to his left, east, down the short block leading to Grand Central, a path darkened by the brand-new Pan Am Building, topped out by the construction workers at fifty-nine stories just fifteen days ago.

The terminal must be quiet now. Splashdown was supposed to come at 1:41 P.M. — that's what they'd said just after lift-off — and 1:41 was twenty-five minutes ago. They'll have gotten him out of the water by now, and the crowd will have dispersed. The thought of being in Grand Central at this hour seems all at once peaceful — the idea of being able to hear his black Flagg Brothers shoes as he takes strides across the marble floor instead of being shuffled through rush-hour crowds at 8:30 and 5:00. The chance to dive into it like a great indoor pool makes him turn left down the dusky block and head for it. He crosses Vanderbilt and opens one of the doors near the hack line. He'll calm down here, maybe call Mary, steady himself before going back to the office.

Once inside, he moves to the staircase that will take him down to the concourse. He sees that instead of being empty the floor is covered. He looks down onto thousands of heads, some bare and some hatted, like a great sea of poppies bent by a breeze, all of them tilted up toward the great screen, which is still lit, still talking. Colonel Powers announces:

A U.S. Navy P2V aircraft in the landing area has received an electronic contact from a device called a SARAH beacon. We do not have any further details at this time except that he has made the contact and has taken a bearing on the source of that signal. He is now diverting his aircraft into that immediate area. This is Mercury Control.

But no word from Scott Carpenter.

Tony DiPretorio says hi to the Puerto Rican mailboy he passes on his way to the projection setups room at CBS, 514 West 57th.

"Ton-ee, Ton-ee," the mailboy sings back, like whoever sings for Natalie Wood in *West Side Story.* He moves his hips a little too, fetchingly, deliberately.

One of the church, Tony thinks, as he's thought before, filing a mental note for future reference, maybe future action. He's back from his after-lunch belt at Over the Rainbow, and he sits down, a little buzzed and ever so faintly horny, a slight, sweet urgency in his belly and crotch.

His eyes go to one of several monitors in the room, most of them tuned to CBS, and he watches Cronkite sweating it out in his ascot and notes the time: 2:05. The screen switches to an overhead shot of the crowd in Grand Central, which is quiet. Tony notices a cute guy in an awful suburban-daddy straw fedora, all wrong for his color, Tony can tell, even in black-and-white. A much older guy, a real sport, must be in his seventies, is also discernible in the none-too-well-focused picture. The old gent is wearing a real straw hat, a boater, something he picked up thirty-five years ago, and looks like he's waiting out news of Lucky Lindy instead of what's-his-name. Now, this guy looks smart, thinks Tony, sending a telepathic message to the sweet suburban daddy to take a tip from the geezer.

Don Louis, more or less a boss of Tony's, though the lines

of authority aren't awfully clear around here, passes Tony's desk and stubs out a cigarette in the ashtray. Everyone in the room, like most of the crowd at Grand Central, smokes.

"So what's the story?" Tony asks Don. "Ya think Superboy bought the farm? Or is he gonna make it back to dry land for din-din?"

Don Louis laughs, as he always does when Tony camps it up. One of the church? Tony wonders for the second time in two minutes. He notes Don's wedding ring, which he's noticed before, and thinks maybe even so. Like maybe he stops off and meets suburban daddy for a quick jerk-off in one of the Grand Central men's rooms.

"The official word is we're supposed to be optimists," Don Louis answers. "Which I guess means you ought to get things ready for nine o'clock."

"*Tout de suite*," Tony answers. So, they're assuming Sky King will make it and that they'll be running the planned half-hour news special, a wrap-up, at nine, preempting a re-run of *Tell It to Groucho*. If he's right, Tony thinks ahead, yawning, that's what he and his mother will be watching from the couch back at the apartment in Bensonhurst. Oh, *Mary*. He wishes it were Friday instead of Thursday.

He goes about the business of setting up the commercials for a *CBS News Extra: The Flight of Aurora 7*, which will be brought to Tony and his mother and millions of others — if Superboy makes it — by Polaroid, "makers of the Polaroid Land Camera"; by Remington, "makers of the new cordless Lektronic II"; and by Philip Morris, "makers of Marlboro, Parliament and Alpine cigarettes." Winding the tapes into position, Tony thinks *he'd* like to spend the rest of the afternoon making the mailboy, or Don Louis, or even suburban daddy. He looks back to the monitor to see if he can find him, but Cronkite is back on the screen. Tony wonders if the boys down the hall are kinescoping this, wonders if suburban daddy will wind up in some film vault, still looking up in his dumb straw hat a hundred years from now.

"I'm going to take your picture." The model in the first commercial, for Polaroid, is Barbara Feldon. Tony doesn't know the chick's name, and no one else does either, though three years from now everyone will know her as 99, Maxwell Smart's girlfriend in *Get Smart*, which will appear, as they still say on 1962 talk shows, "on another network." She demonstrates the new ten-second automatic camera, and though she's got a smart deb's voice, Tony notices, she's got to play dumb. "No focusing: that's for me!" Tony is bored with her before she can go through three or four clicks and pulls and count to ten. "Let's see what we've got. Not bad. Very good, in fact. Want to see? Oh, I guess you'd better go to your camera dealer. He'll show it to you."

"Bye, honey," Tony whispers, when her minute's up and her reel is in position. He goes on to the next one. A jagged electronic sine curve vibrates across the screen and the announcer practically shouts in his nonregional accent: *"Power! The unlimited power of the finest shaving instrument ever made, the new Lektronic II from Remington!"* "Oh, girl, tone it down," Tony says to the announcer's voice, lowering the volume on his projector. He looks for a second toward one of the monitors, which shows a little cardboard capsule being dragged across a cardboard map of Mexico. Christ, thinks Tony, bored by the primitive graphics, you'd think they could do better than this.

(Twenty-five years from today, living with a lover in NoHo and worrying about his health, Tony will be splicing together Cinemax promos with a laser motif in a studio on Sixth Avenue, taking care not to let any image occupy the screen for more than 2.5 seconds.)

The Remington announcer explains that the Lektronic II can give you "shave after shave without a cord, because it runs on powerful rechargeable energy cells." But: "Forget to recharge?" A pair of fingers, taking up the whole screen, snaps in darn-it self-rebuke. Not to worry. Just "switch to reserve power and shave from any standard AC outlet." Tony rolls his eyes. Another dumb-ass suburban daddy, looking a little like Superboy himself, comes on screen, shaving his handsome face with the Lektronic II's "adjustable roller combs" while his little son and daughter brush their teeth and dry their ears in the farther reaches of the oversize bathroom.

"Faggot," Tony says to himself, *sure* that this guy is a member of the church — he's too cute to be anything else. In fact, he could almost swear he'd seen him one night at Over the Rainbow, or maybe the Fawn.

"Two kinds of power in one electric shaver," the announcer sums up. "The Lektronic and new Lektronic II from Remington."

Tony rewinds this second tape, and once it's in the position it will need to be in at 9:17 tonight, he clicks off the projector it's on. As he does so, something from before clicks in his head: all that stuff this morning and at lunch about manual control and fly-by-wire and switching back and forth from one to the other. *Two kinds of power,* and Superboy still may not make it. Oh, irony, thinks Tony, before telling himself, Jesus, it's a handsome face. A monitor is showing a still photograph of Scott Carpenter, not for the first time that day, but for the first time Tony has paid any real attention to it. It's beginning to seep into him; he can feel his emotional motor turning over, the way it does on a Friday night when the drinks kick in.

He puts the third tape into position and tests it. It's for Parliament cigarettes and will be the last to run tonight — if, that is, there's a happy ending and the special runs at all. A man lands his seaplane. He gets out and his headbanded, shirtwaisted girl tosses him his cigarettes. Then she puts on a life jacket, like the one he's got on. He helps her snap the collar shut while she juts her healthy American boobs out at him. They go up in the plane together this time. The announcer (Mike Wallace, still half show biz, six years away from the beginnings of *60 Minutes*) smarms the voice-over: "This man knows the value of an extra margin, in the life jacket he wears, in the cigarette he smokes." The reference is to Parliament's filter, recessed "a neat, clean quarter-inch away." Christ, thinks Tony, beginning to get spooked. If dollface has made it through the atmosphere, he's supposed to be bobbing around on a rubber raft somewhere in the South Atlantic. And if he hasn't, the cute little capsule is just an ashtray now, with dollface's cute scorched remains stubbed out in it.

Somebody's putting up pictures of Carpenter's family on one of the monitors.

Tony looks back to his own projector. Pilot and girl are flying together now; she's in the copilot's seat, puffing a Parliament like she's practically giving it head. Music: "You're smoking neat, you're smoking clean, with Parliament today."

Tony snaps the tape into its final position. He looks back at the other guy's monitor. Another handsome picture of Malcolm Scott Carpenter, in civvies, surrounded by three, no four, kids. Eyes moistening, Tony lets go, whispering to himself as he looks at Carpenter's face: "Oh, baby, it's late. Get home."

Statement by Vice-President Johnson
Regarding the Failure of the Aurora 7
Space Flight, May 24, 1962

Lieutenant Commander Malcolm Scott Carpenter's name will go down in that part of history that records man's noblest efforts to reach beyond himself; his name is first on the list of Americans who went into space and did not return.

As time passes, the names of other astronauts will be added to this roll of honor. For we are going on to conquer the unknown realms around us and harness its power for the use of God's creatures on this planet earth. This is as Scott Carpenter would have wished it. We will not disgrace his honor or his memory by turning back now.

I know I speak for the nation in its sincere but inadequate efforts to console Scott Carpenter's wonderful family and his brave associates who will carry on after him. I hope it gives them some small comfort to know that we will never forget him, and that he did not die in vain. The flight of the *Aurora 7* was a necessary and important step into space that we will be able to stand on as we reach for the stars.

One month ago tonight Scott Carpenter and the other six astronauts went to sleep under the stars, big and bright, that shone on the LBJ ranch outside Johnson City, Texas. Now, at 2:10 P.M., beside an IBM electric typewriter on a secretary's desk in the vice president's six-room suite in the Executive Office Building in Washington, a sheet of paper with the above statement waits to be used, if it's needed.

Jim Noonan has crossed the waiting room floor in even smaller steps than he's used to taking at rush hour. He looks over the seven thousand heads and toward the light coming through the door he entered five minutes ago. Cheated of the peace he sought in here, he thinks about the light that bathed West 44th Street, imagines himself walking back out and into it, disappearing into the vanishing point of his own vision, gone from all responsibility.

A conversation with Gregory from about two weeks ago, when the spookiness really started, comes back to him. He'd found him in the bathroom doing one of his scientific meditations, not upon the swirling tap water but upon the medicine-chest mirror. Standing before it with his mother's compact opened up, he was letting the small and large mirrors reflect each other, and his face, to the point where the picture became infinitesimal.

It gave Jim the creeps. "Trying to make yourself disappear?" he asked. But before he could pat his son's shoulder, the kid had snapped the compact shut and taken off, as if propelled from the bathroom by his own mortified shrug.

He is losing his child, he thinks, as the clock atop the information kiosk reaches 2:15.

"Half a minute to fly across Texas at its widest points! Half a minute!" says the man next to him in a Belfast accent. Joe Kelleher, the super of the building next to St. Agnes's, has come over to the terminal to watch the excitement and to see if he can see himself on TV. Trying not to lose the high spirits that brought him here, he ignores everyone's concentration on Carpenter's apparent disappearance in favor of marveling, to Jim, about the graphic they showed this morning of the capsule flying from El Paso to Houston at the same speed you might trace a long vacation trip with your finger across the road map of an interstate.

"Yeah, it's something," says Jim, wondering how, if the astronaut did make it down, they'll ever find him once the sun sets.

If humans could be connected like dots in a drawing, 123 held hands would bring Jim Noonan to Gregory, who is now on the opposite side of the concourse and looking up at the Kodak Colorama picture over his father's head. He's trying to make out Fifth Avenue and Lowndes Brothers, one of the few New York buildings he knows, though they're impossible to find in the skyline's web.

Gregory thinks, This picture of the city is hanging up in the city itself. He remembers standing in front of the bathroom mirror weeks ago and holding up his mother's compact.

"Trying to make yourself disappear?" his father had asked. *No, trying to go where I'm supposed to. Something wants me in a new world. Why are you tugging me back?*

"You won't find him there," says a woman's voice from behind him. She speaks in perfect, stilted, British-accented English. "If he's found at all, he'll be up there," she says, pointing to the television monitor as Gregory turns around, and directing his attention away from the Colorama display. Miss Kamala Vavuniya, extending a long lunch hour from the Ceylonese mission to the United Nations, smiles at Gregory, her tilak mark like one more eye to make him all the shyer. Shy herself, Miss Vavuniya has been alone in the crowd for half an hour, wanting but unable to speak to anyone until this little boy came along and started looking where no one else was.

"Do you think they will find him?" she means to ask next, but before she can get the words out he is gone.

"If all of the radio-location aids fail," says Cronkite, trying to fill the time with words and hope, "there's a high-intensity flashing light, and there's a sea-marker dye . . ." Unconvinced that Lieutenant Commander Carpenter has much chance of being discovered alive, Miss Vavuniya decides that she will work her way through the crowd, out the Lexington Avenue exit and back to the Secretariat.

———

As Miss Vavuniya tries to leave it, Elizabeth Wheatley struggles to enter the concourse. Once she realizes what the crowd is about, it excites no further curiosity, only annoyance. She and Connie took leave of each other in the East

50s, after Elizabeth decided to hold the matter of Warren in abeyance and call Fred Foy at *The New Yorker* instead. They set up an appointment at his office for 2:45 after she had asked a couple of questions about Kennedy's trip ("Will the Vassar *jeune fille* be going with him?"), and made no promises.

She thought she'd cut through the terminal to East 44th, but after standing on the *Leonardo* and after all the rest of the day's walking she's already as wrinkled as she can bear to be, and she doesn't want to fight her way across the room. Perhaps she can escape via the lower level. She sees the sign near the staircase and heads down, finding the terminal's other marble floor and comb of tracks, the whole place practically deserted, eerily removed from the fourteen thousand feet standing on its ceiling.

The Oyster Bar! She hasn't been there in years. Spotting it, she decides to call Warren MacLeod at his office.

"Did you know I was once a lieutenant on the *Intrepid?*" Those are his first words to her after taking the phone from his secretary. She knows the technique and she likes it. After summoning her with the explosive telegram, he greets her with this man's-man casual remark, as if they've been sitting in the same room for hours and he's just lit a second cigar.

"Yes, Warren, and I was once a Campfire Girl. Is there anything actually *prompting* this naval maneuver in your conversation?"

"Elizabeth, if you weren't such an Italophilic comsymp, you'd know we've got one of our boys up there, showing the flag in the wild blue yonder. And at the moment he seems to be lost. Again, you wouldn't know that, being irrationally opposed to television, patriotism and sentiment, but those are the facts. How are you, cream cup?"

"At the moment I'm standing right under thousands of your compatriots, who are watching the dull spectacle you describe. I'm trying to make my way through Grand Central to see Fred Foy, and I'm being held up by the humanity."

"Christ, Elizabeth, you are a snob."

"Yes. It's got a great deal to do with my talent and a good deal to do with my charm. And if you're still interested in being exposed to the latter, you should think about meeting me at the Oyster Bar at five."

"Sure the wretched refuse will have dispersed by then? We wouldn't want them tap-dancing overhead, cream cup."

"Five o'clock, Warren."

"Okay, we'll have champagne if Carpenter makes it."

"Yes, Warren," she sighs.

Cinematic pause. Warren responds, almost in a whisper, "Hey, babe? We'll have the champagne in any case."

Elizabeth, who has seen every movie Warren has, even if she won't admit it, is thrilled with the staginess of this sign-off.

Now, how to get out of here. It's 2:17, according to her tiny silver watch. Almost a half hour left to get to Fred. She'll stop in the little bookshop down on this level and kill several minutes. Then, she decides, she'll brave her way back upstairs and out onto 42nd Street, so she won't have to cross the whole main concourse.

She heads off toward the bookshop, now even slightly more set against Kennedy; it's his space program, after all, that's disrupted her movements like this. As she walks on the lower level, sound waves from the voices of Shorty Powers and Walter Cronkite are dying on the marble floor above her head. The SARAH-beacon news is repeated by Mercury Control, and Cronkite says, as calmly as he can, that if the SARAH beacon is still transmitting, then there's still hope everything is okay.

But when CBS cuts back to the USS *Pierce*, Bill Evenson has lost his crazy excitement of a half hour ago. He realizes now that the destroyer he's on can't reach the real off-course point of impact — if an impact really occurred — for another six hours.

Of course, the planes will get there long before that. In fact, they should be over the spot well before 3:00. But what will they find? The capsule, perhaps — if that's the shape the SARAH beacon is picking up. But will the man inside it, who's not been heard from in the last forty-nine minutes, still be alive?

———————

Jim Noonan looks through the crowd and toward the dark tube that is track 24, leading into the Park Avenue tunnel. He remembers the story of those three burglars the other week. Christ, an ice pick. Did they ever find them after they got into the tunnel?

He remembers the last time, weeks and weeks ago, that Gregory came to meet the 6:32 at the Melwyn Park station. He hadn't expected him, and he'd been about to start down the steps into the little underpass that would take him over to the southbound side of the tracks and home, when there he was, Gregger, rushing up out of the underpass and greeting him with a goofy, self-mocking smile, wide and straight as a comb, completely unlike himself, as if to say, "Ta-da! Fooled you."

It's been weeks since the weather turned warm, and the sun is once again still in the sky at 6:32 P.M., but Gregory hasn't been back.

———————

Aircraft should be over the scene in twenty minutes, according to the car radio, and Eddie Rodwicki figures he should have this guy to the Yale Club in five.

"Just coming into town?" he asks as they pull away from the East Side Terminal and start up First.

"No. Leaving. I just realized I left a folder in my room. I'm hoping I can get it and still have time to get out to the airport."

"Okay," says Eddie, giving the Checker a little obliging gun.

"They don't know where this guy is," he says, as they get up toward the UN. "Don't even know if he made it back down."

"Mmm," says the guy, starting to flip through the week's *Time*.

"What's your line?" Eddie asks, heading west on 42nd.

"Economist," the guy says, not looking up.

"Oh, yeah? With who?"

"HEW in Washington."

Eddie looks in the mirror, sees the guy again and figures him for forty-five or so, a little pasty, dandruff on the shoulders — not exactly a candidate for one of those fifty-mile hikes. "I thought all you guys were from Harvard," Eddie says.

"No, not all of us," the man replies, still not looking up. "I hope this is the fastest way," he says, annoyed that they're at a red light at 42nd and Third.

"There's no other way to get to Vanderbilt, pal," says Eddie. "I'll get you there." He hits the pedal a little harder than usual when the light goes green. He won't be sorry to be rid of this sourball, who's actually begun to whistle — a habit Eddie's always found ignorant — even as he keeps reading his magazine. Eddie would swear it's a fuck-you gesture, a protest against the radio being on. He's tempted to turn the thing up, but instead he just listens harder through the bursts of midtown interference, wishing he was still with the nice old lady he took to her treatments at Sloan-Kettering this morning, or the French blonde going to the E-E whatever.

The announcer says that Mercury Control is comparing all the data it's got on track and trajectory and estimated landing points — before interrupting himself to allow the voice Eddie now recognizes as Shorty Powers's to come on: "We now have an unconfirmed report from downrange of a visual sighting by a P2V aircraft in the landing zone. We are working to reconfirm that P2V report. This is Mercury Control." Excited but skeptical, Eddie moves the cab forward, west, in the direction of Grand Central, which is coming into view.

Inside it, Cronkite's voice comes down from the screen: "That's the happiest news yet. Let's cross our fingers and wait for that one."

Gregory crosses his fingers and feels the surge within him — the apple tree again — though this time he knows it's for real, knows he's going.

Within two minutes, at 2:26 P.M., Cronkite is giving the audio back to Powers, who has another announcement. "This is Mercury Control." The terminal is silent. "We have just received a report through our recovery operations branch that an aircraft in the landing area has sighted the spacecraft" — CBS switches from a map flashing circles around the newly projected landing point to a shot of the crowd in Grand Central — "and has sighted a life raft with a gentleman by the name of Carpenter riding in it."

Seven thousand people have started to cheer, and some of them to weep, even before Cronkite can shout, "Oh, boy!" Herbert Johnson smiles. Bobby Cancese slaps his nightstick against his thigh, as if a little pain will keep him from blubbering over, but a tear comes anyway when he spots the motherly lady next to him starting to bawl. She sees him and laughs at the both of them and gives him a kiss on the cheek. Marjorie Carson has closed her eyes and is softly humming a Methodist hymn. Waldy Munoz, who has delayed getting on the subway and spent the last forty-five minutes watching the screen, is struggling to leave the concourse, not to go downstairs to the number 6, but back out to 42nd Street, to go to the Port Authority Bus Terminal, alive, at last, with an idea that's taken possession of him.

Only three people seem to be paying no attention at all. One is Joanne Kalkowski, who is smiling at a chocolate cat on display at the Barricini stand. Another is Elizabeth Wheatley, carrying a just-bought copy of *A Nation of Sheep* and making her way, determined not to lose her temper, out the main doors of the terminal.

And the third is Gregory Noonan, who is walking with a half-full bag of M & M's up the terminal's southwest exit ramp, expressionless, slowly, like one of Peter Pan's boys, just captured and ordered to walk the plank.

He can no longer hear Cronkite's voice, which is still cutting through the buzz and applause of the crowd. "Well, that's the longest forty-five minutes we've ever spent. From twelve forty-one to one twenty-five we had no information at all that Scott Carpenter had successfully returned to earth. That's the news now. He's back. He's been sighted. He's in his raft alongside his spacecraft. Now it's a matter of taking him aboard . . . we can only accept their report with gratitude and thanks to God."

Jim Noonan has paid attention, applauded inconspicuously and felt his throat catch. But after the cheering has died into a happy murmur, he still isn't sure what the emotion is. He is anxious, full, and feels the need more strongly than he has yet on this strange, fretful day to shore up his world, gather in what is his, to offer and take from it protection. He put off calling Mary when he discovered what was going on here, but now he can't wait another minute. He stands on his toes, turns around and starts looking for a phone over the ocean of heads.

Gregory emerges from the terminal at the northeast corner of Vanderbilt and 42nd, with no idea where he's going but with perfect certainty he's headed in the right direction. Alas, he has never done the Barnes dance, and when he sees the sign on the south side of 42nd freeze into the Don't Walk position, he reasons that it's all right to cross Vanderbilt from west to east, even though the rules of the Barnes dance say that at this corner all signs will say Don't Walk at the same time. And so, as Gregory puts his right foot into Vanderbilt Avenue, at 2:29:33 P.M., Father Thomas Shanahan, who has reached the opposite corner after walking two blocks on air, is prompted to shout, "Hey!" And Elizabeth Wheatley, who is standing right behind Gregory, and whose maternal instincts are surprisingly strong and quick, reaches out to grab his cotton plaid shirt, hard, by the collar. She tugs him backward at just the moment Waldy Munoz plants a good kick in the right-rear passenger door of Eddie Rodwicki's taxicab, which has turned, legally if too fast, onto Vanderbilt. "Stop, man!" Waldy starts to yell, just as Gregory goes down.

Eddie hits the brakes and bounces the Yale-trained economist against the front seat.

As Eddie jumps out of the cab a small crowd is clustering around the boy lying in the gutter. "Is he all right?" asks a man just behind Elizabeth Wheatley.

Gregory, who has only been grazed, stands up and smiles. For the first time in several weeks he looks like a happy, normal eleven-year-old boy. "He's fine," he says. "The rescue planes just found him."

Inside the terminal, Cronkite's voice has been recapping events with happy astonishment. "It would seem that the capsule had simply disappeared in space." Cutting back from a report by Joe Campbell on the *Intrepid,* now 184 miles from Carpenter and sending out its jet helicopters, Cronkite reports that the paramedics will be there in about ten minutes. He speculates that Carpenter may have kept transmitting throughout what the astronaut thought was a completely successful reentry.

The crowd has hardly dissipated at all. The latest P2V report, that Carpenter is sitting *comfortably* in his raft, is greeted with laughter. It's as if they've had a joke played on them, or lost a round of hide-and-seek. There's a weary party atmosphere, with lots of people deciding to write off the rest of the afternoon. At a quarter after three there will still be thousands watching the screen; a reporter will still be doing interviews from down in the crowd ("I'm proud to be an American," will say a conductor who doesn't have to get on a train until 5:03); and Cronkite will still be explaining, marveling and decompressing from "a flight that gave us forty-six minutes of, I think, the worst time in thirty years of reporting, as we waited along with a breathless world to learn that he was down all right and that he had safely made his reentry . . . it was quite a terrible time for everyone around the world."

And soon Rene Carpenter will be taking a phone call from Scott's best friend in the program, John Glenn. She'll joke about the overshoot: "We just like to do things differently."

But at 2:36 Jim Noonan is feeling no euphoria. Having made it through the crowd to a pay phone, still vaguely heartsick, and having stood waiting in line for a few minutes, and having gotten a busy signal for a few more after that, he now hears himself doing what he never does, shouting: "*Run away?*"

"He never came home for lunch," says Mary, "and he never ate at school either. They haven't seen him since noon, and his bicycle's gone. I've just gotten off the phone with Mrs. Linley."

"Call the police. I'm coming home. Call the police."

He pushes back into the crowd, jostling Marjorie Carson and saying excuse me. He searches the Departures board and finds nothing to Melwyn Park for another hour and fifteen minutes.

Call the police, he'd said. But the police won't find Gregory. An interplanetary Interpol won't be able to locate him. He's disappeared, been carried off; the last weeks have been a gruesome omen. Now Jim realizes what they were about: he *was* losing his son; his son was about to vanish from the world.

Sick with panic, he doesn't know how he will manage to stand, stiff as a swizzle stick in this jolly cocktail of a crowd, for seventy-five minutes. The office makes more sense; he can stay in touch with Mary by phone from there, can talk to the Melwyn Park police himself.

He starts pushing his way in the direction of 42nd Street and the terminal's main exit. The screen shows CBS' Robert Schakne outside the trailer home of Mrs. Florence Carpenter, the astronaut's mother, in Boulder. A family friend, Will Fowler, reads her statement of happiness and relief, which ends with an assertion that her son's flight proves, despite Nikita Khrushchev, that "we shall never be buried."

Jim keeps walking, with difficulty and apologies, moving from Aries to Taurus to Gemini, under which point he sees a skinny boy with a big grin wearing a plaid cotton shirt.

Gregory has trotted back into the terminal. He's never felt better. It's as if his ears have popped for good and all. He's free of the spell that wove its way around him for weeks, and squeezed his ribs this morning in the apple tree, free of whatever reeled him like a fish from the schoolyard and pushed him into the street five minutes ago. But none of this is on his mind now. He's just watching the screen and wondering what the paramedics will say when they reach Scott; wondering whether once he's been flown aboard, the *Intrepid* will go back for the capsule or another ship will be sent to retrieve it; wondering what Scott's color pictures will look like.

Adjusting his viewing position in the constantly moving, milling crowd, he comes face to face with a man whose dazed expression starts to crumble.

The man picks him up and holds him so their heads are inches apart. Gregory looks into a pair of bifocals and sees not his own reflection, and not a series of vanishing mirrors, but the damp, tired eyes of his father.

"Dad," he says, before offering him a happy, baffled hug.

"Let's call your mother," says Jim, taking his son by the hand and leading him toward the main doors. He wants to get out of this crowded tomb. They will make the call from the street, in the light, which is what they now step into, crossing the threshold under the statue of Mercury.

EPILOGUE

Statement by Vice-President Johnson
Regarding the Successful Space Flight
of Aurora 7, *May 24, 1962*

This is a proud day, not only for the United States of America, but for mankind. Once again, a free nation has launched one of its sons aloft from the earth that no longer binds us, and he has come back safely.

The successful flight of Lieutenant Commander Malcolm Scott Carpenter in his *Aurora 7* spacecraft records another encouraging chapter in man's reach for the stars. There will be failures, but the many persons who made today's success possible can be happy in the knowledge that they have helped lay the solid groundwork of a great new age.

I know I speak for the nation in congratulating Scott Carpenter on this joyful event, and in wishing his wonderful family and brave associates all the best for the future. We are still at the threshold, and there is yet much to be done before the unknown realm around us is harnessed for our use. But we are making real progress, as today's achievement has shown the world.

The sheet of paper with this statement, the one Lyndon Johnson actually made, lies on top of the one he never had to, near the secretary's IBM typewriter in the suite of offices in the Executive Office Building. The lights are out; the office is empty; it's almost midnight. Both pieces of paper, years from now and for ages to come, will rest in the same folder deep within the Civil Archives Branch of the National Archives: the Reading File of the Executive Secretary, National Aeronautics and Space Council (RG 220), Mar. 1961–June 1973; Fldr: Chron. File, May 1962.

———————

As midnight arrives Scott Carpenter is once more in the air, in a Navy plane, nine minutes from landing at Grand Turk Island. He's a passenger now, and traveling more slowly than he did this morning: the plane took off from the deck of the *Intrepid* hours ago and has been through not a single sunrise or sunset, just a calm dark night over the Caribbean. Three years from now, Carpenter's explorations in the Navy's Sealab program will make him, in NASA's words, "the first human to experience the two most hostile environments known to man," but right now he is safe and elated. When the plane touches down he'll be hugged by John Glenn, and so full of energy that his first words to Howard A. Minners, the Air Force physician assigned to examine him, will be "What's on the schedule now, Doctor?" He's eager to tell Dr. Minners and the rest of them about his ride, about the morning he was "let in on the great secret."

———————

The *Aurora 7*, which bobbed in the water for hours after Scott Carpenter was hoisted away from it, was picked up by the USS *John R. Pierce* at 7:52 P.M. and is now on its way to the naval station at Roosevelt Roads, Puerto Rico. The center of its name — *UROR* — is gone, burned up in the reentry that dented and singed its shingles. The first and last letters, the *A*'s, have come through, inexplicably, since Cecilia Bibby, the artist who painted them on, used five coats of one kind of paint on the first five letters and only two coats of another kind on the last.

In the years to come the capsule will make more journeys, albeit slower and more earthbound ones: to an exhibition in Japan; to the public library in Boulder; to the Museum of Science and Industry in Chicago. Two years from now it will be revisited by Scott Carpenter at the 1964 World's Fair in Flushing, Queens, a few miles from Eddie Rodwicki's apartment.

———————

Pad 14, scorched from the morning fire of the departing rocket, lies deserted and cool in a bath of moonlight. It will be four more months before another rocket pours flames down upon it. No cameras are trained on it tonight, just as no reporter carrying a flashlight is anywhere near the cove where the loggerhead turtles have peacefully gestated themselves one day closer to their July emergence.

In Audley End, Cambridgeshire, England, the Friday morning sun will soon be up, but Sally Rodwell, worn out from fear, is sleeping soundly. Inside her, a legless boy, now just twenty-nine days from his birth, a boy who will be remarkable for the beauty of his face and the serenity of his disposition, quickens and shifts, with a stunted thrust that she still cannot feel.

Bill and Penny Hatfield's healthy unborn daughter, who will die in a car crash on April 11, 1979, sleeps soundly in her mother's womb in Omaha, Nebraska.

———————

The light will also soon be up over Coventry Cathedral, ready to shine on its reconsecration, but on East 43rd Street in Manhattan, Tommy Shanahan, sitting on the steps of St. Agnes's Church, depends on what neon and fluorescence the streetlights afford for the pushing back of midnight. He sits on the Bronx edition of the *New York Post* —

CARPENTER IN ORBIT!

— brought home to the rectory this afternoon by Father Francis, who'd been up in Morrisania, visiting an ancient former parishioner.

News of this pastoral house call reminded Tommy of his mother's cousin Annie in Inwood, though he has no intention of going back up there for at least another week, and no intention of feeling guilty about it either.

The church steps are still wet and are gradually soaking through the *Post*. A couple of hours ago the skies were howling, as millions of raindrops hit the pavement like steel ball bearings. All the priests got up from the TV to look out the rectory window. "You wouldn't think such a lovely day could end like this," Father Francis had said, a remark whose triteness had sent Tommy from the room.

It wasn't even true. The ferocious storm was over well before midnight. The day, which Tommy doesn't want to be over, is only ending now, peacefully. The light from the neon cross attached to the wall of the church near Adolph's Locksmith is shining through air that's calm and dry. Tommy looks from the electric crucifix to the silver gargoyles of the Chrysler Building across the street, at the corner of Lexington Avenue, up which Carpenter's motorcade will travel a week from Tuesday. Tommy thinks that the gargoyles look more like ornaments on a cathedral than St. Agnes's neon marker, crass as a pawnbroker's golden balls.

It was the same way this afternoon, he thinks, looking down the street toward Grand Central. When he was in there nine hours ago, after the rescue had occurred and the crowd was just beginning to disperse, he'd looked up at the ceiling, at the painted stars, and felt they were not only more beautiful than the stars in the sky but more beautiful than the figures on the Sistine ceiling, which he'd stared at, bored and cranky and unmoved, in the summer of 1956 with a dull group of seminarians on a two-week tour of Italy. (Bishop Fulton J. Sheen, an early riser, is just now getting up — not far from the Sistine Chapel. There was never any chance that he'd drop in to hear Tommy preach this afternoon. What Tommy didn't know is that Sheen is in Rome, getting ready for his private audience, now just hours away, with Pope John XXIII.)

Is God more present in the things of this world than in the supposed signifiers of His own? Tommy looks to the Chrysler Building and back to the station and thinks he feels more at home in their sight than he has in all the churches he's passed through in the last ten years.

He looks up into the sky and thinks of Scott Carpenter, with more kindness and awe than he did this morning. There's no man in the heavens now, no one cartwheeling the globe as there was just before his own glorious hour this afternoon. Now the astronaut's ride seems a splendid thing, a part of his own miracle, and Tommy has to wonder if prosy old Father Francis wasn't right this morning when he said that God wanted us to meet Him halfway.

On the eve of rebellion, on the eve of sin, Tommy feels more prayerful and holy than he has in years, certain somehow that he will soon be getting closer to God, just by kissing one of His lovely, forbidden creations.

Dwarfed by the steel bones of the Pan Am Building, which are still being fleshed out, the statues of Hercules and Minerva, flanking the aspirant Mercury, seem curiously cowed in the dark, just-washed air of midnight. Meant to crown Grand Central with the "moral force" and "intellectual energy" they respectively represent, they seem instead to preside over a building that is running out of both. Trains are not planes. Warren MacLeod is scheduled to fly next Tuesday out of Eero Saarinen's TWA Terminal at Idlewild, which will be dedicated the day before. The days when he might have reached his California business on the Santa Fe Chief are long gone, though Mercury, bravely extending his arm into the night, seems not to have noticed, or to know that fifteen or so years from now his survival, and the whole terminal's, will depend to some extent on the good efforts of Mrs. Jacqueline Onassis, who has been in bed, upstairs in the White House, for the past two hours.

At two minutes past midnight, unnoticed by any of the four cleaners sweeping up the last butts and wrappers from the afternoon crowd, a ten-watt bulb, the light signifying Pollux on the Grand Central ceiling, pops and dies.

CARPENTER ORBITS EARTH 3 TIMES SAFELY,
BUT OVERSHOOTS . . .

Before Elizabeth Wheatley can get through the twenty-two word headline of the *Times*'s bulldog edition, which she and Warren MacLeod picked up a few minutes ago after a steak dinner at Elmer's, she's lost interest. She scans the page for news of Kennedy, about whom she'll have to start reading again — she'd ignored him entirely in Italy — if she's going to be ready for this Mexico trip.

"Entire Nation Gives Thanks When Astronaut Is Sighted."

Don't overdo it, thinks Elizabeth, moving her eyes back to the left of the front page, which carries a story about the Senate's upholding a Kennedy veto of some farm bill. Hopeless, thinks Elizabeth, wondering why she ever said yes to Fred Foy. She'll never get interested in the assignment.

Pushing the paper to the other side of the double bed in Warren MacLeod's company suite in the Mayfair Regent, Elizabeth closes her eyes and lies still, flat on her back, palms facing upward, just as those of Bellini's Saint Francis are posed in the darkness of the Frick, several blocks northwest of here.

It's been a long day, she thinks. She hears Warren in the next room, putting ice into two tumblers. She hadn't really expected the two of them to make a night of it, to "pick up where we left off," as he put it, somewhat to her discomfort, after calling home with a lie to his wife in Locust Valley. Still, it will be nice having him in Mexico, where he's promised to come after his business in California, and after Kennedy's gone. Imagining a couple of sunny afternoons in Sonora, Elizabeth stretches luxuriantly and, after this long day of walking, kicks off her Delman shoes, noting, curiously, that out from under one of their bows has fallen a small piece of what appears to be candy — an M & M, it proves to be. Now how long has she been walking around with that?

Tossing it into the wastebasket, she lies back down, turns on her side and feels herself falling asleep, thinking about the morning breeze she felt on her face while she stood on the deck of the *Leonardo* — which, twelve hours from now, will be picking up anchor and sailing back toward Italy.

At the White House, the President, who has just gotten into bed — with his wife — is not thinking about Mexico, or about the Tariff Classification Bill he will sign tomorrow, but about the anniversary tomorrow will bring — namely, of his pledge to get to the moon and back by 1970. The editorial writers will no doubt take note of it and ask how much progress has been made over the past twelve months, so it's a damn good thing Carpenter isn't lost in the stars tonight.

Last year the President also said that "life is unfair," a remark Joan Anderson Linley, having listlessly turned on the Channel 7 late movie in her White Plains apartment, is now recalling. Kennedy had been talking about the reserve call-up over Berlin, why some men had to go and some didn't. Jack Linley was one of the ones who didn't. But Joan supposes another call-up could come at any time, and feels guilty that she's the one holding off on having a baby. Being a father might keep Jack exempt, and for that reason alone, she thinks, she ought to be getting pregnant.

The thing she can hardly admit to herself is that she rather likes the idea of Jack's being called up and sent away — not to anyplace dangerous like the Korean border but to where it would much more likely be, some Army base outside a nice little German town. She pictures him spending most of his time there drinking beer and playing cards and being bored with his buddies until tensions died down and he was sent home. Meanwhile, here by herself, she'd have the chance to figure out not only if she really wanted a baby, but if she wanted to be married to Jack at all.

It's one of the days when she thinks the answer is no. He's asleep in the bedroom now, a half hour after the two of them had fast and hardly furious sex. He's bored and boring and angry these days, resentful he's selling footballs at Herman's instead of tossing them for the Titans. It was a long shot that he'd make it, and he didn't, but he won't forget about it.

She's got the sound down low on some picture about Indians. She'll never stick with it, but she's glad to be out of the bedroom for a while. She's usually up at this hour, trying to get something ready for tomorrow. But that's not necessary tonight. Tomorrow she'll just do all the stuff she never got to this afternoon. The kids spent most of it watching the space-flight on a TV they wheeled into the audi/gym while she was on the phone with the cops, in the office with the school psychologist, and later on her way over to Mrs. Noonan's. Grand Central, of all places. She seems to be the only one who doesn't think it's the end of the world. It's sort of funny, actually: poor little Gregory trying to hide his transistor earphone all morning and then all the rest of the kids getting to watch the flight on television because he went and disappeared. Anyway, she's determined not to treat him like a case, which the school psychologist, who's got too little to do in the district, seems bent on doing. In fact, when he comes into class tomorrow she's just going to give his head a light-hearted tousle and ask, "Everything A-OK, Gregory?"

God, isn't that what's-his-name, Ben Casey, playing Hiawatha?

Waldy Munoz lies on the sofa bed in the front room of the railroad apartment on East 117th Street. His transistor radio, playing "Travelin' Man," a "solid-gold" hit from Ricky Nelson, sits for better reception on the wet window ledge.

The telephone rings and he grabs it, knowing it's crazy Ramón and that his mother will kill him if she hears one of his friends calling at this hour.

"Fourth floor, ladies' lingerie," falsettoes Ramón. "Did ya get the job?"

"Yeah, I got it. But I ain't taking it."

"How come, man?"

"Because I'm gonna go up, up, up. And away, away, away. That's how come. Now get off the fucking phone before my mama hears me on it. I'll talk to you tomorrow."

If Ramón doesn't remember his up-up-up from this morning, Waldy does. As Ricky Nelson finishes singing, he looks out the window and down to Garfein's Tile and Linoleum, where he starts work tomorrow at 10:00. He remembered the Help Wanted sign as soon as he left the bus station this afternoon, holding the piece of paper on which he wrote the one-way fare to Miami.

(On January 28, 1986, as the *Challenger* explodes over Cape Canaveral, Waldy, standing near the Vehicle Assembly Building and wearing his twenty-year service pin, will look up from the paint gun he has operated faithfully and well for so long, and know what the flash and plume signify as having finally happened.)

Down the hall, through the wire-mesh pane of frosted glass on the kitchen door, he can see the fuzzy silhouette of his mother, making a sandwich for his sister to take to school tomorrow. When Alicia moves to the other side of the room, she leaves visible through the pane only the soft-edged light of a sixty-watt bulb, shining its steady haze, south of Waldy's eyes, like a nebula.

To the east, just over the Triborough Bridge, Eddie Rodwicki sits in his Astoria living room and feels grateful that Jan Murray is hosting *The Tonight Show*. What a relief from Jack Paar, that name-dropper and crybaby who's always seemed to Eddie just a little bit that way, if you know what he means.

The electricity went out with the storm a while ago, but it's back on, and Eddie, drinking some of the red wine left in the bottle his brother-in-law brought over last Friday night, is finally beginning to relax. He should have been in bed half an hour ago, but he's felt jumpy ever since this afternoon, over that kid. "It came *this* close to happening," he told his wife, aware, even as he said it, that he was refusing to put it bluntly: *I came this close to killing him.*

He wasn't himself all evening. When his son asked for money to see *Journey to the Seventh Planet* on Saturday, Eddie had not only said sure, but asked if he couldn't go with him, too, an offer the kid described as "kind of weird." The kid was right, of course. It's just that the little guy suddenly seemed in danger of every moving car and weirdo in the city. Eddie just wanted to protect him. His wife could see what he was thinking. As soon as Eddie Junior was out of the room she turned around and said, "Take a load off, will you? It *didn't* happen. That's the point."

"Kind of weird" is a phrase also used tonight in the Herlihy household, behind the Noonans' in Melwyn Park.

"So what do you think?" Ellen Herlihy had asked — meaning, about Gregory's running off. The question was meant for her husband, Ted, but got answered by her son, Georgie. "I think it's kind of weird," he said, before adding, after a pause, "but kind of neat, too." This remark annoyed Ellen, indicating as it did the possibility that the unlikely figure of Gregory Noonan might temporarily have surpassed her own son in derring-do.

There are raindrops beaded up on the Herlihys' new air conditioner, which before the storm was installed at the back of the house, in the master bedroom window, largely by Ellen, whose hopeful lookout for signs of additional commotion at the Noonan house were met with her husband's asking whether she was trying to strain her eyes.

Mary Noonan, who has not made love to her husband and not conceived another child, sits in the dark by her kitchen window, smoking a cigarette and regarding the Herlihys' air conditioner, whose raindropped surface shines in their porch light.

It was too big for the trunk, so it sat on the back seat all the way home from Montgomery Ward, as Ellen kept saying, "It's probably just a kid who looks like him" and "Maybe he just wanted to play a little hooky," both of which assurances Mary knew to be false.

She knew then that it was her son, knew he had gone there to fulfill some purpose, and that it was connected to climbing the apple tree this morning. She also knew, as Ellen's Buick went past the lumber yard, that it was a bad purpose, not Gregger's but God's, that something was about to happen and that he would never come home. And that's why she didn't urge Ellen to hurry: she didn't want to get home any sooner than she would have, didn't want to call the school and find he wasn't there.

And then, just as the car came within sight of the railroad station, she knew with equal — no, this time *real* — certainty that everything was all right.

She gets up and goes to the back door, checking the lock one more time, looking through the glass and screen at the apple tree, the Venus's-flytrap that failed to get Gregory into its clutches.

Is God to be thanked for that? If He is, then who is to be blamed for making the danger in the first place? It's the old story. "Prayer is the lifting up of our minds and hearts to God" — so says the Baltimore Catechism — but as Mary looks into the sky, she is not looking for God, only for the stars, which are still hidden, though the storm has passed. There was a time when, every night, she'd taught Gregger to wish upon a star, sang him the Disney lullaby she now whispers as she straightens the café curtain, puts the ashtray in the sink, climbs the stairs and passes his room on the way back to bed.

Mary does not find Jim in bed, because he is in Gregory's room, having stepped through the door, which was on a crack, on his way back from splashing his face at the bathroom sink. He hears a couple of raindrops sluggishly plop their way through a downspout and is amazed at the tranquility of things now that the storm's howls are over.

He'd gone up to bed, where he couldn't sleep, after hearing the late news say Carpenter probably got lost not because he fired his retro-rockets late but because his capsule came in at the wrong angle. A few degrees more in the wrong direction and he might have skimmed off course like a stone, been marooned in a loop-the-loop orbit until he suffocated and died.

"I'm glad he got home." That's all Gregory said about it on the train, not because he was withholding something, or addressing his father from that hostile frozen planet he'd been on for weeks, but because that's all that seemed necessary to say. Far from being remote, Gregory seemed to have come back into the atmosphere, to have returned from the outpost he'd been stationed at, having somehow declined or been excused from moving farther and forever away. He and his son were breathing the same air again. They chatted about everything from Moose Skowron's batting average to why Corvairs have the engine in back, and not once, either in the terminal or on the 3:48 home to Melwyn Park, did he ask Gregory what he'd been doing in the station, twenty-five miles from school and home. Whatever he'd had to do he'd done, and he'd come through.

He looks down at his sleeping son's pink feet, dimly aglow in the room's rocket-ship night light. They stick out, not from under a brown coat, but from a blanket. They are serene, alive. He knows the child to whom they belong.

His father has withdrawn from the room. Gregory's right foot twitches. He is dreaming, not of space, but of a beach. He is lying on warm Florida sands, an image kinescoped into his brain a few days ago, by a black-and-white TV report on the upcoming mission of *Aurora 7*, and released now, in living color, by his active, sleeping mind. In the dream he is happy, possessed of an animal contentment, once more riding the earth, but secure this time, with no need to hold on.

For whatever reason God made him, He doesn't yet wish to share with Gregory His everlasting happiness in heaven.

Tomorrow he will go to school and learn certain small facts — the year of the Homestead Act, the spelling of "incredulous" — that will stay with him for the rest of his life. Kenny Kessler will greet him loudly by saying, "Hey, Greg, I hear you overshot your house by twenty-five miles," but the other students, out of puzzlement, respect and short attention spans, will refrain from teasing him.

Like everyone connected to him on May 24, 1962, he too will begin living a future, because however in doubt it was for a time today, one has been vouchsafed him by God. Over the next seven years he will grow toward manhood as man grows toward the moon, and on the late evening of July 20, 1969, he will be in a nearby state park, not watching television and not even looking up at the sky, but making out with his first serious girlfriend. Some six weeks later he will go off to college, where he will be a mediocre student, though considered remarkable for a sunny, talkative disposition and, in a time of widespread insolence and generational tension, for a conspicuously friendly relationship with his parents.

The noisy boys down the street have long since gone to bed, and Winifred Woodward has fallen asleep on her porch. Above her the North Carolina sky is calm, marked only by its usual twinkling dots of light. Looking up at the stars tonight, she had the idea that she was seeing great distances, which is true, of course, but not the whole truth. What Miss Woodward didn't realize is that she was also looking back in time.

The light of Supernova Shelton, for example, has traveled 16 billion miles today, leaving just another 150 trillion until it makes its appearance on earth in the early morning hours of February 24, 1987. Had God, at the moment He created the universe, flung the stellar dust ever so slightly to the right or left and made that star companionless, it would, upon reaching the end of its life, have collapsed into a white dwarf and probably never been remarked upon. But the stars fell where they did, and Supernova Shelton 1987 had a companion, the acquisition of which led to the explosion of light that is traveling earthward.

As Gregory once told his mother, the day will come when men will see the moment God snapped His fingers and made the world. The "great secret" that Scott Carpenter pondered today will give itself up when the ultimate telescope, powerful enough to see through six billion light-years of "lookback" time, catches God in the act, thereby giving men knowledge not only of His original intention but also, perhaps, of His daily moods. (Unless God smudges the mirror.)

He killed a man in Waterbury, Connecticut, tonight. The storm He let loose — for all we know in a regretful snit over His decision to let a thirty-seven-year-old man and an eleven-year-old boy live through the afternoon — injured another twenty-five people and destroyed forty-five homes. He hadn't intended to reunite the boy and his father. He had intended for some weeks to send this one of His field's lilies, this one of His sparrows, whom His eye is always on, to his death, under the wheels of Checker cab number 7D22, just as He had planned to let Carpenter skip off the earth's atmosphere and keep orbiting until he suffocated. But His moods change. Five days from now the papers will report that twelve-year-old Kenneth Shickley, Jr., while chasing a squirrel near Shamokin, Pennsylvania, has fallen down a 550-foot mineshaft to his death. "Mercy" is not a word expounded upon by the Baltimore Catechism, and as such is not an idea that Gregory Noonan ever pondered before falling asleep and into his dreams tonight. But he did say his prayers before going to bed, and he did make the customary petition that God's will be done on earth as it is in heaven.